TIGHT-LIPPED

ERIK CARTER

ISBN: 9798478344115

CHAPTER ONE

Breckenridge, Colorado
The 1990s

SOMEHOW, when Elliott Bell saw the gun in the man's hand, he knew he wasn't about to be assaulted—he was going to be murdered.

Elliott was no firearms expert, but the pistol reminded him of the 9mms with which he'd trained during his time in the Army. By itself, the gun could mean one of several things: a home invasion; a disgruntled individual related to one of Elliott's cases; a wandering lunatic, perhaps.

But in the man's other hand was another item that changed the equation entirely.

A large stun gun.

It was the combination of the two weapons that told Elliott that the man had come not to rifle through his CD collection or pressure him into giving up the location of his safe.

No, whoever the man was, this stranger standing in his doorway, he meant to kill Elliott.

And, given the stun gun, Elliott was most likely going to be tortured, too.

Elliott's next thought was of Alexandra, his girlfriend. She'd be there in an hour. She'd find his body.

This was a sickening notion.

Further solidifying the notion that the stranger had murderous intentions was the man's expression, an ominous sneer, glinting from the mystery of his half-concealed face, draped in shadows created by Elliott's front porch light and shrouded by the hood of his thermal winter coat. The man was on the short side with an average build. Dark brown, medium-length hair poked from beneath his hood.

As Elliott watched the man in a moment of awkward but dreadful stillness, his impulse wasn't to flee or to shout out to the neighbors—he simply steeled himself to the notion that he was going to have to fight for his life.

The sneer on the man's face grew wider as he inched closer to Elliott, and while he kept the pistol aimed forward, he used his other hand to brush the hood from his head. The warm light that streamed out of Elliott's door and onto the snowy porch washed over the man's face, illuminating the mystery.

Aside from the near-psychotic expression, his visage was quite plain. His cheeks bore an oily, unwashed sheen and two days' worth of stubble. Only one characteristic kept the man from being completely forgettable: his eyes. One was very dark brown, almost black; the other was pale blue.

Suddenly, the man pulsed the stun gun. A spark arched between the two electrodes, and a *ZAP* barked into the dark quietness beyond, echoing off the pines. The sound was so loud, so piercing, so unexpected that it made Elliott jump. The man's sneer didn't change. He'd gained no grim satisfaction from Elliot's fright. There was only icy determination pouring out of his dark stare.

He motioned for Elliott to go inside, and when Elliott's attention flashed to the left, to the baseball bat he kept by the door frame, the man gave a knowing shake of the head and said simply, "No."

The man's voice was as plain as his features, but there was fury in it, barely contained. While the pistol had clearly been around for years, the stun gun in the man's hand looked brand new. The plastic was clean and unmarred. The metal components were shiny, spotless. Elliott eyed the electrodes, and he pictured the blue-white spark he'd seen a moment earlier, the piercing sound it had created. Elliott's flesh bristled at the imagined sensation of the electric current on his skin.

As Elliott backed away, the man pushed inside, shut the door behind him, buffeting a final gust of cold air into the warmth of the cabin. The pleasant glow of copious varnished wood glistened on the oily shine of the man's filthy face. His mismatched eyes flicked to the corner, saw the baseball bat, returned to Elliott with a smirk.

"Who are you? What ... is this?" Elliott said. His voice was tiny, shaking, and shame immediately poured over him. Elliott had never thought himself a particularly brave man, but he wasn't a weakling either. Yet here he was, at what might be his end, trembling like a coward. Pathetic.

"You don't remember me?" the man said in his plain voice. He gestured to his eyes, one then the other, highlighting the discrepancy. "C'mon, man."

Elliott had seen maybe two people in his life with mismatched eyes—vague memories, not specific faces. Still, when he'd opened the door moments earlier, met the man's gaze, obscured in the shadow of his hood, there had been a sense of recognition, almost familiarity.

It was as though he knew this man from somewhere, at some time. But—

Then he remembered...

And his expression must have given him away because the man's lips curled up in a slight grin.

"Hard Sprint?" Elliott said. "That's it, isn't it? You were with me at Operation Hard Sprint. One of the officers."

"That's right," the man said. "Tristan Pike."

Pike. Yes. His eyes. Of course.

The briefing room. Before the group went into the field. Elliott remembered staring at the incongruous eyes, transfixed, as Pike had given the group its directives.

Later, in the swamp, the flash of the explosion had lit both of Pike's eyes, washing away their differences, painting them both fiery red. The screaming. The smell of blood everywhere. You couldn't see it, not in the blazing fire, not in the surrounding darkness, but you could smell it. A thick, coppery scent. Pike had been in the front, those newly uniform eyes staring back in terror at the others, before he rushed to help them, the gallant leader.

Now, years later, in Elliott's luxury cabin on the other side of the country, Pike's eyes looked cold and determined as they scanned left and right, up and down, absorbing the surroundings.

"You've done well for yourself, Bell," Pike said. "Damn. Guess I shoulda been a lawyer."

Elliott glanced at the pistol. But, once more, his gut feeling told him that the stun gun was the more immediate threat. The electrodes glistened, a metallic mouth open wide, ready to attack.

"What is this, Pike?" he said, his voice shaking again, damn it all.

"You're the first," Pike said. "Then it'll be Artiga's turn tomorrow. I know where he is. When did you last speak to the others?"

"What others? What are you talking about?"

Pike narrowed the mismatched eyes and jabbed the stun gun into Elliott's chest.

ZAP!

The shock was as much a neutral sensation as it was searing pain. While there was the feeling of hot needles impaling him, there were also undulations, innocuous, pulsing waves that clenched his muscles tight. His limbs froze, immobile. Time seemed to freeze as well. All that existed was Pike's sneering face, his extended arm, a general sense of the golden-warm haze from the surrounding cabin.

And then it ended.

Elliott's body jolted, and he stumbled backward.

"Don't screw with me, Bell!" Pike hissed. "Horn, Davidson, Milano, Langstaff. When did you last contact them?

Elliott's heart pounded. His skin, his entire body tingled from the shock. He felt something strange, looked down, and saw his fingers shaking violently. He balled his hands together, squeezed against the shake.

"I don't know those names. What the hell are you talking about?"

Pike turned to the side, exhaled loudly. "Horn's in Louisville, Kentucky. Davidson's in San Francisco. But Milano and Langstaff—it's like those two just disappeared."

The stun gun inched forward, and Elliott's retreat matched the slow and steady pace, nearing the threshold to the dining room.

"Man, I'm telling you," he said. "I don't know..."

He trailed off.

One of the names Pike had given was familiar, but the others were completely foreign. Only for a moment, though. A logical conclusion quickly coalesced.

Again Pike recognized Elliott was putting the pieces together, and once more the man gave a bitter grin.

"They're the others, aren't they?" Elliott said. "The other survivors from Hard Sprint."

Pike nodded as he continued forward with his two weapons, matching Elliott's backward progression into the cabin.

"Man, I knew those folks for one night. *One night.* Hell, only a few hours. How the shit would I know where they are now?"

"Liar! You've been organizing with them. For months."

Elliott was shaking. "This is insane..."

Pike sneered. "Are you willing to die for them, Captain?"

Elliott's bare feet padded onto the gray herringbone rug beneath his oak dining room table, and then his ass bumped the table's edge. His backward movement came to a halt.

Moments earlier at the front door, he'd decided against calling out to his neighbors in the tightly spaced group of luxury cabins on the side of a Colorado foothill mountain; the armed lunatic he was facing might have done something rash.

But now, he had another means of seeking help. He wasn't about to blow a second chance. To hell with staying quiet.

He slowly slid his right hand under the table, locking eyes with Pike, distracting him from what was happening below.

Elliott's fingers found a small bulb of cool plastic tucked behind the front lip of the table. He pressed it, held it for the required three seconds.

The cabin burst with piercing noise—a blaring, pulsing alarm pouring out of three sirens positioned strategically throughout the building.

Pike looked up, bewildered, his brown-and-blue eyes darting. For only a second. Then he glanced to the side, out the window.

Elliott's neighbor's cabin was only a few feet away—Steve

Marshman, a retired dentist from Illinois. The two windows on the side of Marshman's cabin were pitch black.

Pike's attention snapped back to Elliott. "That was stupid."

A flash of movement, and another warbling wave in Elliott's chest, pouring into the rest of his body. Pike had jammed the stun gun inches away from where he'd shocked him before. The pain crackled through Elliott's ribs, his lungs. His muscles quaked, stomach contracted.

Pike yanked the stun gun back, ready for another strike, giving Elliott just a taste of relief.

But then he quickly pivoted to look out the window again.

Elliott followed his gaze.

One of Marshman's windows was alight. Marshman leaned into the glass with his hands on the sill, peering toward Elliott's cabin.

Though he couldn't hear the man, Elliott clearly saw the words on Marshman's lips: *What the hell?*

Marshman darted off to the front of his cabin.

Sensing the urgency of the situation, Pike turned back to Elliott and immediately brought the pistol to Elliott's head.

His finger tensed on the trigger.

Elliott's thoughts went to Alexandra, how much he loved her, and once more the knowledge that she was going to find his dead body made him feel sick.

His muscles tensed. He waited for the crack of the gun.

Nothing.

He opened his eyes, found Pike staring at him.

"I'm not letting you off that easy, traitor. You're going to suffer," Pike said. "I'll find Milano and Langstaff. And you'll have suffered for nothing."

He jammed the barrel of the gun into Elliott's stomach.

And fired.

The blast roared through the cabin, over the golden timber walls, up to the heights of the lofty ceiling, louder even than the blaring siren.

And the pain eclipsed everything he'd suffered in the last few minutes.

He fell to his knees, looked at his stomach.

Glistening red on his fingers. Warm, sticky, wet. His T-shirt was soaked in it, the circle of crimson growing larger, a rapidly spreading, asymmetrical sphere devouring the light blue cloth. With the wheezing sounds coming from his lips, and the rotten, burning feeling in his stomach and lungs, it was clear that his earlier prediction was correct.

He was going to die tonight.

He fell farther forward, onto his stomach, which brought another shock of pain through his body. His face dropped to the rug, and as he looked up, saw Pike aiming at him again.

Except this time it wasn't a gun he was aiming.

It was a Polaroid camera.

Click.

The flash blinded Elliott, making him jolt, a little prod to the pain in his body. When his eyes squinted open, he saw Pike's feet dashing off across the hardwood toward the foyer.

But before Pike could open the door, it flung open. Marshman entered, wearing a robe and rubber galoshes. Pike jabbed the gun toward him, and Marshman gasped, came to a quick stop, hands up.

For a moment, it looked like Pike would cut Marshman down. But then he just said, "Get out of my way" and rushed past him, slamming the door behind him.

Marshman rushed over to Elliott, his galoshes thwacking on the hardwood.

"Elliott! *Shit!*"

A car engine fired up outside, followed immediately by the sound of tires crunching in snow.

Marshman's robe was a fuzzy mass, his face an indistinct smudge. The peripheral of Elliott's vision faded and blurred. Beads of sweat on his forehead, the back of his hands. Another flash of pain shivered through him.

He saw Alexandra. She smiled at him, said something, but no sounds escaped her moving lips.

It was Marshman, not Alexandra, before him, speaking. Elliott sensed a hand on his shoulder.

"Elliott, I..."

The words faded to echoing nothingness then pulsed back into reality.

"...can you hear..."

Black spots flashed over Elliott's vision, blotting out Marshman's face. Another wave of shivering, sweaty pain.

Only seconds left. Then he'd be gone.

"Do you..." Sound vanished again, returned. "...calling 911!"

The vague mass that was Marshman swept to the side, revealing a golden, fuzzy haze before him. Elliott's hardwood floor, of course.

But it was more than that.

It was the golden glow of the hereafter. He was almost done.

Another wave of pain folded him, pinching his knees to his chest, pulling his line of sight away from the golden beauty. A grayish, fuzzy bloom enveloped everything. Only a tiny circle of visibility left, a patch of the herringbone pattern of the carpet, a blood-spattered, shaking hand.

Marshman's footsteps became far-distant tapping sounds as he scuttled off to the telephone in the adjoining living room and spoke rapidly to a 911 operator. The man's voice faded away once more. And this time, Elliott knew it would not return.

There was silence, a hollow, reverberant nothingness.

And the golden glow again. The wooden beams of the ceiling far above. So far above.

Yes, this was it.

Nothingness.

All was black. For only a moment. Then a fireball lit the darkness. The explosion. Only years earlier, but so, so far in the past. The forest was aglow, the swamp water sparkling orange-gold. A woman beside him, slumped against a tree. Her face was split open. Blood poured onto her plain, insignia-free battledress uniform. Screams. The smell of copper wafting through the wet, oppressive air.

That was his principal memory, the most vivid detail. He rarely thought of the incident, but when he did, it was this single moment. The woman's split-open face. The way the skin splayed. The clean, pale bone beneath shining in the firelight.

Elliot died thinking of the woman's face.

CHAPTER TWO

MENDOCINO, CALIFORNIA

SILENCE JONES SPRINTED toward the massive building, a soaring affair of decaying red brick and shattered banks of windows with an arched roof at its lofty peak. Unruly bushes clung to the side. A half-dead arborvitae shot out of the crumbling asphalt and ascended the corner of the central tower, nearly to the peak—a scraggly, brown-and-green flagstaff without a banner.

Waves crashed on the rocks behind him, and even as he ran as fast as he could, focused on his deadly task, Silence couldn't help but be reminded of his childhood. He'd spent his early years in this area of Northern California, not fifty miles from his current location.

It was the closest he'd been to his birthplace in years, and he was there to murder a guy—the one who was a hundred feet away, sprinting for the abandoned factory.

Upon first glance, you wouldn't think a man like Simon Ramsey would be a ruthless leader capable of running a criminal organization that held an otherwise peaceful town in its grip. Ramsey was on the short side with a soft, slight build. His face was dopey, his eyes were droopy, and his skin was way too white for that of a Californian, its milkiness amplified by his dark hair and eyes and the gross little soul patch on his lower lip.

But everyone, no matter how unassuming, has a few talents, and Ramsey had two: an uncanny knack for mass-producing methamphetamines and the ability to convince small-town types to follow him.

These proficiencies led to the explosive growth of his small-time criminal empire and inspired look-the-other-way attitudes from way too many local police and government officials.

And Ramsey's proficiencies were ultimately what brought Silence Jones into town. To right a few wrongs. Silence had been in the Mendocino area for four days. He'd eliminated everyone who was complicit in Ramsey's scheme.

Now only Ramsey himself remained.

As Ramsey slowed slightly at the door, he stole another glance over his shoulder. His eyes, which stared through a pair of small, gold-rimmed glasses, went wide with fright as they found Silence barreling toward him. He also wore a white wife-beater, baggy jeans, and a dark brown fedora that had somehow stayed on his head throughout the chase; Silence had noted that the hat looked at least one size too small.

Ramsey disappeared into the building and slammed the rusty metal door behind him. A few moments later, after crossing the last stretch of crumbling asphalt, Silence approached the door.

He stopped, pulled his Beretta 92FS from its shoulder holster, and in the moment it took him to screw the suppressor onto the end of the barrel, he closed his eyes and took a deep breath from his stomach. A one-second meditation, a technique that came courtesy of his dead fiancée, C.C.

A moment of calm.

And then explosive action.

He kicked the door, cleared the entry, and went into the building. He squinted his eyes, adjusting to the change in lighting, a slight change—it wasn't bright outside, nor was it very dark in the building, with its massive banks of shattered, dust-smeared windows on the upper levels. The change in the air, though, was drastic—from a moist sea breeze fragranced by flowers and grasses to dry, dead, stagnancy, the smell of decades-old machinery, bygone times, and failed dreams.

Silence brought his hand to his mouth to stifle a cough as the dust tickled the back of his throat. His Chelsea boots scuffed on the debris-strewn concrete as he approached a corner, stopped, and listened.

Footsteps in the distance. Echoing. Running away.

Silence adjusted his grip on the Beretta and cleared the corner, then entered the main floor of the structure.

It was a wide expanse of decaying metal. Whatever devices the factory had once housed had long since been removed, their faint footprints remaining on the grimy, diamond-pattern steel plane. In the back were a set of colossal doors, open, the type one expects to see in an aircraft hanger. They divided the space in two. The ceiling was high, maybe forty feet, with large steel beams traversing it at regular intervals. Metal stairs and landings led to offices and other spaces higher in the building.

But no Simon Ramsey.

Silence held perfectly still. Listened.

The footsteps had stopped.

Shit!

Maybe Silence had underestimated the guy. Maybe Ramsey's resourcefulness extended further than simply fooling some rubes with a few clever words and a decent recipe for meth. Maybe the guy was a true survivor. Every second that passed vastly increased the chance that Silence had lost him. He pictured Ramsey slithering out some side door or through a broken-out window.

Silence plastered himself against the wall, eased into a doorframe, and then—

There!

Footsteps again. Beyond the towering doors.

Silence took off.

He dashed into the open space, toward the other half of the building, and even at a full sprint, the doors seemed to remain in the distance, never drawing nearer. The place was *that* massive.

When he finally reached the doors and slowed slightly to clear the threshold, he saw Ramsey, halfway across the wide-open space in the other half of the building, a tiny figure in an orange-red expanse of rusty metal that was bisected by a beam of light that skewered the dusty air via a hole in the ceiling.

Ramsey was about a hundred feet away. A thirty-three-yard moving target, one trying desperate evasive tactics, juking left and right. A challenging shot. However, Silence's Beretta was fully loaded—fifteen in the mag, one in the chamber—and he gave a moment of consideration to throwing some lead downrange.

Ramsey was slowing. Rapidly. No matter how much of a survivor Ramsey was, he was in poor shape. Adrenaline and the sheer, animalistic will to live can only do so much before impartial limitations set in. Silence had witnessed this many times. Just before he eliminated a person.

But even though Silence's trigger finger was getting itchy, and even though the gap between him and Ramsey was shrinking, he couldn't risk eliminating Ramsey. Not yet.

There was one more step Silence needed to accomplish first.

Ramsey whipped around, chest heaving, footsteps clomping, growing slower. He made eye contact with Silence...

And he pulled a small revolver from his front pocket.

Silence pushed his reservations aside and sated his anxious trigger finger.

Survival indeed.

Three quick rounds, muffled by the suppressor but amplified by the factory's massive steel walls.

Bang! Bang! Bang!

He aimed for center mass, slightly to the left—Ramsey's right side, where he held the revolver. One of the rounds missed Ramsey entirely, but the other two tore into his torso, one by the shoulder and the other lower, in the ribs. The combined blows spun Ramsey around, sending the revolver clattering across the metal flooring and dropping Ramsey into a mound.

Silence approached cautiously, Beretta aimed at the other man, who was face down on the metal, his torso rising and lowering and quivering with quick but deep breaths. A low and steady groan and the sound of something wet.

Silence stopped, put his boot on Ramsey's shoulder, and gave him a good shove, rolling him onto his back. Ramsey screamed, eyes closed. His face glistened with sweat. Blood dripped from the corner of his mouth. The front of his tank top had little white coloration remaining; it was now almost pure crimson.

His eyes blinked open and found Silence's. "What do you want, man? You've won. You killed 'em all. I'm finished. You know that. What more do you want?"

Silence raised his Beretta, leveling it with Ramsey's forehead. Ramsey gasped.

"Talk," Silence said.

Ramsey gasped again, louder, and even shuffled his ruined body back an inch on the rusty metal. His mouth gaped, and his eyes bounced across Silence, as though searching, making computations.

This was the first time they'd met face-to-face. People always had a powerful reaction to Silence's voice, which was an unnatural mix of depth and crackling torment. They just couldn't comprehend that a human being could sound the way Silence did.

Ramsey sucked in his lower lip, cleaning the blood from it, and studied Silence more. He seemed to be considering Silence's command now, not his voice. His eyes flicked to the Beretta, still aimed at his head.

"Talk?" Ramsey said. "You mean, about the money?"

Silence didn't respond.

"If I tell you, you'll let me live, right?" he said, nodding, as though answering his own question.

Silence didn't respond.

"It was all cash, man. All of it." His eyes flicked to the Beretta again, and then he suddenly coughed, fist going to his lips, bloody spittle speckling his knuckles. "Two hundred grand. I got it in a gun safe in a basement. A shitty house out on Mondelez Street. 932 Mondelez. Okay? That's it. I swear. Have it! Just take it, man. Take it!"

"Thanks," Silence said.

He fired twice. Into Ramsey's forehead. A double tap.

Ramsey's head dropped to the metal. Eyes open. Looking up to the lofty ceiling. Slight movement. The head rolled to the side, open eyes staring at Silence.

Silence observed the reverberant nothingness of the moment.

And then he heard footsteps behind him.

CHAPTER THREE

THE SOUND HAD COME from behind.

In that sliver of frozen time, a sense of dread swept over Silence. He was standing in the middle of a wide-open space. No corners to turn. No walls to duck behind. The nearest cover was yards away. Completely exposed, entirely vulnerable.

He exploded into action, diving to the left.

As his body rolled to the side, he had another fraction of a moment to ponder the situation. Who the hell was behind him? He'd eliminated all of Ramsey's minions. Tracked them down over several days of investigation.

But had he missed one?

Of course, it could be someone else, someone not related to Ramsey at all. Maybe it was a local who'd seen the two men sprinting toward the empty factory. Or it could be a cop. Hell, it could be a vagrant to whom the rust-riddle shell of a building was a home.

If any of those scenarios were true, Silence couldn't fire. Not until he confirmed identity. Not until he got a visual.

He rolled onto his chest, sliding over the dusty metal, and

in one solid movement he planted a foot to stop his momentum and aimed his weapon.

A hundred feet away was a man staring at him as he casually strode in Silence's direction, hands in pockets.

And the man was smiling.

"Show me—"

Silence's bellow came to an abrupt halt as pain sliced his throat. Speaking was torturous to the mangled scar tissue inside his neck. The more syllables he used, the more pain he felt. Especially when he raised his voice.

He swallowed and finished his sentence. "Your hands!"

"No need to, Suppressor," the man said in a tone that matched his smile. He kept his hands in his pockets.

Silence felt his steely grip on the Beretta slacken.

Suppressor. Silence's codename.

"Why don't you get off the dirty floor?" the man said as the taps of his dress shoes echoed off the towering walls in the distance. "I'm just here to chat, Asset 23."

The man had used Silence's codename and his number. Only the confirmation remained.

"I hear..." Silence said and swallowed. "Seattle is beautiful..." He swallowed. "This time of year."

"Just don't forget your umbrella," the man said, now only a few feet away.

Confirmation. The man was a Specialist.

Silence lowered the gun entirely. The Specialist offered a hand and helped Silence to his feet. The man's eyes craned up, and he raised his eyebrows as Silence extended to his full six-foot-three height.

With safety reestablished, Silence's thoughts drifted to a new concern, one that had been pushed out of his mind during the action. He looked down and began furiously brushing the dust from his jacket and shirt and pants.

The gray jacket and black turtleneck were both heavy-duty. His trousers, however, had yet to be tested in the field, and he was uncertain of their durability. Prophetically, his eyes fell on a small tear on the cuff.

Damn.

The cloth was black, though, and the tear was discreet. His tailor back in Pensacola could fix it easily enough, make it disappear.

He looked back at the Specialist and found the man smiling still, but now the grin was smaller, less overt, ready for business. The man was about six foot tall and lean, early thirties or so. His hair was dark blond, perfectly parted and rather short on the sides, framing a face that was small and angular.

A messenger bag hung from the man's shoulder, and he wore a white polo shirt and khakis. The shirt bore no insignia, which meant he didn't work for a car dealership or a pool sales company or a lawn care outfit. The clothes were clean, new, and looked expensive, which could mean—

"Stop that," the Specialist said.

Silence's eyes went back to the other man's, and he gave a confused grunt. For the sake of his throat, Silence used non-linguistic communication when possible.

"Don't try to figure out who I am," the Specialist continued. "You know how this works."

Silence took in a breath to clear his momentary anger before replying. C.C. had taught him that one of the easiest ways to get oneself into a better state was to take a deep breath, from the stomach, a diaphragmatic breath.

Of course Silence knew how things worked in the Watchers, the vigilante organization of which he and the Specialist were a part. Assets like Silence—the field agents, the blunt instruments, the lowest on the totem pole—were never to know the identities of the people in higher positions.

But not only was it part of Silence's job to suss out the

truth, it was in his nature. Before being conscripted into the Watchers, he had been a police officer, working toward a detective slot, and prior to that an academic. He'd spent his life deciphering things.

Right now, though, Silence needed to remember his place, so after his deep breath, he repressed his ego and said, "Yes, sir."

The Specialist nodded, narrowing his eyes at Silence for a moment, then strolled a few feet to the side, hands in his pockets once more, looking at Ramsey's body.

Silence followed.

The Specialist tsked. "Another one bites the dust." He turned to Silence. "No need to call for cleanup. I'll get it taken care of."

Silence nodded.

Usually after a kill, Silence had to request "cleanup." He would call a direct number from his cellular phone that would connect him immediately with a Specialist.

Specialists, like the man standing with Silence now, were the lifeblood of the Watchers. While the higher-ups made the decisions and the Assets like Silence worked in the field as assassins correcting failures in procedural justice, Specialists provided weaponry, channeled money secretly around the globe, surreptitiously navigated the legal system, and provided all other logistical needs for the Watchers' mission.

More importantly, aside from logisticians, among the Specialists were the individuals who delved through judicial records and news stories to find people who had escaped the justice they deserved, the people who needed to be eliminated.

The Specialist, still grinning, shook his head as he looked at Ramsey's corpse. He tsked again then turned back to Silence and opened his messenger bag, took out a file folder, and handed it to Silence. "Falcon asked me to deliver this to you personally. Time-critical."

Silence opened the folder. On top of the stack of documents was an 8x10 color photograph—a steely-faced woman posed before a blue backdrop, an American flag to the side. She wore a dark pinstripe dress suit, white button shirt beneath. A badge hung from a lanyard halfway down her chest. She was in her late thirties or early forties, fair complexion, light auburn hair, dark eyes, and a heart-shaped face.

Silence glanced up at the Specialist, and when he did so, the other man took his hand from his pocket and checked his wristwatch. "You should be getting a call any minute now from—"

Silence's cellular phone rang. He fished it from his pocket, flipped it open. "Yes?"

"There he is!" the jovial, familiar voice exclaimed. It was Falcon, Silence's boss. "How the hell are ya, Si? Did you finish off Ramsey?"

Silence looked at the body. "Yes."

"Is the Specialist there?"

Evidently, the speaker on Silence's phone was loud, because before Silence could respond, the Specialist shouted out, "I'm here, sir!"

The Specialist laughed.

Falcon laughed.

Silence remained quiet.

"Good to hear your voice, buddy!" Falcon shouted.

Silence pulled the phone away from his ear.

"Likewise, sir!" the Specialist shouted back through his grin.

It had always amazed Silence at how jolly Falcon maintained himself in this world of underground, murderous vigilantism. Clearly he'd found a kindred spirit in this Specialist.

In a normal tone, Falcon continued. "I know this is a little unorthodox, Si, handing you an assignment so quickly after you wrapped up your latest, but time's of the essence. Do you have the file?"

"Yes."

Silence sighed. Typically he got a bit of time off between missions, a chance to recuperate his body, mind, and spirit.

But often not.

The corpse on the floor next to him hadn't even cooled, which made the file folder in Silence's hand—and the contents it surely contained, the dark deed he was about to be tasked with—feel unnaturally heavy.

"The photo on top," Falcon continued. "That's your contact. Special Agent Viola Gibbs, Florida Department of Law Enforcement. This morning, her boss put her on administrative leave for asking too many questions, the wrong questions. This flagged one of our Specialists, who looked into it and discovered what Gibbs had been investigating: a pair of murders. Flip to the next photo."

Silence did as directed, turning over the photo of Gibbs and finding another 8x10 photo, this one a gruesome crime scene—a man with a massive bloody wound to his stomach, wearing a T-shirt and pajama bottoms, curled in the fetal position on a gray herringbone rug that was soaked in his blood. Mouth open in a grimace. Eyes squeezed tight.

"Breckenridge, Colorado," Falcon said. "Victim's name: Elliott Bell. Lawyer and former Army JAG. Gunshot wound to the stomach, left to bleed to death in his living room. Next-door neighbor saw Bell arguing with an armed man, rushed over before Bell was shot, looked the guy in the eye. And saw one distinguishing characteristic: heterochromia."

"Huh?"

"Mismatched eyes. One blue, one brown. Otherwise the

neighbor described the guy as white, average height, average build, square-jawed, brown hair, parted."

"Colorado?" Silence said, squinting at the details of the image—the man's hands pressed into his wound, the hardwood floor surrounding the rug. "Why Gibbs..." He swallowed. "Investigating there?"

Investigating was a big word, lots of syllables. He grimaced at the pain in his throat.

Falcon chuckled. "Yes, why indeed. Why would a Florida *state* investigator dig into a recent murder outside of her state, way on the other side of the country? That was the detail that propelled our Specialist to look into the matter.

"Turns out, Gibbs only started looking into the Colorado killing after a murder closer to home. She's an investigator for the FDLE's northwest region, working out of your town."

The FDLE, Florida's state-level investigative agency, divided the state into seven regions, each with an operations center located in a major city. The northwest region's operational center was in Pensacola, the city where Silence lived.

"Gibbs was investigating at the far west end of her region, Panama City Beach," Falcon said. "Next slide, please."

Taking his meaning, Silence turned to the next photo in the folder.

Another dead man. And even more blood. A massive head wound with a blast-pattern puddle dotted with brain and skull sprayed onto blacktop and white parking lot stripes. From what remained of the man's face, Silence could tell that he was Hispanic. Dark hair. Dark eyes. Olive skin. A strong, square jaw. He wore a polo shirt and slacks. Muscular physique. Similar age to the first victim.

"Meet Derek Artiga," Falcon said. "Another former Army officer. He wasn't left to suffer like Bell; after he took a .45 to the temple, I imagine he was out instantaneously. Gibbs discovered a link between the Artiga's murder in Panama City and Bell's in Colorado. Seems both of them were the survivors of a failed training exercise at Eglin Air Force Base a few years back. The powers that be tried to say it was a routine exercise, but we've uncovered a codename: Hard Sprint."

Eglin was also in the northwest area of Florida, between Pensacola and Panama City.

"An explosion," Falcon continued. "Eglin's been involved in military testing since 1939, and so you'll still find UXO buried out in all that wilderness. Unexploded ordnance. Which is what Bell and Artiga's group stumbled on—a big, 500-pound World War II son of a bitch. The triggering mechanism had corroded with age, and when they set it off, ten of the seventeen people were killed. Now, years later, two of the seven survivors were murdered a day apart. Interesting, huh?"

"Yes," Silence said.

"Agent Gibbs thought so too. That's why she started poking around. Evidently she asked too many of the wrong questions. She was put on administrative leave yesterday afternoon. From 1 pm yesterday through 7 at night, she placed a total of thirty-seven phone calls from her home phone, all over the country—Illinois, Arkansas, Tennessee, Idaho, California, you name it. And she also booked a flight for later today, non-stop from Pensacola to SDF."

Silence recognized the three-letter airport code. He had hundreds of them memorized. SDF was Louisville International Airport in Kentucky.

He flipped past the photos to a stack of papers— biographical reports on Gibbs, Bell, and Artiga, something that a Specialist would have prepared. He let the full contents of the folder drop back into place, and the top photograph stared at him once more.

Special Agent Gibbs. He noticed again that steely countenance, but as he studied it more intently, he detected subtler details. There was a bit of pride at the corners of her lips, sparkle in the eyes. C.C. had often told Silence that he had an empathic quality, that he was good at reading people—deciphering their stories, connecting with their vibration. Viola Gibbs gave Silence the impression of a person who had climbed higher than anyone thought she would, who had clawed her way to success inch by inch.

"Any questions?" Falcon said.

"No."

"Good luck, Suppressor."

Click.

He was gone.

Silence closed the folder, looked up, found the blond-headed Specialist staring at him with that grin of his. The man motioned with his head toward the opposite end of the warehouse. "Drive you to the airport."

The Specialist turned, and Silence caught up with him, fell into step beside him. Their footsteps echoed off the rusty metal vista that engulfed them, sounding hollow and resonant.

Two figures inching across a ruined industrial expanse, like a dystopian version of a John Ford panorama.

The Specialist took out a mobile phone, pressed and held a button for speed-dial. Almost instantaneously, Silence heard a greeting from the speaker, and then the Specialist said, "Cleanup needed. Mendocino, California."

A pause as he listened.

"An address? Hmm…"

He looked at Silence, who shrugged.

"Old factory off Shoreline Highway. Use the Asset's GPS dot."

Silence, like all Assets, had a GPS dot embedded in his right arm.

The Specialist chuckled as he listened to the response from the other end of the phone, and his eyes went to the opposite side of the massive building, their destination, far in the distance. "We'll be here for a bit longer, not to worry."

Another pause.

"Very good."

He ended the call, collapsed the phone, and dropped it in his pocket.

Again their footsteps echoed off faraway planes of rotten metal. The Specialist gave Silence a once-over, scanning him up and down.

"Looks like you and Ramsey had a little bit of fun there at the end of the mission, huh?"

Silence grunted.

"You can clean up on the jet," the Specialist said. "Grab a shower. Nice meal. Change of clothes. In the meantime..."

He reached into his messenger bag.

"I understand this is your brand."

He handed Silence a green bottle.

A Heineken.

Ice-cold. Dappled with moisture.

Silence tore off the cap, threw it into the nothingness surrounding them, and swigged greedily. Three big gulps, and half the beer was gone.

He pulled the bottle from his lips. Panting. Smiling.

Generally, the Watchers treated him, and all the other field agents, like tools, like pawns. Indeed, that's why they were called "Assets." Each of them was a criminal, a righteous individual who had committed a heinous act, liberated from their judicially imposed sentence and conscripted into a society of murderous vigilantism until their debt had been paid off. The Watchers instructed their Assets to perform unthinkable acts that had slim chances of survival.

Paradoxically, the Watchers also treated Assets like

royalty with many fringe benefits such as the luxurious private jet that Silence was about to board to cross the country.

And they paid attention to Assets' personal tastes, expressed through small but unbelievably endearing gestures.

Like bringing a tired man who'd just been pushed to the edge for three weeks a cold bottle of his favorite beer.

The Specialist watched as Silence took another swig, then clamped his hand on his shoulder, gave it a squeeze.

Silence walked with this person—someone he just met, a superior, a man he wasn't supposed to have ever seen, a friend who wasn't a friend—and readied his mind for another foray into the dark and deadly.

CHAPTER FOUR

PENSACOLA, FLORIDA

As VIOLA GIBBS rushed through her house, grabbing clothes and toiletries and other bare essentials, a bizarre, almost surreal notion struck her—she might never see this place again.

The major ramifications of what she was about to embark on had already crossed her mind, of course. Yesterday, at the moment she decided to head across the country on an unlicensed investigation—doing so as a special agent from a state law enforcement agency, one who had recently been placed on administrative leave—she knew that she could very well be forfeiting her career, her reputation, and her very future.

What she hadn't considered were the small details.

If her life was to be forfeited, so too were the incremental components that constituted her life. Such as her house. It was a nice place, a few years old. Three-bedroom, two-bath. In a quiet, safe neighborhood brimming with shady oaks and, in the patches of sunlight that the oaks permitted, lush green lawns and lazy palm trees.

Gibbs had never needed status symbols, but as she grew older, she realized she'd spent far too many years and expended way too much energy trying to stay grounded, to be humble. She'd subconsciously convinced herself that money and success were bad things, and she'd held herself back. Being humble was one thing, but if you keep yourself too grounded, you're never going to soar.

So she loved this house—a place that her prior, years-earlier self would have labeled as "snooty"—and it broke her heart that she now felt unsafe within its walls.

The previous night had been spent at a motel. She'd paid in cash. And now she was trying to spend as little time as possible in the home before she left Pensacola.

To leave Florida and face this bizarre mission she'd forced upon herself.

She leaned over the kitchen sink, peered through the sheer drapery to the street beyond. Mrs. Longworth's minivan and Tom's Celica and other neighborhood regulars. Right in front of her house was the yellow taxi, waiting for her. She'd left her car in a parking structure downtown last night and had been using taxis since, the better to shake off anyone who might be following.

No pitch-black cars with pitch-black window tinting waiting on her street. No ominous looking panel vans. Nobody looking toward her house with a finger pressed against an ear-worn listening device.

But maybe Gibbs was thinking about this all wrong. Maybe she was looking for too many Hollywood stereotypes.

Maybe they'd come in a plain-Jane, ho-hum vehicle—something like Tom's Celica over there—and when they approached the house, maybe they wouldn't be wearing dark suits and sunglasses but rather street clothes—T-shirts and jeans, trying to blend in with their environment. That made more sense.

Hurry.

She stepped to the refrigerator, grabbed a half-full bottle of Gatorade and two Aquafinas, tossed them in her duffel bag, and went back to her bedroom.

She'd forgotten underwear. There could very well be government men after her, ready to whisk her away to "an undisclosed location," and she had to make a U-turn for panties of all things, dammit.

She yanked open the drawer with a *clunk*, grabbed a handful of her unmentionables, threw them in the bag.

And halted.

Thump.

Something from the other side of the house. A small thud. From the floorboards? The front door?

Her breath shuddered, and she cursed herself once more for locking her gun in the safe already. That should have been her *last* step before leaving the house, not the first.

She listened.

The *tick, tick, tick* of the clock in the living room.

And her heart. Thundering in her chest.

Most people were afraid of spiders or murderers or ghosts or demons.

Gibbs, though, was afraid of only one thing in this world.

Men in black.

Individuals from government or quasi-government organizations. Dark-suited, sunglass-wearing men who had the mission of silencing people who asked too many questions.

These were the shadow characters of 1950s and 1960s lore —both science fiction and supposed real encounters. As a child in the '60s, Gibbs's father had been a fan of sci-fi novels and film and television, and so she'd been the unenthusiastic consumer of such tales during many of her formative years.

But while her father had been unsuccessful in fostering a love of sci-fi in his daughter, he had brought forth a prominent phobia, which had followed Gibbs into adulthood, fueled by Hollywood's continued obsession with shadowy government characters. Recently her fears had only been exacerbated by that new show, *The X-Files*.

This phobia was an integral part of Gibbs's decision to become a special agent herself, which she treated as an exercise in facing one's fears. She'd needed to show herself that governmental institutions were manned by *real* people, not shadowy figures.

And as a state agent, she'd had several direct encounters with federal agents—typically from the FBI but also other agencies like the DEA and ATF. These had been nerve-racking encounters for her, but she'd seen that the government men and women were indeed real people, not specters.

She'd faced her fear.

And fully convinced herself of how silly she'd been all her life, even if she still got the heebie-jeebies sometimes.

Then *this* happened—her investigation suddenly getting called off after pressure from unknown sources, being placed on administrative leave.

There were forces after her. She could feel them.

She was living her own nightmare.

Another breath. Deeper. Through her nose.

Quiet, she told herself. *Listen.*

The clock ticked. The muffled sound of laughter from a neighbor somewhere in the distance. A car slowly drifting past the front side of her house.

Tick, tick, tick.

One more deep breath.

Then she sprinted through the house, eyes going shut of their own accord. Through the kitchen door.

And outside.

She sucked in a deep breath of warm Florida air.

The sun was painfully bright, and she threw on her

sunglasses then rushed down the sidewalk toward the idling taxi. Only a few feet ahead, but it looked a mile away. Trees. Bushes. A park bench. People she didn't recognize looking in her direction.

She waited for the sensation—hands grabbing her arms, a quick thrust and a change of momentum, tossed into the back of one of the blacked-out vehicles that she'd imagined when she looked through the kitchen window minutes earlier.

But before that could happen, she was in the taxi's frigid air conditioning and stale cigarette stench.

"Let's go," she told the cabbie.

The car took off, and Gibbs purposefully declined a backward glance at her beloved little house.

Now, one more stop to make in Pensacola.

––––––––

Martin, the security guard, gave her a bizarre look as he took the plastic tray holding her keys, purse, and sunglasses and waved her through the metal detector.

There were more bizarre looks as she crossed the lobby— her heels *click-clack*ing on the polished marble—and headed for the elevators. She could feel their eyes, every last one of them. They knew she wasn't supposed to be there, and they knew *why* she wasn't supposed to be there. Men in suits and women in dress skirts, staring but trying to be inconspicuous. Whispers that carried up the stone walls.

As she entered the elevator and turned around, she looked back into the lobby, her gaze roaming, finding the gawkers. Their eyes darted away as if they hadn't just been staring at her. One person tried, and failed, to conceal a snicker.

The doors closed, squeezing her view of the lobby out of existence.

A fresh wave of stares came as she exited the elevator onto the third floor, these more intense and more puzzled than those in the lobby. The whispers were more plentiful, a bit louder.

She traversed the open work area full of cubicles, using the pathway that traced the far side of the space, by the offices. She breezed past her own office—its door closed, the window darkened with its blinds closed tight—and to the back of the office space, where she threw open the door of room 317.

Lance Caldwell bolted from his chair, eyes momentarily going wide behind his half-rim glasses, before his shock was replaced with exasperation.

"Viola..." he sighed. "Why are you back here?"

Gibbs pushed into the office, which had an aesthetic as blandly utilitarian as the rows of binders and training manuals lining the shelves on the back wall. The only splashes of life were a single houseplant in the corner and a train of framed personal photos behind the desk, and these details seemed as regulated as the memorandums and criminal reports thumb-tacked to the bulletin board, as though Caldwell had felt obligated, not inspired, to include them.

She shoved a chair out of her way and stopped a foot away from the desk, planting a fist in her hip.

"'Viola,' is it? You always use first names when you're trying to smooth things over with someone whose ass you just reamed, don't you 'Lance'? Did they teach you that in how-to-be-a-douchebag-leader school?"

Caldwell stuck his hands in his pockets and slowly moved around the desk, his head bobbing in that birdlike manner of his. With his flyaway hair—cut short but still untamable—and the loose skin on his neck, Caldwell's physique and mannerisms made him as much avian as human. He certainly liked to strut around like a peacock. And when real danger arose, he flew far, far away.

He repeated himself, using a tone that was quieter but sterner. "Why are you here?"

"Because it's not right, and you know it's not right, and I want a damn explanation. Whatever I stumbled on—somebody wants it to stay quiet, otherwise you wouldn't have shut me down immediately. Who was it, Caldwell?"

"That's Special Agent Supervisor Caldwell."

"What happened to 'Viola' and 'Lance'? Who *was* it? FBI? The statehouse? *Tell me!*"

Though she was questioning him so emphatically, almost screaming, part of Gibbs *didn't* want an answer. For the director of an FDLE operations center—even a worm like Caldwell—to place one of his agents on sudden leave without a full explanation, the outside force must have been extremely potent.

Her mind flashed on men in dark suits with dark glasses. Stern stares. Someone being beaten in a dark, windowless room. A woman. Her.

Caldwell plopped his ass on the edge of his desk, crossed his arms, his legs, casual but stern, mediating but administrative, more wannabe leader posturing.

"You know I can't do that. I have people I answer to just as you have to answer to me."

"I answer to no one now. I'm on leave, remember? Last chance. *Who. Was. It?*"

"You crossed a line. There are certain questions that just don't get asked, not even by us." Caldwell sighed again, and this time it came out almost as a grumble. "Viola, I know you well enough to know that you're not going to let this thing go. Just ... tell me you're not gonna do something stupid. Please, tell me that."

"I'll do whatever I want during this vacation that's been

thrust upon me." She stepped even closer, close enough to see that her boss hadn't shaved that morning, white whiskers twinkling on his turkey neck. "Right is right, Special Agent Supervisor Caldwell."

She spun around, crossed the room, flung open the door, and left.

———

Two minutes later, after a quick nod to Martin, the security guard—whose befuddlement hadn't diminished while Gibbs was upstairs—she threw on her sunglasses as she descended the granite steps outside the building's revolving entrance and went to the taxi, which had waited right outside.

The cabbie looked at her from the rearview as she climbed back into the air conditioning.

"Airport," she said.

CHAPTER FIVE

AN HOUR LATER, in a different area of Pensacola—the quirky, quiet, quixotic neighborhood of East Hill—Silence let out a small sigh as he took the concrete steps up onto the oversized porch of his mid-century home.

Stepping beneath the overhang brought instant relief from the blazing sun, though the tomato-soup-thick humidity was still bothersome. There would be an even bigger rush of relief momentarily, once he opened the door in front of him and stepped into the air conditioning, which he always kept cranked sky-high.

He glanced to the left, to another porch, the one belonging to the much older home a few feet away, separated from his own by a gravel drive. The other porch was deserted—no one in the rocking chairs or porch swing.

Good.

He loved Mrs. Enfield, his blind, ancient, next-door neighbor, but sometimes her reciprocal love was overwhelming, particularly when Silence needed alone time. And right now he needed some alone time before he embarked on his upcoming assignment in earnest.

Because something had been bothering him since he left California.

He peered around the corner and through his neighbor's window. There she was. A tiny black woman with a shock of white hair, slumped in an antique armchair, chin at her chest, which lifted and sank slowly, rhythmically. Asleep.

Silence couldn't see it, but he knew that on the small table in front of her would be her CD player, offering up a radio program from decades earlier. "Listening to her stories," as she called it. She had a copious number of these compilation discs, which she'd collected through the generosity of her friend and former caretaker, Lola.

Silence turned the key, and the deadbolt thunked out of the way, and as he pushed through the door, the air conditioning struck him as a magnificently frigid blast. His 1955 house had a shotgun-style layout, the boundaries of the living spaces ill-defined, what would be called, in 1990s terminology, "open-layout." The dining area was just beyond the door, and past that was the kitchen. On the opposite side was the living room area. At the back, a hallway that separated two bedrooms and led to a storage space.

Though the house was several decades old, the Watchers had updated it to Silence's chic tastes. Everything was grays and blacks and whites with accents of polished chrome, stainless steel, brushed nickel. Splashes of color came in the form of bright greens—big tropical indoor plants that local nurseries had assured him were neglect-resistant. Silence had neither a green thumb nor the time to care for needy flora.

He stepped around the shiny dining room table and dropped his jacket on one of the stainless steel chairs that surrounded it. Into the kitchen, past the dark gray cabinetry that he had installed shortly after he moved in, and to the gleaming black refrigerator.

Throwing open the door, he got another gust of cold air.

A six-pack of Heineken sat dead-center on the top shelf. Beside it was a stack of three cartons of eggs. On the shelf below was a pack of pudding cups. Otherwise, the fridge was empty.

His adventures in Mendocino had kept him away for two weeks, so naturally his supplies were low, but even when he was home, readily available provisions were scarce. He was hopelessly feeble in the kitchen. Once he'd triggered a smoke alarm while making popcorn.

Microwavable popcorn.

He eyed the egg cartons. He ate a lot of eggs. His dead fiancée, C.C., was a vegetarian, and since much of Silence's life was in honor to her, he consumed much less meat than he had before her death.

But C.C. hadn't simply abstained from eating meat; she hadn't eaten animal products of any sort. She predicted that this would be a new trend in the twenty-first century, a subset of vegetarianism called "veganism."

But while Silence skipped out on a lot of opportunities to scarf down mouthwatering ribs and juicy steaks to appease the deceased love of his life, he simply couldn't avoid eating *any* animal products at all. Just couldn't do it.

Hence the reason he ate so many eggs.

At the moment, though, he was too tired to whip up eggs. So he opened the freezer. One item. Centered on the top shelf, upright, as though on display, waiting for him.

A microwavable hamburger.

Sorry, C.C.

It came complete with two patties, bun, cheese, and pickles. It was even pre-loaded with ketchup and mustard. Silence grabbed the small box and was about to turn it over to check out the nutrition information before quickly stopping himself. The thing had to be a cornucopia of man-made additives—preservatives and food colorings and fillers. Ignorance was his best bet.

He popped it in the microwave.

One minutes and forty-five seconds later, the kitchen smelled scrumptious, and he retrieved the steaming bit of chemical heaven from its paper box, grabbed a Heiny from the fridge, and headed to the couch.

In the few feet of travel, his mind again went back to Mendocino.

He'd completed the assignment. He'd eliminated Simon Ramsey. But it had been dicey at the end, which was why Silence had to chase the guy into the abandoned factory.

And the situation had only gotten dicey because of Silence's misstep.

During the last couple of days in California, Silence had felt that Ramsey was about to leave town, but he'd ignored that instinct. It was only when he'd passed Ramsey on the highway—their cars going in opposite directions—that he'd known Ramsey was indeed trying to leave town. Had it not been for this chance encounter, Silence would almost certainly still be hunting the man down, trailing him through California or somewhere else in the U.S. or anywhere in the wide world.

Or...

Silence could have lost the scumbag altogether. He could have failed his mission.

He should have listened to his gut.

C.C. had always told him to do just that—to trust his instincts, to follow his intuition. She'd said that while Silence regularly utilized his ability to read people, doing so was the only way in which he put faith in his humanistic side. And she was right. Silence let cold, hard facts guide him in the field.

Typically, this was exactly what was needed. But there

were other times when things went south because he didn't listen to his center, that part of him that C.C. tried to get him to connect with via meditation and other esoteric means.

The times he hadn't listened to this part of himself often ended poorly. Like almost losing track of Simon Ramsey.

He plopped onto his sectional sofa, a long, gray, squarish stretch of non-tufted fabric with firm but comfortable cushions. He leaned forward and thumbed a slate coaster across the coffee table—the felt feet making a soft but harmless scratching sound against the glass surface—then deposited the scalding-hot box, taking another deep inhale of the alluring steam.

He twisted the cap off the beer and threw back a swig. The experience wasn't quite as wondrous as the Heineken that the Specialist had given him back in the warehouse at Mendocino, but damned if it didn't taste good, this tiniest respite of tactile enjoyment, a fraction of joy and normalcy before returning to his life of violence.

He brought the rim back to his lips.

RING!

The phone on the end table beside him.

The Watchers almost never called his house phone, opting instead for his cellular. They certainly wouldn't call him when at home while he was working an assignment, and he most certainly was on assignment again with this new Viola Gibbs job.

The phone call could be from only one person...

RING!

He exhaled. And answered.

"Hello?"

"Si?"

It was a voice as minuscule and wrinkled as its bearer.

"Thought that was you I heard a few minutes ago," Rita Enfield said. "You woke me up."

"Sorry."

Blindness had amplified the old woman's hearing. Silence wasn't sure if this was the reason she was such a light sleeper or if it came naturally. He suspected it was a bit of both.

"Whatcha doin'?" Mrs. Enfield asked.

"Having late lunch."

"Oh... Well, bring it over here. You don't need to eat alone."

I like eating alone, Silence thought.

But he said, "Yes, ma'am."

You don't argue with a little old blind lady who adores you.

He looked at the beer in his hand. When Silence had first met Mrs. Enfield years earlier, when he moved into this house, he was living in a state of drunken denial over C.C.'s then-recent murder. Mrs. Enfield had taken it upon herself to curb his drinking habit and had done so successfully. But she'd also done so excessively, to the point where she believed that *any* drinking on Silence's part meant he was slipping back into his old habits.

This wasn't the case at all. Silence hadn't been drunk once since he had agreed to Mrs. Enfield's insistence so many years ago. He'd rarely even gotten tipsy. But he enjoyed his occasional Heineken.

He rubbed his thumb along the cold green glass.

She'd smell it on his breath, the one gulp he'd had before he answered the phone.

He squinted at the bottle, watching as the beer undulated gently with the movement of his hand.

Might as well.

He downed the rest of it.

————

"You've been drinking, haven't you?" Mrs. Enfield said.

"One beer."

Mrs. Enfield grumbled.

Her house was a Victorian beauty, but while its charms could have been an asset in the right design-conscious hands, somehow the antique quality of the place had taken on a creepy vibe under Mrs. Enfield's ownership.

It was always too dark, which made logical sense, being the home of a blind lady, and while she was a tidy person and kept thing spotless, there was still a feeling of dustiness about the place. The decor was eerie and old, and Mrs. Enfield's own ancientness only served to amplified the vibe to a level of macabre.

There was one tiny, glass-shaded lamp alight in the living room. Mrs. Enfield sat in a clawfoot chair, and Silence was across from her in a musty loveseat. On the table between them was the CD player, still relaying her "story," volume lowered.

Though the chair was small, it still dwarfed Mrs. Enfield. She was as tiny as she was frail. Though age had done nothing to diminish her spirit, it had completely enveloped her physical vessel, wrinkling her dark brown skin into a contour map, bleaching her hair as white as her functionless eyes.

A massive orange tabby with a head like a linebacker covered the old woman's lap. Baxter purred and stared at Silence through squinted, happy eyes as a string of drool dangled from the corner of his mouth, glistening in the muted lighting. The little guy was seldom without his cat smile, and his drooling was just as much a constancy.

"I'm glad you're home," Mrs. Enfield said.

"Leaving again soon," Silence said and grimaced when the last syllable hit his destroyed throat the wrong way. He swallowed, lubricating. "Sorry."

Mrs. Enfield's shoulders drooped. "That job sure does keep you busy."

"Yes," Silence agreed.

As with Mrs. Enfield's monitoring of Silence's drinking problem in the first days of their association, Mrs. Enfield had also, very early on, perceived that he was in a violent line of work. She was an incredibly intuitive individual and also street-smart; therefore she understood that if her new neighbor wasn't a cop, wasn't military, wasn't a martial arts instructor, then she probably shouldn't ask too many questions about the violence in which he was involved. It was a self-preserving policy, but she still cared. So while she didn't ask *specific* questions, she still asked many questions.

"You seem distracted," she said.

More of that unnaturally keen perception of hers. She might not have been able to see, but she never missed a thing.

There was no use in trying to elude her. She was too damn good. So he simply said, "I am."

"How so?"

Silence thought for a moment. "Because I almost..." He swallowed. "Messed something up." He swallowed. "Because didn't listen to gut."

Mrs. Enfield's blank, white eyes gazed at him. She nodded as she absentmindedly rubbed Baxter's head. The cat leaned into this simple pleasure, eyes closing, the volume level of his purring increasing a couple of degrees.

"You can't always trust what you see, Silence. Remember that."

Silence felt like being a smartass. "You can't see at all."

Mrs. Enfield gently pushed Baxter aside, straightened out of her chair, leaned over the table, and flicked Silence's ear.

A sharp pulse of pain, and Silence jumped in his seat. On a daily basis he witnessed Mrs. Enfield's hands struggle to find doorknobs and glasses of water and even Baxter, but when it came time to flick Silence's ear—which she did more often than one would think—she had amazing accuracy. The precision of a laser-guided missile.

Silence put a hand to his ear. The flesh was warm from the impact.

"Don't sass me, boy," Mrs. Enfield said as she settled back into her chair. There was a little blip in the purring as Baxter settled back into place on her thigh.

Silence gave his ear one final rub and placed his hands across his lap. "Yes, ma'am."

Mrs. Enfield gave a curt nod of the head and a self-confirming, "Mmm-hmm."

There was a moment of quiet, just the ticking of a pair of gothic, nightmare-inducing clocks from the opposite side of the room and a sound to which he was unaccustomed in her house: dripping water.

Then Mrs. Enfield said, "You'll be around for the rest of the day, at least?"

"No. Leaving..." He swallowed. "In an hour."

Mrs. Enfield's shoulders dropped again. "Oh." She scooted Baxter a little closer. "Well, do you have time to fix my sink?"

She pointed a bony finger to her right.

Through the open doorway, Silence saw the source of the dripping sound: the kitchen sink.

"Of course."

CHAPTER SIX

RHETT, the bartender, walked up—bottle in hand, smile on his lips—and glanced dramatically at his wristwatch.

"Three hours..." he said. "I'm thinking you either really like hanging out at the airport, or you just like my company."

He gave Gibbs a grin, big and toothy, effortlessly charming. His cologne was apparent but not overpowering, sweet but masculine. He was no older than twenty-two or twenty-three, which meant he was about fifteen years Gibbs's junior. And the fact that he continued to be so friendly, so borderline flirty, for hours on end, even after Gibbs had remained unapproachable, meant that this was all an act, one that he surely gave to every female who fell into a barstool at this corporate bar and grille at Pensacola International Airport.

It was a compact version of the restaurant chain's standard offerings, with slight changes to the decor in the form of superimposed images of airplanes and Pensacola landmarks adorning the walls. Menu cropped, prices hiked.

Rhett raised the bottle of rum, gave it a little shake that he paired with a lifting of the eyebrows, a non-verbal: *One more?*

Gibbs glanced over his shoulder, to the clock mounted on the mirrored wall behind him, flanked by rows of liquor bottles. Only forty-five more minutes.

She shook her head, slid off the stool and reached into her purse, took a fifty from her wallet, and dropped it on the bar. Three overpriced rum-and-Cokes and a decent tip for young Mr. Charming.

"Thanks, Rhett."

"Enjoy Kentucky," he said. And then, through another glistening smile, he added, "See you soon."

As she stepped out of the relative darkness of the restaurant and into the bright hallway, she wavered slightly. She'd had one too many, and Rhett had been pouring them strong.

And she hadn't eaten in over eighteen hours.

She straightened up, brought her shoulders back, recomposed herself. The Gate 9 sign was ahead, at the far end of the airport's single terminal. Her two-inch, chunky heels clacked on the polished flooring as she navigated the crowd. Pensacola International wasn't a big airport, but the Pensacola region was a vacation destination, and it was early spring break season, so the crowd was thick, full of chatter and laughter and the smell of sunscreen.

After maintaining her composure for the entire brief walk, she wobbled again as she dropped into one of the vinyl seats near her gate. Her stomach churned with alcohol, nerves, and hunger. She'd get something to eat on the plane, an eight-dollar sandwich, perhaps.

But no ten-dollar glass of wine, that was for sure.

She looked through the wall of windows to her left—the tarmac beyond, bright in the sun, a palm tree close to the glass, listing in the breeze—then glanced to the monitors above the desk a few feet away, the flight information and boarding times.

Before her eyes made it to the screens, she met someone's gaze.

He was across from her, in the row of seats facing hers. Massive proportions, long arms and legs that toppled over the thin seat cushion and the minuscule polished tubing of his chair, a spider poised on a web. Cheeks hewn at sharp angles. A harsh line of a jaw. Exotic. Attractive.

And staring right at her, dark eyes unblinking.

Gibbs knew who he was. Who he *had* to be. She'd dug into the murders too deeply and way too quickly.

Caldwell's words flashed through her mind: *There are certain questions that just don't get asked, not even by us.*

She'd thought Caldwell was a coward. Now she was beginning to respect his wisdom.

Because this person in front of her was some sort of governmental professional. A no-man. A man in black. A killer from the CIA's Special Activities Division, perhaps.

She'd almost made it. She'd gotten all the way to the airport before they tracked her down, right to her terminal, forty-five minutes before she was to leave.

She studied the man's suit.

A black suit.

Shit...

Yes, he was one of the infamous men in black, though he wore the dark suit differently than the clichéd image in her mind. It was well-tailored and form-fitting, not boxy and by-the-books bureaucratic. And he wasn't wearing a tie. In fact, his white shirt was splayed open several buttons, the collars lying over the lapels, revealing a silver chain that draped down his chest. The shirt's material looked expensive with a subtle texturing—herringbone, maybe. Stylish shades peeked out of his jacket pocket.

Maybe he was a bit cooler than your average governmental shadow figure, but there was no doubt in Gibbs's mind that he was from a clandestine agency.

As evidenced by the stare he was giving her.

And entirely confirmed when he stood up and moved toward her.

She had to crane up to continue their unbroken gaze. The man was easily six-foot-three. In two steps, he'd crossed the space between the rows of seats.

Before he sat, he gave a concerted glance to a man in the row of seats by the windows, who was staring at him. The guy was in his thirties, blond, and the bright yellow tank top, turquoise shorts, and cheap plastic sunglasses said he wasn't quite ready to leave Florida. When the large man's gaze found the nosy tourist, the latter quickly hid behind his magazine.

The man in black slid into the seat beside her and finally looked away, momentarily, as he plunged a hand into his pocket.

Gibbs's heart jumped, mind raced—*knife, hypodermic, pistol, muzzle*—and she immediately admonished her foolish paranoia. Whoever the guy was, he wouldn't pull a weapon in the middle of an airport.

He retrieved his wallet, produced a card, and reached it toward her, his dark gaze returning. She hesitated before taking it.

At first she thought it was a swipe card—it was plastic with the right proportions and rounded corners—but as she turned it over, she found no magstripe on the back. The plastic was opaque; she could see her palm through it. A pair of dark blue stripes cut diagonally down the left side, and dark blue, raised lettering gave a message:

MY ORGANIZATION IS AWARE OF YOUR SITUATION.

WE UNDERSTAND NORMAL CHANNELS HAVE FAILED YOU.

WE HAVE THE MEANS TO ASSIST.

PLEASE EXCUSE THIS FORM OF INTRODUCTION.

I AM NOT MUTE, BUT SPEAKING IS PAINFUL.

I AM HERE TO HELP.

The first two words...

My organization

Oh God... Oh God...

Gibbs's heart thundered. She looked back up, found the cold brown eyes waiting for her.

"Talk," the man said.

Gibbs jumped in her seat. The man's voice was alarming. Horrendous. He sounded like a cement mixer. Deep and awful, crackling.

A scare tactic. Throwing a person off-guard was a powerful technique, one used by interviewers and police interrogators and torturers alike.

The man's bizarre voice was over-the-top. *Way* over-the-top.

But effective.

Because he had definitely thrown her off-guard.

She tried to speak. Couldn't. Her lips moved, but only puttering sounds came out. She felt weak, pathetic.

"You're not—" the man said, his terrible voice coming to a sudden halt. He grimaced and swallowed—a pronounced action that made his Adam's apple bob. "Boarding this flight."

He'd pointed to the jetway outside as he said it. Then he

returned his attention to Gibbs while leaving his arm extended and pointing in a slightly different direction.

"We have alternate…" Another swallow. "Flight to Louisville."

Gibbs followed his finger. In the distance, away from the commercial airliners, a lone Learjet glistened in the Florida sun.

Gibbs gripped the armrests. Her palms were sweaty against the vinyl.

Oh, shit!

The man's eyes remained locked on her. His expression was cold yet blank.

She tried to speak. Still couldn't.

The man motioned with his head toward the window again. "Will explain outside." He swallowed. "Please come with me."

She broke away from his awful stare, looked down the hallway, teeming with people. Moments earlier, she'd determined that the man wouldn't draw a weapon.

No, this guy wouldn't make a scene. He couldn't risk it.

She turned back to him and finally found her voice.

"Up yours," she said.

She grabbed her purse and bag and hopped out of her seat and into the aisle.

Yes, she could find another way to Louisville. Hell, she could just drive. It would only take ten hours or so, not a horrible delay.

She looked over her shoulder.

And found the dark eyes.

He was following, right behind her, only a few yards back, his tall figure towering over the others, casually shouldering past a group of laughing, luggage-laden tourists as he closed the gap.

She spun around, picked up the pace, heels cracking on the floor.

"Excuse me!" she said, nearly shouted, as she dodged a stationary elderly couple.

She stole another glance to the rear.

Gone.

The man was nowhere to be seen.

What the hell?

She slowed down, pulled to the side, searched the crowd. But couldn't find the handsome, cruel face bobbing over all the other heads.

A couple of breaths, and she refocused, coaxing rationality.

The guy must have pulled away to place a cellular call. Reinforcements. Which meant there would be others outside, waiting for her.

And probably *inside* too...

She scanned the crowd again, looking for any other sinister, suit-wearing men or women, anyone with a finger to his ear, listening to a secret communication device, anyone with a cold stare aimed in her direction.

She took off.

A cab. She'd get a cab.

Yes, she'd pay in cash, have the cabbie take her to a car rental place. But not one at the airport. She needed to get away from here.

Then she'd rent a vehicle, paying in cash once again, and head toward Kentucky, at which point—

An arm jutted in front of her, the hand smacking into the wall hard.

She stifled a scream and came to an abrupt stop.

The dark man stood before her, looking down at her.

"Be cool," the man said, still using the growly voice. "We're a couple." He swallowed. "We're having argument."

He reached into his pocket, retrieved a small notebook, and extended it to her. A handwritten note.

The man swallowed. "Read this."

But she didn't take the notebook. Instead, she swung her elbow sharply to the side, shattering a glass display window—a jewelry store that had not yet opened shop for the day.

An alarm screeched, piercingly loud. Screams from the others surrounding them. And a split-second look of astonishment from the shadow man.

She used this fraction of a moment when she'd turned the tables on him—caught *him* off-guard—and swung her knee up hard into his crotch.

He didn't buckle. He hardly even bent. But it was enough to get her free.

She darted away, through the crowd, turned into a short hallway. The door at the end bore a push bar and a red warning sign: *EMERGENCY EXIT ONLY*.

She crashed through the door, into the blazing sun, the thick humidity. Instantly a new alarm blared, even louder, even shriller, drowning out the store's system.

An alarm worthy of an international airport.

She glanced behind. Just before the door shut, she caught a glimpse of pandemonium in the terminal.

And the dark man bolting down the short hallway toward the door.

She was on a small landing with a set of metal stairs that led to the tarmac below. She scuttled down the steps, one of her heels catching on the diamond-pattern grip, nearly falling.

Bang!

The heavy metal door slammed open behind her. The man came after her, bounding down the steps.

Wailing sirens. Four police cars, blue lights flashing. One came from the parking lot, another from the parking structure, and a pair of them were on the runway.

She sprinted, stumbling in her heels. The man's presence loomed behind. She couldn't hear him, not over the screaming sirens and blaring alarm, but she could feel him.

She looked over her shoulder.

He was there. Only feet away.

Faster. Faster, dammit!

Heavy footsteps behind her, approaching rapidly. He was so close she could hear him even over the sirens.

Suddenly, the siren sound spiked, making her reach for her ears. One of the cars was right in front of her, headed toward her, lights flashing.

Shit! She was stuck between the two of them—the man in black and the squad car.

Something brushed her back. The man. His fingertips. Tugging at her suit jacket. She bounded forward, avoided him.

The cop car twisted to the side, pulling to a screeching lateral stop right in front of her. Smoke billowed from the tires, the pungent smell of scorched rubber.

Powerful arms, machine strength, grabbed her from behind, around her waist, lifted her off the ground.

She swung, kicked, pummeled.

In front of her, the cop car's passenger-side window went down with a mechanical buzz.

And revealed a smiling face.

Smiling!

"Need a ride?" the cop said.

In a flurry of motion, the rear door came open, the shadow man wrangled her into the backseat, and the car took off, inertia plastering her into the seat.

The car rocketed away from the airport.

Gibbs panted, caught a whiff of the car's musty interior —old vinyl and stale sweat. The shadow man was beside her on the bench seat. In the front seat, the cop whistled and patted his hand on the steering wheel as they zoomed away.

Then Gibbs saw where they were headed—the Learjet that the shadow man had pointed at earlier.

She turned in her seat, looked out the back window. Chaos at the main terminal, which grew smaller in the distance. Cops and emergency vehicles, hysterical throngs of people visible through the walls of windows. All the energy was focused at the far end of the building, by Gate 9.

Except for this single cop car barreling away to the Learjet.

This was it. Gibbs was done for. Whoever these people were, they were whisking her off to somewhere that was sure to be awful.

As she faced the front again, the cop silenced the siren, which made his whistling more pronounced. Gibbs turned to the man beside her, found that now-familiar stare.

"Who are you?" she said.

The man didn't reply, just reached into his pocket and handed her the small notebook he'd tried to show her back at the airport. It was open to the same note she'd seen moments earlier.

I know who you must think I am. I'm not with the govern-ment. My group works within the government. I'm investi-gating the same murders you are. Let's collaborate.

An extra-governmental institution that investigated murders? No, Gibbs refused to believe it.

She looked up. "FBI?"

The man shook his head.

"CIA? That's it, isn't it? Special Activities?"

The man shook his head again. "Not government. *Within* the government."

Gibbs scoffed. "Yeah. Right. So, what, are you like the A-Team or something?"

She'd said it with oozing sarcasm, but the man was unaffected, shrugging it off.

"But with more..." He swallowed. "Resources."

A cold sensation flashed over Gibbs, prickling the hairs on her arms.

The guy was serious.

If she wasn't in the back of an apparently commandeered squad car, lights flashing, barreling across an airport to a waiting Learjet, she would have assumed the man was a lunatic.

But something told her this was all real.

She looked at the note again, the last sentence.

"'Let's collaborate,'" she read and met the man's stare again. "And if I refuse?"

The man took the notebook back and with a twist of the wrist closed it, swinging the plastic front cover around the spiral binding and into position.

"You have no choice," he said as he slipped the notebook back into his pocket.

CHAPTER SEVEN

SILENCE WATCHED the woman sitting across from him in the plush leather chair, which was bone white and overstuffed, part of the plane's black-and-white-themed interior.

Viola Gibbs.

By the time he'd gotten her to the plane, her ferocious and tenacious resistance that had created the chaos back at the airport had waned. It was as though she had accepted her fate. Resistance had turned into hesitance.

She had avoided eye contact with him the entire time—from when they went up the air stairs into the cabin, when he took his seat and instructed her as to which seat to take, through takeoff, and for the first few minutes of the flight. And while she was rigid with discomfort and undoubtedly a shit ton of fear, she also surreptitiously glanced about the cabin, and her eyes couldn't hide how impressed she was with the opulence of the jet, which led Silence down a line of deductions.

She was clearly a successful individual. Making one of the state agencies was no small task, so she was surely educated, and she was surely making a decent paycheck. But something about her reaction to the plane also told Silence that she wasn't used to such luxuries, despite how large her paycheck might be. He imagined she had a humble upbringing and that she didn't take too many vacations, didn't allow herself too many fancy meals and fancy clothes. Indeed, the clothing she wore was high quality but not extravagant, professional but not personal.

Of course, he couldn't be certain about any of this, but he was seldom wrong about such things. It was his analytical nature, what C.C. had called his "empathic abilities."

In his previous life—before C.C. was murdered, before his face was destroyed and reconstructed, before his voice was stolen from him, which led to his being conscripted into the Watchers—he had been on his way to becoming a detective in the Pensacola Police Department. Even with all the heartache he'd suffered, it still pained him that he'd never made detective. Maybe in his older life, after the Watchers, after his debt was paid and he was set free, he would become a private detective. Or write mysteries and thrillers. Who knows.

For now, though, he would continue to use his analytical skills to aid his mission as a righteous killer, analyzing people such as the FDLE agent on the other side of the table. Back at the airport, he'd seen in Gibbs's eyes a look of compliance...

Right before she gave him a crushing blow to the junk and attempted an escape.

Silence had let his guard down. He'd foolishly accepted the false impression that Gibbs had given.

Instinct, though, had been telling him that this woman was incredibly savvy, that she wouldn't give up so easily, that she *wasn't* complying.

But he'd relied on his eyes, not his instinct. He hadn't listened to his gut feeling.

Again.

Just like he'd failed to listen to his gut in Mendocino.

He watched Agent Gibbs, who finally seemed to calm down. Her breathing had slowed, reaching a normal rate, and she'd stopped glancing around the plane and was now looking right back at Silence.

The jet was at cruising altitude, and the engines hummed smoothly outside. Silence and Gibbs were a few feet apart, their white swivel chairs separated by a small, black table. On Silence's side of the table was the manila folder he'd gotten from the Specialist in California.

He took his NedNotes brand PenPal notebook from his pocket, opened it to a message he'd jotted shortly after take-off, and placed it on top of the folder. He poked a finger on the notebook/folder combo and slid it across the table.

Gibbs eyed him skeptically.

Silence gave a small nod. *Read.*

Another moment of pause, and then Gibbs complied, reading the note, which said:

We know about your investigation into the murders, their connection to the old Eglin incident, and that you were investigating when you were placed on administrative leave. We know you're going to Kentucky to continue your investigation alone. We also want to figure out what's going on.

Her reaction was blank while she read, morphing into a raised eyebrow by the time she'd finished. She placed the notebook on the table.

She looked at him, waited, as though expecting him to say something. When he didn't, she went on to the second item he'd shared with her—the folder. She opened it, and her eyes widened as she flipped through the contents.

If there was one way to win her trust, it was by showing her the materials, proof of his legitimacy.

"How did you get all of this?" Gibbs said.

"We have connections," Silence said and swallowed. "But you know more than us." Another swallow. "Talk."

Gibbs chewed her lip as she studied him. She was clearly weighing her options, how much she should tell. Finally, she spoke.

"You have here a list of the seven survivors' names, rank, and military branches. What you don't have is a list of phone records." And in a pointed tone she added, "Other than mine."

Silence didn't respond.

She continued. "Elliott Bell—who'd been an Army first lieutenant at the time of the incident—was killed on Monday in Breckenridge, Colorado. Two days later, all the way in Panama City, Florida, Derek Artiga—who'd also been an Army officer, a second lieutenant—was murdered. Someone broke into Artiga's house. He escaped, called both 911 and a friend before the guy chased him into a Walmart parking lot and put a slug between his eyes. Guess who the friend was, the man Artiga called."

Silence shrugged.

"Elliott Bell."

Interesting, Silence thought.

"Of course, Bell was already dead by the time Artiga called him. Pretty bizarre, no?"

Silence nodded. "Very."

"And it gets weirder," she said as she grabbed the folder and started thumbing through the materials again, quickly, a second pass. "Other than Bell and Artiga, none of the people had met before. Seventeen individuals from every branch except the Coast Guard—eight Army, four Air Force, three Navy, two Marines—with a disproportionately high number of officers. Seven. Two of the officers were stationed at Eglin, but the rest of them were from bases all over the country."

She paused with a look that said she was awaiting a reaction. When he didn't give her one, she said, "You don't talk much, do you?"

Silence didn't respond.

She narrowed her eyes. "The card you showed me earlier, the message written on it—does it really hurt when you talk?"

Silence nodded.

A pause. "What's your name?"

"Troy."

Gibbs gave it a moment and then said, "Is that your first name or your last name?"

Silence didn't respond.

As a security precaution, Silence gave an alias to every person to whom he offered his services. As a means of lowering the number of syllables he had to run through his painful throat, he always chose a one-syllable name.

When he'd given this new pseudonym, Troy, he raised an eyebrow slightly. Just enough to tell Gibbs that it wasn't *really* his name. A display of trust. Or, perhaps, a peace offering. It was clear that Gibbs understood. She was a pro, after all.

She studied his latest non-reaction for a moment, then quickly, as though catching herself in a moment of weakness, she looked back to the folder, flipped a page. "And I see you have Bell's neighbor's description of the killer along with the one Artiga gave in the 911 call—multicolored eyes; one brown, one blue."

She snapped the folder shut, slid it back across the table. Silence stopped it with a finger.

Gibbs eased back into her seat, releasing a fraction of her guard, infinitesimal relaxation.

"Tristan Pike and Donnie Langstaff. Those are the two officers who were stationed at Eglin. Both Army. Both company-grade—Pike was a captain; Langstaff was a first lieutenant. And Pike was the officer in charge, the one who took the group out into the field that night." She pointed to the folder. "Did you guys happen upon Pike's most distinguishing physical characteristic?"

Silence shook his head.

"Pike had heterochromia, multicolored eyes," Gibbs said. "One brown eye; one blue. Just like the descriptions of the murderer. Less than one percent of people have heterochromia." She paused. "Which means the person murdering the Hard Sprint survivors is the officer who led them into the field."

———

As Silence blinked out of his nap and back into reality, he looked across the table at the person in the other overstuffed leather chair.

Gibbs stared out the window, hands stacked on her lap, head leaned back into the cushy depths of the headrest. Her face bore an expression somewhere between blank and defeated as it lulled gently with the movements of the jet. Silence had perceived a small reaction—a slight twitch in her eyes—when he'd awoken, but she never fully looked his way.

As with how he'd immediately—albeit subtly—let her know that "Troy" was not his real name, he'd thought that allowing himself a nap would be another show of trust, lowering his guard.

But he continued to get a vibe from her that she not only distrusted him because he'd essentially abducted her but also because of some underlying, deeper fear. Since she worked in government—as a state-level investigator, an agent—Silence found it hard to believe that her distrust was related to his admitted involvement in a subversive agency. But that was the vibe he was getting.

He stretched his arms over his head, yawned. There had been zero opportunity to unwind since his confrontation with Simon Ramsey, and he was damn sore. And still drowsy, even after the nap.

Gibbs finally acknowledged him, turning away from her window to give him a small, polite smile, before resuming her daydream.

A returning of the favor. A small show of trust. Miniscule.

Yet Silence could still tell she was holding back. She knew more than she was letting on. He could feel it.

But he wouldn't press her on it.

Not yet.

The folder was open on the table in front of him, and there was a page of information about heterochromia that the Watchers had provided. He reread the first paragraph.

Heterochromia iridum is a variation in eye color, which can be complete or sectoral. Onset is genetic or acquired. Only about six out of every 10,000 Americans are affected.

Gibbs had said that less than one percent of the population had heterochromia. According to the information in Silence's file, the number was considerably less than one percent. Six one hundredths of a percent.

Gibbs had also said that the officer who led the Eglin exercise, Tristan Pike, had heterochromia, and the two eye colors—brown and blue—matched the descriptions given at both the Bell and Artiga murders.

Of course, it would be easy enough to fake multicolored eyes. Just pop a colored contact lens on one eye. In his previous life, Silence himself had worn colored contact lenses to help shield his identity when he worked an undercover case as a police officer.

But why would anyone want to frame Pike? And since information about the Eglin disaster was proving so elusive, there were surely only a few people who even knew that the officer in charge had multicolored eyes.

It would seem that Tristan Pike was most certainly the killer.

But that brought about more *why*s.

Why was an officer murdering service members whom he'd led into the field? Why was he killing people he'd only known for one night?

Why had he waited years?

Another yawn formed, and Silence tried to stifle it, couldn't. He didn't know exactly how long he'd napped, but his internal clock was impeccable after years as an Asset, and he'd timed his slumber to coincide with the flight time. Right on cue, he felt the jet begin its descent.

Gibbs glanced away from the window and met his gaze. The flat yet distrusting expression remained on her face.

Silence waited, hoping for something more from her, some clue.

But she simply turned away.

CHAPTER EIGHT

LOUISVILLE, KENTUCKY

Tristan Pike took several deep breaths, trying to steel himself for what he was about to do, but the wretched shithole in front of him derailed any attempt at mantric, pre-violence calm.

The cottage style abode had surely been a bright-eyed young couple's "starter home" decades earlier but now looked like a crackhouse, replete with overgrown trees and bushes, a weed-filled lawn, bars on the windows, bars on the door, and a gabled roof that was shedding its shingles.

This? This was where Kurt Horn had ended up?

The Kurt Horn he had met years earlier was successful, intrepid. Pike had known him for only one night, the sole individual with whom he'd interacted prior to the briefing. Horn had been a Navy puke, enlisted, and he'd recently started an investing firm, a side job that he'd planned on making his full-time gig soon enough, hiring several additional brokers once he separated from the service.

It was inconceivable that Horn had gone from those

heights to these depths in a few years. And yet Pike had gotten confirmation earlier on the phone.

This was Kurt Horn's home.

Just unbelievable.

Not that it mattered. Pike was about to murder the guy.

In a city the size of Louisville, Pike had assumed it would be a challenge to track down the correct Kurt Horn, which seemed to him a rather common name. But it had only taken a few hours, a pleasant surprise.

After placing unanswered calls to all the *HORN, KURT* listings in the phone book, he was just about to hit the street, to knock on doors, when he considered something else—he hadn't called the *HORN, K.* listings. It was a long shot, but one worth taking before he started showing his face, with its easily recognizable eyes, all over town.

The first *HORN, K.* had been a female. And rather irritable.

But the second one, a man, had answered in the affirmative to all three of Pike's questions: *Was he Kurt Horn?* and *Was he in the Navy at the beginning of the decade?* and *Did he take part in a training exercise at Eglin Air Force Base?*

That's how Pike had ended up at this shithole.

His gun was in his hand, rolled in a T-shirt. He uncovered it, bounced it a couple of times, feeling its weight. Another deep breath. And then he bolted up the creaking steps and kicked in the door.

Chunks of rotten wood exploded onto matted carpeting, which was strewn with litter and filth. There were no screams, as one would expect from a sudden, violent home invasion. Instead, the two people inside barely acknowledged him.

A man lay on a chair, face-up, arms outstretched, mouth open. African American, fair-skinned, with prominent freckles and a mass of reddish-hued hair. He wore a stained white tanktop. A crack pipe was on the end table beside him. He looked at Pike, blinked his wet eyes, said nothing.

There was no resemblance to the man Pike had briefly known years earlier. None. This person was taller, thinner, lighter skinned, and a goddamn loser.

He was *not* Kurt Horn, despite the confirmation he'd given.

Aside from his chair and the small table—where his crack pipe perched on a haphazard mountain of magazines—there were two other armchairs, the only other furniture in the space. A mound of dirty clothing engulfed the striped one. The other held a second human.

A woman. White, rail thin, and curled into a tight, knobby-spined ball on the chair's stained cushion, so unresponsive as to seem dead were it not for slow movements in the chest. Skin lesions as bad as those of the man beside her. Greasy, orange-red hair in a sloppy mound atop her head, fashioned with a rubber band. Her filthy tanktop was almost identical to her companion's, a morbid uniform.

Pike looked back and forth between them. The man continued to stare back, blinking rapidly but otherwise completely oblivious.

Pike's eyes fell on the crack pipe, and a notion crossed his mind, a glimmer of hope. Maybe this *was* Kurt Horn. Maybe the poisons had changed the guy's appearance—lightened his skin, eaten his muscles. Pike knew little about the effects of crack cocaine, but he knew they were horrendous.

Pike aimed his gun at the man, "Are you Kurt Horn?"

The eyes looked at Pike, but the body didn't even twitch, just as unresponsive as that of his lady friend. The man laughed. "Huh?"

"Are you Kurt Horn?" Pike repeated.

The man finally moved. The armchair creaked and

groaned as he leaned forward a couple of inches, and the man grimaced intensely, like he'd just pulled a muscle.

Then a smile.

"You're the dude who called earlier!" the man shouted. A bout of laughter. "Sure, man, I'm Kurt Horn. Just like I told you on the phone. And I was in, like ... the Navy or something, right?"

More laughter.

Pike exhaled, lowered his gun slightly. "But not really?"

"No, not really."

The man guffawed.

"I'm Kendrick, man. Kendrick Horn."

With great effort, Kendrick raised his right arm, offered a handshake from five feet away. His hand swung precipitously. Pike ignored it.

More laughing. "Who're you, bro?"

Pike brought the gun back up. "I'm the man whose time you just wasted."

BANG!

A slight pause, a moment of consideration. Then he fired again, three more times.

BANG! BANG! BANG!

Kendrick Horn's torso hopped twice on the filthy chair, slid off the front, and came to an awkward, twisted halt on the floor, beer cans clattering, plastic bags crinkling.

Pike would kill not only the people on his list but anyone else who got in his way.

And this bastard had certainly gotten in the way.

Still, something played at Pike's insides, and he felt his chest rising and lowering, rapidly. For a moment, he couldn't believe what he'd done, and this bewilderment froze him in place. He sensed a prior version of himself somewhere in the hazy remoteness of his soul.

Screams in the distance. Neighbors. Pike had to get out of

there. Fast. Cops would be there soon. But not too soon. Shithole neighborhoods were never a priority.

The Polaroid camera dangled against his back, its long strap slung over his neck. He grabbed it and snapped a photo of Kendrick Horn's body.

He turned for the door and stopped. Motion. The woman. Eyes blinking open. Minuscule movements in her arms.

Four 9mm rounds, fired only a few feet away from her, and it was a camera's flash that had awoken her from her stupor.

Strung-out piece of shit.

She looked at Kendrick Horn's bloodied, dead form. Barely registered it. The glazed-over eyes found Pike. Blinked. And she smiled.

"What's your name?" she slurred.

Pike raised his gun. He'd killed one pile of human garbage. He could rid the world of another.

His finger tensed on the trigger.

And the tension released.

He lowered the gun. A drop of sweat rolled down his temple. And that same abstract sensation moved through him, the one he'd felt moments earlier after killing Kendrick, something from the past.

The crackhead blinked at him. Blank-faced. Sores and acne. Head teetering. Eyes beginning to close again.

Pike jolted.

The sirens were growing louder.

He sprinted out of the house.

CHAPTER NINE

GIBBS SAW AN OPPORTUNITY TO ESCAPE.

She and Troy descended the Learjet's air stairs, heading to the tarmac. A black Mercedes was ahead and to the left, about a hundred feet away from them. As soon as they'd stepped into the bright sunlight, Troy had, with a grunt and a point, indicated the Mercedes as their next destination.

From the plane, Gibbs had seen that they hadn't arrived at Louisville International. Her father had been an aviation enthusiast and passed on much of his knowledge—way too much. With her memory bank of unwanted aviation trivia, she suspected that this smaller airport was Louisville's famous Bowman Field, the oldest continually operated commercial airport in the U.S., a suspicion that was confirmed upon arrival.

During descent, she'd also seen a large group of people milling about stationary aircraft. Now, on the ground and outside the Learjet, she noticed that the congregation was outside the airport's administration building—a massive and stately brick-and-concrete Art Deco beauty—and that the aircraft were biplanes and other old things with glistening chrome components.

Maybe a hundred people, all dressed in regal yet outdoor-appropriate clothing with an eclectic flair, reminding Gibbs of the attire one sees on TV during the Kentucky Derby. In fact, several of the ladies even wore the outlandish hats—wide-brimmed with ridiculous bows the size of schnauzers.

Wait staff in white tops and black pants milled among the guests and the airplanes, balancing silver trays on perched, gloved fingers. Long tables with ice sculptures and hors d'oeuvres. Large tripod stands held signs with elaborate script font announcing that this was an annual charity event for the Northern Kentucky Horse Rescue and Adoption Society.

She studied the layout, developed a plan. Twenty tables—ten on either side of a pathway that went through the middle of the antique aircraft collection and led up to the front steps of the stunning admin building.

There were pathways she could exploit, yes, but she'd have to avoid that main pathway through the center. She'd already rejected the notion of creating a scene, trying to draw in police or security officials. Troy had proven in Pensacola that he could handle such a scenario.

She'd have to do something different this time. She'd make her escape through one of the groups of tables. The left side, yes. The aircraft were larger on that side. More visual obstructions, more corners to turn.

But first she had to put space between her and Troy, and so—

Her thoughts came to an abrupt halt.

She felt someone's stare.

And slowly turned, finding Troy's dark eyes waiting for her. He scowled.

Then took her hand.

"No time, darling," he said as they stepped off the air

stairs and onto the tarmac. He gestured to the Mercedes, swallowed. "Don't want to be late."

Gibbs exhaled.

It had been a foolish plan, anyway.

Troy's hand was warm, coarse, a bit dry, and it completely dwarfed hers. And it told her something: Troy was strong as hell. Even though he wasn't squeezing at all, she could feel energy in his thick fingers, meaty palm, like an electric current waiting to be switched on.

It was late morning. The sky was blue and full of big clouds, and there was a slight chill in the air, or at least it felt that way after being transported from the humidity of Panhandle Florida. As she looked over her shoulder, she saw that the party guests weren't bothered at all. The only jackets were sport coats. Many of the ladies' dresses were sleeveless.

A raffle drum sat beside one of the ice sculptures—a rearing stallion, naturally—and a good half of the drinks clenched in the attendees' hands were mimosas. A brunch. Something in Gibbs yearned to be over there. She wasn't exactly a charity auction sort of person, but the laughter and the general pleasantness of it reminded her of how dark of a situation she'd gotten herself into.

And how it was her own damn fault.

They reached the Mercedes, and Troy finally released her hand. He opened the passenger door for her, which was likely another precaution against an escape attempt, but she also suspected he was naturally chivalrous. Something about this man kept insisting to her that he wasn't the man in black that she feared.

He was dangerous. That much was very clear. The insane strength she'd felt in his hand was enough to prove that.

But there was more to this guy. She could sense it.

She settled into the leather interior, which bore a strong new car smell. Troy climbed in beside her, put the gear selector into drive, and they took off. A few moments later, they pulled out of the airport and onto a busy city street.

"Where are we headed?" Gibbs said.

"Three Louisville Kurt Horns." Troy swallowed and slowed the vehicle, flicked the turn signal, merged onto a new street. "Which one?"

It took Gibbs a moment to decode what he'd said—he was asking her about her research, asking which of the Louisville area Kurt Horns she had planned on visiting before he intercepted her.

In the same way that she'd sensed there was something deeper to this mysterious man, she was also starting to understand that he hadn't been lying about his throat condition. She would need to learn how to decipher him.

"The one on 125 Maisel Court," she said, pulling the address from memory.

Troy nodded, looked to the rearview, and pulled onto a side street lined with short flowering trees, bringing the Mercedes to a stop. He popped open the center console and retrieved a small plastic box—an electronic device, buttonless with a screen covering its front side. He took a power cord and a black plastic cage that turned out to be a holder for the device. After assembling the unit, attaching it to the dash, and plugging it into the cigarette lighter, he pressed a button, and the screen came to life.

A pixilated map appeared.

Troy pressed the letters on a graphical keyboard at the bottom of the screen, and suddenly a small, tinny, female voice came from the device, making Gibbs jump.

In five hundred feet, make a U-turn.

Gibbs's lips parted, and she pointed at the device, which immediately made her feel childish. "That's a GPS device!"

Troy's eyes flicked over to her. He didn't respond.

And suddenly she was suspicious again...

Next-century tech like this signified that he worked for someone ahead of the curve. CIA. NSA. Some top-secret military unit.

The Mercedes took off again, and after a few feet, Troy turned into a median opening and made the U-turn that the device had requested.

The device spoke again.

In three point one miles, turn right.

"You called him?" Troy said.

This time, she couldn't decipher him. "Huh?"

"Kurt Horn."

"Of course I called. I got the wife. She told me she wouldn't discuss her husband's military service. When I insisted it was urgent, she got flustered and hung up on me."

"And the others?" Troy said.

"With Bell and Artiga dead, that leaves four survivors: Horn, Davidson, Milano, and Langstaff. I've found nothing on Langstaff and Milano, but I know that Davidson's somewhere in San Francisco. She was a sailor like Horn. Enlisted. There are several possibilities in the city, but I could only reach one by phone the other night.

"Since I have a lock on Horn, that's why Louisville was my first stop—to get past Horn's wife and convince her that her husband's in mortal danger. Then I was going to rush to San Francisco and track down Davidson before it's too late."

She stopped and faced Troy.

"Which means *we're* going to San Francisco after this," she said.

She wanted to test him, to poke at his stone-faced, in-command facade. She waited for him to assert his dominance, to tell her that he would need to relay the intel she'd given him to his "organization."

Instead, he simply nodded his agreement.

Interesting.

She looked out the window. They were on a four-lane highway, and as they zipped past a side street, a sign revealed the thoroughfare's in-city designation: Taylorsville Road. The trees were robust and emerald green. The thick, lush grass lawns were equally green. This stretch of the city had a decidedly country vibe. There were even long, low fences that reminded her of the classic Kentucky horse farms you see on TV.

As Troy followed the electronic woman's flat-voiced commands, the Mercedes left the fields behind and turned deeper and deeper into suburban niceties. Soon they were at an upscale neighborhood called Lake Heights, slowing to a stop in front of a picture-perfect middle-American house with a gabled roof and dormer window, architectural shingles, a cozy porch with upscale lawn furniture, and surgically clean landscaping. Though it was lovely, it looked much like the houses surrounding it, aside from one defining feature: the deep blue color of the wood siding.

The address was 125 Maisel Court.

Kurt Horn's house.

Troy got out of the car without a word, headed for the house.

As Gibbs rushed to catch up with him on the sidewalk—which was lined with crushed marble and solar path lights—the absurdity of what she was doing suddenly struck her.

This was *real*.

She was approaching the house of the woman who had hung up on her phone call the previous night. From the other side of the country.

And if this was real, so too was the administrative leave. Which meant she was *really* disobeying Caldwell, that she was *really* conducting an unsanctioned investigation.

And she was *really* following this tall, dangerous, handsome man who had essentially kidnapped her at an international airport.

This was all way too real...

A pair of tall concrete planters overflowing with flowers flanked the front door. Arborvitaes traced the outside corners of the porch area, stretching high into the sky. When Troy pressed the doorbell button, there was the muffled sound of a melodic chime from within the house.

As he waited, Troy flicked back his suit jacket, shoved his hands in his pockets. Gibbs caught a glimpse of a shoulder-holstered Beretta.

A few moments passed. No sounds from the house. Just birds in the trees. A lawnmower in the distance. Troy turned to her. He didn't smile, but he gave her a small pump of the eyebrows over his sunglasses.

He jingled the keys in his pocket. Then he tried the glass outdoor door. Unlocked. He opened it, and rapped on the main door, which was painted forest green with a peephole and a small window at the top. His hands returned to his pockets, as the glass door slowly returned to position on its pneumatic door-closer.

More waiting, then Troy suddenly turned back toward the car.

———

As Gibbs settled back into the Mercedes' passenger seat, she said, "And now?"

Just as she asserted herself earlier, she wanted to make a clearly deferential statement now. A show of her growing, but hesitant, trust.

Troy gave another look to the house, then started the engine, adjusted the air conditioning controls.

"We wait," he said.

And instead of putting the car into gear, he reached to the side of his seat, reclined all the way to a lying position, and settled in, crossing his arms over his chest. Though Gibbs couldn't fully see his eyes through his sunglasses, it looked like he'd shut them.

He was displaying a bit of trust in her as well. Two forces, testing the waters.

Or he was just damn tired.

Gibbs arched an eyebrow. "We wait?"

Troy didn't turn to her, didn't open his eyes. "Have better idea?"

It was a moment before she could formulate a response. "No, I suppose I don't have any better ideas."

And, suddenly, there she was—in the middle of Kentucky, in the passenger seat of a Mercedes, with a stranger who might be a spy, might be an assassin, might be a lunatic ... waiting.

She just looked at Troy for a moment, paralyzed by the oddities, by the realness in which she'd found herself, blinking.

Then she recomposed.

Troy was right. There was nothing else to do but wait for Kurt Horn or his wife to return.

She searched for her seat-recline lever.

An electronic chime pierced the quiet of the Mercedes' cab—a cellular phone's ringer.

Troy reached into his pocket, retrieved a phone, flipped it open.

"Yes?" He listened. "Negative."

Another, long pause, during which Troy fished his notebook from his pocket, which Gibbs now noticed to be a NedNotes brand PenPal. Before joining the FDLE, a detective at her local department had carried the same style of notebook. They were pocket-sized with plastic covers that came in a variety of colors. This one was sky blue.

Troy scribbled a note while the person on the other end of the phone spoke. Finally, he said, "Yes, sir."

He collapsed the phone, returned it to his pocket, glanced at the note, and entered a new address into the GPS device.

Head west on Maisel Court, the electronic woman said.

Troy pulled the Mercedes into the Horns' driveway, backed out, and then they took off, heading in the opposite direction from which they'd arrived.

"Who was that on the phone?" Gibbs said.

No reply.

"Where are we going?"

In response, Troy pointed to the GPS device.

Gibbs sighed. "Oh, yes, I see. We're going to 702 Heflin Street." She rolled her eyes. "Let me rephrase. What are we doing, and why the hell are we leaving Kurt Horn's place behind?"

"Three Kurt Horns in Louisville." Troy said as he slowed the Mercedes for a stop sign. He checked traffic, turned left as the GPS commanded, and swallowed.

"Also two *K. Horn*s listed in..." He swallowed. "Louisville phone books." Another swallow. "One was just murdered."

CHAPTER TEN

GIBBS WAS over 500 miles from Pensacola, but suddenly she felt at home.

There was a crime scene before her.

Troy parked the Mercedes two blocks back from a dilapidated house with barred windows and doors, rotten siding, and a half-dead tree. Police tape circled the overgrown lawn, outside of which was a collection of idling vehicles—three police black-and-whites, an ambulance, and a news van.

At the sidewalk, a cameraman stood behind a four-foot tripod, filming the house. Cops kept the gathering neighbors at bay. A group of uniformed personnel slowly, carefully egressed from the front door, rolling a stretcher that was draped with a white blanket. Two more cops at the far corner of the porch patiently listened to a scrawny, rough-looking, redheaded woman as she gesticulated wildly between animated words and bouts of tears.

Gibbs leaned forward, onto the Mercedes' dash, getting a better view. She took off her sunglasses. Daylight was fading. Her heartbeat went up a notch, as it always did with a big turn in one of her investigations.

Pike had made a mistake.

She was positive that she had the correct Kurt Horn back at Maisel Court, which meant that Pike had killed the wrong man here.

Which further meant that Pike was fallible, not a criminal genius.

Which further meant Gibbs could bring his ass down.

She turned to her massive, taciturn companion. Troy had one hand on the steering wheel, looking blankly toward the house.

"Okay, we're here," Gibbs said. "What now?"

Troy opened the door and stepped outside.

"Well, okay then," Gibbs said.

She exhaled.

This was getting old fast.

She hurried to catch up with Troy, who was approaching one of the gawkers, standing alone a block away from the action. An older woman—Hispanic, plump, short, and wearing an oversized, faded sweatshirt commemorating the 1978 Indianapolis 500.

"What happened?" Troy said to the woman as they stepped up.

At the sound of his voice, the woman jumped back, hand going to her chest, eyes flaring wide.

Troy just waited, blank-faced.

"Someone shoot him. Oh, *Dios*, they shoot 'im up." The woman bit her lip. "I heard it. Three shots. Maybe four."

Gibbs moved closer, asserting herself. If she and this shadow man were conducting an investigation together, she needed to up her game. She'd been in enough bureaucratic pissing matches to know that if a person didn't establish authority and respect earlier on, they never would, especially as a woman.

"Who was shot?" Gibbs said. "Mr. Horn?"

The other woman nodded. "Yes. Kendrick."

Troy looked at Gibbs and then back to the older woman. He pointed to the house. "Who's that?"

The woman followed Troy's outstretched finger. Gibbs did too. He was pointing at the scrawny redhead on the porch, who was still in hysterics.

As she looked down the street, a glint of light caught Gibbs's eye—a reflection from the TV news camera. The cameraman was swinging his camera around, a shot of the neighborhood surrounding the crime scene. The lens swung toward her. She quickly turned, averting her face.

"Is Ruby," the woman said. "Kendrick's ... um, 'friend.' Know what I mean?"

"Yes," Troy said.

The woman squinted at him for a moment, as though trying to make sense of his bizarre voice, and then she said, "Ruby has many friend, but she and Kendrick real close, *sí?*" The woman looked back to the house again and brought a fist to her face, bit a knuckle, fighting off tears. "She come banging on my neighbor's door, screaming. About ten minutes after the gunshots. Musta been high. She always is."

"Did you hear anything she told your neighbor?" Gibbs said.

"That some white dude shoot Kendrick. White dude with two different colored eyes."

Troy and Gibbs exchanged another look.

"Thanks for your time," Troy said and immediately turned, heading briskly for the Mercedes.

Gibbs scrambled to keep up with his long, loping strides. She looked up at him and gave a small raise of the eyebrows. He nodded.

And that was all that was needed.

It was creepy how quickly she was falling into a natural,

unspoken communication pattern with a strange man who'd snatched her from an airport.

Could this be what they call Stockholm syndrome?

Troy, too, sensed the unacknowledged communication, answering the unspoken question: *What's our next move?*

"We get back to Kurt Horn's place," Troy said and swallowed. "Fast."

CHAPTER ELEVEN

SANTA MONICA, CALIFORNIA

Austin Huber sat at an ornate, wrought-iron table, awaiting his companion, and took another sip of his Long Island iced tea. His lips gave a small, almost involuntary smack at the tartness. Some might say The Blue Corner had put too much sour in their Long Islands, but not Austin. He liked them nice and tart.

He adjusted his heavy metal chair, pulling it another inch or so out of the sunlight. It was another perfect California day—seventy-four degrees, low humidity, gentle breeze—but the sun was making him feel ever so slightly too warm.

The Blue Corner was an upscale place with upscale prices. A red velvet rope barrier—dangling from glistening chrome stanchions—separated the outdoor seating from the adjacent sidewalk, where people strolled by, toting expensive shopping bags, sunglasses on their faces, smiles on their lips. Just past the foot traffic was the street, a quiet affair lined with boutiques and other Blue-Corner-esque restaurants and tall, majestic palms that moved fractionally, gently, slowly in that casual breeze that Austin was enjoying. The trees exhibited the same easy, no-stress, California energy as the people on the sidewalk.

The Golden State had been a promised land for Austin his entire life, long before the success of his novels, but it wasn't until after he became a bestselling author that he finally made the move. As he absorbed the opulent perfection of his surroundings, the energy of success and ease and prestige, he wished he'd moved west far earlier than he had, a notion that crossed his mind on an almost daily basis.

He tried to burn this moment into his memory, because with what he was about to do, the task he was embarking upon, his life was going to get very chaotic and it might be awhile before he got to enjoy simple pleasures like this again. His plan would begin in earnest as soon as his companion arrived at the restaurant, so for this brief moment, he could savor his remaining bit of peace.

Too late. Austin spotted him.

Otis Watts twisted his way through the tables, looking terribly out of place in his bargain-basement, discount-rack, short-sleeve shirt and slacks. Austin could see tension on the older man's face as he glanced down at the tables he was passing—very clearly Otis was already fretting over the prices of The Blue Corner's cuisine.

The heavy chair screeched against the concrete as Otis pulled it out and dropped into it. He immediately looked to his right, at the nearest table, more apprehension written all over his face.

"Don't worry, Otis," Austin said with a sigh. "I'm buying."

Otis did nothing to hide his relief, sitting up taller in his chair, even smiling. He was mid-fifties with nearly all-white hair—both his medium-length haircut and his old-guy beard. The only bit of color was a speckling of grays in the mustache.

Otis dropped a folder on the table. "The information you requested. "

Austin found a single sheet of paper with a list of addresses and phone numbers from all around the country, organized in groups that were labeled with people's names.

Otis spoke while Austin scanned the data. "Took some work to track all those folks down. Several of the names turned up multiple phone numbers, addresses. I skipped Pike and Milano, as per your request, and I found possible hits for everyone except Langstaff. Sorry, brother, just couldn't find the guy. It's like he just vanished after the incident at Eglin."

The list was long and exhaustive. Otis's work had never disappointed Austin. He was a good private eye. And he looked the part, too. Like a classic LA private detective. Frumpy clothes. Grumbly but well-meaning demeanor. Yesteryear attitude and mannerisms.

"Good work, Otis," Austin said as he stuck the paper back in the folder.

No response. Only a bizarre expression in Otis's basset hound eyes, something like suspicion.

"Something on your mind?" Austin said.

Otis hesitated. "You know I love digging into things for you. Doing research work for a novelist sure beats cheating wives and deadbeat husbands, but..."

He trailed off. Austin had never seen the man like this. While Otis could seem on the outside a bit bumbling, he was actually deadly competent.

This was bizarre.

"But what?"

Otis rubbed his beard. "While I was researching, I found something ... uh, bizarre. Two of these folks have been murdered. Recently. In the last few days."

Otis looked at him then, clearly awaiting a response,

wanting a lightning-fast assurance that his long-time client had nothing to do with the murders.

In response, Austin just took off his Gucci sunglasses, placed them on the table, narrowed his eyes slightly.

Otis removed his hand from his beard and placed it on the other one atop his stomach, began rubbing them together. Though he fidgeted in his seat, his eyes never left Austin's.

Suddenly he stood.

"I gotta hit the john."

Otis's chair moaned again, and then he plodded away, past a potted palm, around a waiter, and into the exterior men's room.

Hmm...

Austin had known that involving Otis would be a risk. But he hadn't thought the man would get *this* rattled, that he would come at Austin with a semi-accusation.

He would need to monitor the guy.

But first things first.

He looked at the list Otis had just given him, found the right listing, then reached into his pocket and retrieved his cellular telephone. He entered the number and waited.

A man answered his call.

"Hello," Austin said. "May I please speak to Kurt Horn?"

CHAPTER TWELVE

LOUISVILLE, KENTUCKY

PIKE MOVED past a row of cracked plastic seats, orange, one of several rows in the bus station in a bad part of Louisville. A light drizzle tapped on the blue-tinted plexiglass overhang that shielded an expanse of broken concrete that was speckled with discarded gum. A plastic bag spasmed in the faint breeze, caught in a tuft of dead grass that had sprouted from a fissure in the pavement. There was the smell of urine.

Once upon a time, this must have been a nice place. Clearly, some thought had been been given to the aesthetics. The city planners and architects and transit officials must have believed it would have been a bright spot in a rough neighborhood, a beacon for change and hope. Somewhere along the line, the destitution of the surrounding neighborhood had overpowered the good intentions.

Pike hadn't come for a ticket. Fate had brought him here. After fleeing Kendrick Horn's shack, a chance look out his window had shown a line of televisions suspended from the bus station's ceiling. As he checked his watch, he'd seen that it was a little over an hour until the five o'clock news would play. Since he needed to stay in Louisville—as he'd yet to eliminate Kurt Horn—and having just committed a murder in the city, he needed to keep a very low profile. If he was going to catch the news, he could think of nowhere more inconspicuous to watch than this urban hellhole.

The TVs hovered over one of the rows of orange chairs, where a homeless person lay on his side, German-pretzeled through the chairs' chrome arms—legs above, torso beneath, one arm dangling off the side. The man snored.

As the news program began, with closed-captioning playing at the bottom of the screen, Pike stepped closer, listening for the audio. Nothing. All he could hear was a pair of vending machines humming in the distance, vying for auditory dominancy with a Motown class that crackled out a few battered speakers spaced out among the rafters. The ceiling mounts holding the televisions bore a strip of metal across the front of each unit, blocking access to any buttons, volume or otherwise. Pike would have to make do with the closed-captioning.

The initial story related to local politics—a city councilman with a marred reputation. A few minutes of this, and then came the story Pike was awaiting.

Kendrick Horn's shithole house appeared on the screen, surrounded by police tape, emergency vehicles with flashing lights, and a spattering of locals. The headline in the lower-thirds read:

VIOLENT, BAFFLING MURDER ON EAST SIDE

Below that, the close-captioning said:

POLICE AND AREA RESIDENTS ARE STUNNED BY A SEEMINGLY RANDOM MURDER ON THE

CITY'S EAST SIDE. FOUR GUNSHOTS SOUNDED
FROM KENDRICK HORN'S HOME THIS AFTER-
NOON, STARTLING NEIGHBORS. AS NOTHING
WAS STOLEN FROM THE HOME, POLICE OFFI-
CIALS HAVE INDICATED THAT THIS COULD
POSSIBLY BE A CRIME OF PASSION OR AN
ENTIRELY RANDOM ACT OF VIOLENCE.

While the closed-captioning played, there had been a variety of shots of Kendrick Horn's home—a wide shot of the house, where two uniformed cops interviewed the red-haired crackhead whose life Pike had spared; artful closeups of the flapping police tape and the overgrown lawn; a shot down the street; and finally, when the closed-captioning ended, another wide shot, this one panning from the house to the surrounding neighborhood.

As the image continued to move and bring more of the neighborhood into view, Pike saw another pair of police. Plain-clothes cops.

He took a couple of steps closer to the screen, narrowing his eyes. The crunch of his footsteps on the concrete made the bum stir in his sleep.

The cops were far away from the immediate crime scene, making them tiny figures on the screen. They wore dress clothes, not uniforms—which meant they were detectives—and they were clearly interviewing someone, a middle-aged Hispanic woman in a shoddy dress. Had they not been talking to the woman, Pike would have taken them as two more neighbors drawn to commotion, ones wearing dispro-portionately nice clothing.

Pike reached around his back, grabbed the Polaroid camera, leaned toward the screen, and snapped a photo of the investigators just before the image on the television changed, returning to one of the anchors.

The flash lit the surroundings, glinted off the glass screens, and the sleeping man stirred once more, rubbed his eyes. "What the hell?"

Pike pulled the photo from the camera, gave it a couple of gentle shakes. The gray square began dissolving into an image, ghostlike details emerging in the haze, revealing the pair of detectives.

The man was tall with dark hair and a black suit, white shirt, no tie. It was another few seconds for the woman to materialize. Attractive with a toned figure and reddish hair. In the moment of time preserved in Pike's photo, she was the one talking to the witness, while the tall man watched, stony-faced, hands clasped at his waist.

"Shit," Pike hissed.

He'd assumed little would come from his actions at Kendrick Horn's crappy neighborhood. But with detectives involved, this meant that Louisville's police department was taking the murder seriously.

Killing Kendrick Horn had been a foolish mistake, one of pride and emotion. A damn idiotic mistake.

And now Pike was paying for it.

More of the detail had emerged from the photo's gray haze, a clear look at both detectives.

The tall one, the male, looked more and more intense as the image focused. Borderline psychotic. One of those "not on my watch" type of cops.

Yes, Pike had committed an absurd blunder. But now that he had a Polaroid photo of the detectives to add to his collection, he had a tactical advantage: he knew what they looked like, but they didn't know what he looked like.

And he'd be on the lookout for them.

CHAPTER THIRTEEN

SANTA MONICA, CALIFORNIA

THE MIRROR WAS a massive S-shaped affair lined with tiny, glistening, black tiles, immaculately clean. Otis Watts watched his reflection as a drop of water rolled from his brow to the tip of his nose.

He took a deep breath and willed his hands to relax. Obediently, his fingers released their grasp on the edge of the sink, which was as spotlessly clean as the mirror. Its black color was also in line with the mirror, matching the little accent tiles.

He brought his hands to chest height, turned them over. Color slowly faded back into his palms, which were moist from sweat or water or both, glistening in the bright light coming in through a stretch of frosted windows that circled the bathroom, way up there at the top of the ten-foot walls.

"Are you all right, sir?"

The restroom attendant. A handsome Asian kid of maybe twenty-one years wearing a white linen shirt, sleeves rolled, unbuttoned halfway down his chest, as uber-cool as the rest of this ridiculous restaurant. He had the look of a Hollywood hopeful, as did so many people in the area aged sixteen to fifty-five.

Otis gave him a nod and a weak smile.

But this non-verbal response had been a lie. He wasn't all right at all.

What was he going to do? He had always thought his client, Austin Huber, to be a good man.

But now he was thinking he was a murderer.

Shit! What to do?

At the moment, the only thing he could do was to go back and finish his lunch. At least he'd get some fancy food out of this, though in his experience, fancy food was hit or miss—it tasted like crap as often as it tasted divine.

He took another breath, accepted another towel from Mr. Cool, wiped his face, gave a tip, and left the restroom.

The sunlight squinted his eyes, and he threw on his aviators. At the far corner of the outdoor seating area, by the red velvet rope barrier, Austin sat staring at him from behind his own sunglasses, a designer pair. His button-down shirt was splayed open, halfway down his chest, even farther than the restroom attendant's. And he was grinning—almost smirking, it seemed.

Or was Otis's imagination, his nagging suspicion, turning a harmless, even friendly smile into something sinister?

He pulled out his chair.

"You were gone a while," Austin said.

Otis patted his belly. "I've had the shits lately."

He gave Austin a queasy face.

Austin shrugged. "Whatcha gonna do? I took the liberty of ordering for you."

"Fine."

They looked at each other. Two tables over, a pair of women burst into laughter. Cars hummed by on the street beside them. A bird chirped nearby.

And Otis and Austin just kept staring at each other.

Finally, Austin said, "Yes?"

Evidently Otis's trip to the bathroom—with its water-splashing and five-dollar-tip towels—had done little to change his outward appearance. He'd always had the annoying tendency of wearing his heart on his sleeve, an unfortunate trait for someone in his profession.

"What is this, Austin?" He pointed to the folder. "This isn't research for one of your novels, is it? Seven survivors from a disaster at a military base years ago. Two of them are murdered within days of each other, right at the same time you're having me dig up information."

Austin didn't budge, but when he spoke, his voice was sharper than usual, a dangerous edge. "I write crime fiction, Otis. What exactly are you implying?"

"I'm not implying. I'm exploring."

Austin folded his arms on the table. "The protagonist of my new novel—you know, the one I've been working on for two months, long before the murders you mentioned—is also the survivor of a military training disaster."

He reached into the leather messenger bag leaning against his chair, dropped a stack of white paper in front of Otis. It landed with a solid thunk, the impact quivering the metal table. An oversized rubber band loosely held together the pages. Centered on the front page, clearly typed with an old-fashioned typewriter, was:

AN ABUSE OF POWER
by Austin Huber

Otis slid back the cover page, found the first page of Chapter 1, which bled profusely with red editorial marks— slashes and scribbles and notes. Opening paragraphs of a tale of military intrigue. The very first line was a damning rebuke of Otis's subtle quasi-implications.

```
The  incident  at  Fort  Riley,  Kansas,
left  thirty-one  people  dead,  and  it
also left Lieutenant Sam Drummond with
two  lifetime  afflictions:  a  piece  of
shrapnel  buried  in  his  left  shin and a
whole lot of nagging questions.
```

Otis looked up, saw his reflection in Austin's two-hundred-dollar sunglasses.

"It's a bad coincidence, Otis, my hiring you to look into the incident at the same time as the murders." He leaned in closer, laying his arms over the table's crisscrossed iron bars. "But if you're implying something horrible, think about this —when we met two nights ago, when I gave you this gig, that was the same night the first person was murdered in Colorado."

Otis hadn't thought of this, felt silly for not having looked at the cold, hard facts.

He rubbed the back of his neck. "Yeah, man. You're right. I'm sorry." And he would have left it at that, but something compelled him to add, "Still ... it just seems weird."

Austin didn't respond immediately. "I want to remind you, that any work you do for me is confidential."

The words had come out cold, almost deadly, and Otis jolted back in his chair, a slight movement but one that was hard enough to make his heavy iron chair scoot back.

Suddenly, Austin retreated from the table, easing back

into his own chair and turning his head with a smile. The waitress had arrived.

"Wonderful!" Austin said, and as a plate slid in front of Otis, he added, "I hope you like *salade niçoise*."

CHAPTER FOURTEEN

LOUISVILLE, KENTUCKY

THE MERCEDES CAME to a quick stop, tires chirping, and before Gibbs could even open her door, Troy had already hopped out of the car and started crossing the quiet street toward Kurt Horn's house.

Gibbs chased after him again.

Screw the new exercise plan she'd started last month. She could just follow this guy around all the time, try to keep up with him.

They rushed up the pristine sidewalk. The sky was going pink and dark. The solar path lights had activated, a string of earthbound stars lining the path. A few crickets were warming up for their evening chorus. Ahead, lights were on in the front bay windows.

Someone was home.

Gibbs sighed out a bit of relief. But the work was far from over. When she'd spoken to Mrs. Horn the previous day on the phone, the woman had assumed Gibbs was a lunatic. Gibbs couldn't blame her. If some stranger phoned Gibbs asking about her husband's service record from years prior, asking about his whereabouts, she would also assume the person was crazy.

She took a big step and cut in front of Troy. She'd dealt with Mrs. Horn already; she needed to take the lead here. More bureaucratic pissing match maneuvering.

"I have an idea," she said.

Again, Troy didn't protest. If anything, his ever-present blank yet cold expression seemed to warm with a bit of intrigue. *What's this lady up to?*

She liked that.

Just before she stepped onto the porch, she felt a presence and turned. A man stood on the corner, in the darkness beyond the sphere of light offered by a streetlamp, looking in her and Troy's direction. He wore a T-shirt and jeans. His hair was blond. And he looked a lot like the tourist she'd seen at the airport in Pensacola, the one with the goofy sunglasses who'd been watching her and Troy from behind a magazine.

She glanced behind. Troy was looking at the other man.

They stepped onto the porch, and Gibbs rang the doorbell.

A moment later, the door cracked open, and a hesitant face peered out. Diane Horn was black with pale skin, large eyes, and straightened hair that fell past her shoulders, parted in the middle. She wore a purple turtleneck and pajama pants, caught in the limbo between work clothes and lounge wear.

"Diane Horn?" Gibbs said.

"Yes?"

The woman narrowed her voice as much as she did her eyes.

Gibbs hesitated ever so slightly. This was the first truly illegal action she'd committed during this "investigation."

"My name is Special Agent Viola Gibbs with the Florida Department of Law Enforcement."

And with that, Gibbs was a criminal, using her position in an unauthorized manner while on leave.

She released a shuddering breath, through her nose, tried to conceal it.

Troy gave her the tiniest of nods. Respect. He understood what she was doing. He got it.

Gibbs turned back to Diane Horn and gestured toward Troy. "And this is my consultant, Mr. Troy."

The other woman was incredulous. "Florida?" A small laugh. "I think you have the wrong house, lady."

"Is your husband, Kurt, available?"

A tentative pause. "He's not home."

"May we have a word?"

Suddenly Mrs. Horn's eyes flashed wide, then narrow. "Wait a minute! You're that chick who kept calling me last night, aren't you?"

"Yes."

"Get off my property!"

"But I—"

"I said go away, you crazy bitch!"

She slammed the door.

But it stopped three inches short of closing.

Troy's hand held it open. His arm had punched out to stop it so quickly Gibbs hadn't even seen it, not even a blur.

"Please," Troy said. "Kurt's in danger."

Mrs. Horn's lips parted for a moment before she replied. "Danger?"

"Life or death."

The woman shuddered.

Gibbs inched closer, and in a quiet tone, she said, "Ma'am, every moment is critical. Three people have been murdered so far, and we believe your husband is the next target."

Mrs. Horn's eyes danced between Gibbs and Troy. There was a small crunching sound, and it was a moment before

Gibbs located it—the woman's fingernails, clenching hard on the edge of the door.

Another few seconds.

And then she opened the door.

————

Inside, the place radiated with the feeling of home—memories and good meals and the steady pulse of facing life's challenges. In this way, it reminded Gibbs of her little house back in Pensacola. But there was a stark difference. This place sheltered a married couple, a family. Her place was home to only herself. No one else. Not even a dog or cat. These last several hours with Troy were the most time she'd spent with someone outside of a work setting in months.

No...

Years.

If she weren't in the middle of the most critical juncture of her life, this notion would have depressed the hell out of her.

The Horns' living room was eclectic-chic. One wall pale lilac; the other, bright yellow. A few whacky adornments complimented more traditional ones. The design juxtapositions flowed perfectly, and Gibbs suspected it was Diane Horn, not Kurt, who had spearheaded the work. Men just didn't have the eye for such things.

Diane's legs were folded beneath her on a firetruck-red loveseat, and Gibbs and Troy were across from her on a full-size sofa—wicker with off-white cushions. Untouched glasses of water were on the table in front of them. Even in her current state, Diane had insisted on being a gracious hostess.

Still, she couldn't look at them. She just stared at her knees as she rubbed them with both hands, over and over.

"I just don't understand why anyone would kill the

survivors of the Eglin explosion," Diane said. "They weren't a unit. They were from different branches. All veterans of the Gulf War. It was just a two-day TDY."

In her line of work and with her background, Gibbs was accustomed to the way military families frequently used abbreviations without explanation. *TDY* stood for *temporary duty*, a service member's short-term work at a place other than his or her permanent duty station.

Diane shook her head, still watching her knees as she continued to rub them. "But maybe there was more to it than what Kurt told me. They never tell you everything, ya know. Sometimes they'll only share with other military members. And some things they'll never talk about, just keep in their head until the grave."

"Two of seven survivors killed," Troy said and swallowed. "Last two days." He paused. "Pike. Name familiar?"

Diane nodded. "Yes. Pike was the officer in charge that night, right?"

Troy nodded.

"It looks like Pike is the one committing the murders," Gibbs said.

She allowed this statement to float in the air, giving Diane a chance to absorb it.

The other woman gasped, shook her head more vehemently as her eyes glazed over. Then she suddenly sat up straight; her hands stopped circling her knees.

"Wait," she said, looking at Gibbs. "At the door you said three people had been murdered." She turned to Troy. "But a moment ago, you said that *two* of the Hard Sprint survivors have been killed."

"Third murder today," Troy said. "Here. Louisville. Kendrick Horn."

The woman gasped. "Horn. You mean ... You mean ... Like, a mistake? Like Pike was trying to kill Kurt?"

"Yes, ma'am," Gibbs said.

Mrs. Horn wailed, and her head fell to her hands.

"Where is he?" Troy said, and Gibbs immediately shot him a look. He hadn't given Mrs. Horn *nearly* enough time to process her emotions.

The woman pulled her face from her hands. Mascara streaked the curves of her cheeks. Between sobs she said, "Where's ... Where's Kurt?"

Troy nodded.

"He's out of state. Montana. Annual hiking trip with his brother." She looked past them, to a clock on the far wall. "Won't be back until tomorrow, about this time. No cellular reception up there, and he won't have it turned on during the plane ride tomorrow."

She ran a shaking hand across her forehead.

"You have to leave, ma'am," Gibbs said. "Do you have children? Pets?"

Mrs. Horn shook her head.

"Then just go. A hotel. A friend's place. Anywhere but here."

Diane was shaking now. Her head darted left and right, scanning the house frantically. "How ... How can I reach him? I can't call him. And he never leaves the damn thing on anyway. I ... I ..."

"We'll watch for him," Troy said.

"I'm not leaving here without him!"

Troy leaned forward. "His car?"

"His car?" Mrs. Horn said. "It's a dark blue Ford Taurus."

"Plate number?"

"I can look that up, but ... why?"

Troy took his notebook from his pocket, retrieved a mechanical pencil from the spiral binding, and wrote a quick note that he put on the table, facing Mrs. Horn.

Gibbs twisted to read it.

Fontaine Street is the only way into this community, correct?
We will position ourselves at Fontaine and intercept a blue
Ford Taurus with the license plate number you provide.

Mrs. Horn nodded, and the tension in her face slackened fractionally. "That's right. Fontaine's the only street that leads into Lake Heights."

She stood and walked over to a desk on the opposite wall, rifled through some papers, and returned. She pointed at the notebook.

"May I?"

Troy handed her the notebook and pencil.

"Here's the license plate number," she said as she wrote. "And I'm also writing Hubert's address and phone number. Hubert Tremble, Kurt's Navy buddy. They met here, in Louisville, long after the war, but you know how that military bond can be. Like I said, I know Kurt doesn't tell me everything about his military experience, but he and Hubert share it all. Plus, they've both had Gulf War Syndrome symptoms all these years, so there's that connection too."

"Wait..." Troy said and looked over to Gibbs for a moment before looking back to Mrs. Horn. "Kurt has GWS?"

Gulf War Syndrome was an elusive and mysterious set of chronic health issues that affected a significant number of service members who returned from the war. The symptoms were wide-ranging: rashes, insomnia, diarrhea, cognitive issues, respiratory issues, muscular issues. As varied as the symptoms were, the hypothesized causes were just as varied, things like exposure to pesticides; exposure to nerve gas; exposure to nerve gas pretreatment pills; and exposure to depleted uranium.

"Well, yeah. Of course he has GWS," Diane said. "Everyone did."

There was something strange about her tone. So matter-of-fact.

"What do you mean, 'everyone did'?" Gibbs said.

Diane just looked at her for a moment before replying, head cocked.

"I assumed you knew..." she said, trailing off. She frowned and looked at both of them.

Troy shook his head. "Explain."

"Everyone who took part in the exercise that night—everyone who died in the explosion, all the survivors—every single one of them had Gulf War Syndrome."

CHAPTER FIFTEEN

THE WORDS RACED through Pike's head, the ones he'd just heard through the staticky speaker in his earpiece, what Kurt Horn's wife had said.

Gulf War Syndrome.

Everyone at Operation Hard Sprint had suffered with GWS symptoms upon returning to the States. Of course. That had been the entire point of the exercise.

The exercise that Pike himself had led.

And yet ... he'd forgotten that detail until he heard Mrs. Horn say it.

How could he have forgotten something so crucial?

Focus.

He'd allowed his mind to stray from his mission several times since he parked a couple of blocks away from Kurt Horn's house—not the imposter in a crackhouse, but the *real* Kurt Horn.

The one Pike was going to murder.

He glanced at his knee, where one of his Polaroid photos rested. It was the photo he'd taken at the bus stop when he'd photographed the news program playing on the muted television.

There, on the far left side of the photo, speaking to one of Kendrick Horn's neighbors, were the two Louisville detectives—the towering, dark man and his partner, an attractive, auburn-haired woman.

They'd only remained a mystery for a few hours.

Now Pike knew their names. The man was Troy, and the woman was Gibbs.

The listening device was providing more than just crucial intel for his mission parameters; it was also informing him about his adversaries. The detectives had been at the Horn house for several minutes now, and the wife—whose name he also now knew; Diane—had allowed them in.

The male detective, Troy, did little speaking, and when he did, it came through a monstrous growling voice with which he produced chopped, broken-English sentences.

Quite odd.

There was a pause in the conversation down at the blue house at 125 Maisel, and Pike put a finger to the device in his ear, straining to listen through the gentle hum of static. He glanced out the window as he did so, and this was enough to distract him again, to pull him away from righteous murder and Gulf War Syndrome and the explosion at Eglin Air Force Base years earlier.

A pang of disappointment flooded through him as he took in the beautiful neighborhood. In another life, he could have lived somewhere like this.

The peaceful community had a perfectly peaceful name, Lake Heights, and it blanketed a few dozen acres of rolling Kentucky hillside. Stately homes, mostly two stories in height, with lawns that were well tended and landscaping that was fresh and tidy. An ever-expanding place, by the looks of it, with swaths of fresh concrete, open lots with realtor signs, and new construction.

He stared at the streetlights, which stretched before him like a chain of stars across the blushing sunset, dwindling into the distance, down the hill, illuminating immaculate lawns and processions of flowering bushes and decorative grasses.

Pike could picture himself, in a different reality, walking the neatly trimmed sidewalks by the lush green lawns under those pretty streetlights. He would be well dressed. Maybe there would be a woman on his arm. A girlfriend. No, a wife. In front of them would be their golden retriever, tugging his leash, making them laugh. Maybe there would be a stroller too.

Before his mind could make any more additions to his mental image, a flash of logic brought the fantasy to a sudden halt.

Shit, he *had* lived somewhere like this.

Only a few years ago. When he was still a military officer. Before the explosion. Yes, he remembered. It had a name, something cutesy, something just like "Lake Heights." What had it been called?

How had he forgotten?

Rita.

Had that name, Rita, been in the community's title?

The Orchards of Rita Ridge, perhaps.

Or, *The Village at Rita Meadow.*

There was a small burst of static in his earpiece, bringing him back to the moment, to his mission, refocusing him. He pressed a finger to the earbud, adjusted the volume dial, and looked through the windshield where, two blocks away, sat Kurt Horn's house, a well-lit, bright blue piece of suburban perfection.

Earlier, in the daylight, Pike had rung the doorbell. And knocked. And rang the doorbell a second time. And waited.

Nothing. No sounds from beyond the door and no flashes of movement behind the drapes. So he'd taken a calculated risk, slipped to the side of the house, and installed a tiny listening device on the window, another gift from his unseen friend, the Benefactor.

His calculated risk was now paying off.

He grimaced at another pulse of static. Diane Horn's voice faded out, replaced by warbling distortion, and Pike thought he'd lost reception for good.

Then a voice faded back in.

"Ma'am, it's time," the female detective, Gibbs, said. "You must leave now."

Pike could hear Mrs. Horn's little stammering breaths even through the distortion. "But ... I can't leave. Not ... not without Kurt."

"Now," said a deep, horrible voice.

Pike shook his head.

Not only was Detective Troy a massive man with cold facial expressions, but he had a voice like a broken rototiller. One creepy dude.

Pike put the Polaroid photo aside, grabbed the legal pad from the passenger seat, and placed it on his knee, glanced over his notes, the pieces of intel he'd gathered.

Kurt Horn gone until tomorrow night

Detectives' names: Gibbs, Troy

Blue Ford Taurus. License plate number ???

THEY KNOW ABOUT THE GWS CONNECTION

He focused on the last note.

These Louisville detectives now knew the overarching purpose of Hard Sprint. Gulf War Syndrome.

This was bad.

But not catastrophic. Not yet.

Because there was a silver lining to this situation. The fact that the detectives seemed to have been completely unaware of the GWS connection prior to a few moments ago meant they didn't know the *other* details about Hard Sprint.

The much more crucial details...

That was a relief. But only a small one. Because these two detectives were tenacious as hell.

He studied another note.

Blue Ford Taurus. License plate number???

Pike now knew the make, model, and color of Kurt Horn's vehicle, and he knew the approximate time Horn would make his return to Lake Heights tomorrow.

But he didn't have the fully revealing piece of intel: the plate number. Mrs. Horn had written it down for the other two, not spoken it, so Pike hadn't heard it through his listening device.

Which complicated matters.

Another complication: Kurt Horn drove one of the most common cars in America.

Of course he did...

Damn it all to hell.

But Pike would get this figured out.

A voice in his earpiece. Gibbs.

"We'll watch for your husband, Mrs. Horn. And we'll intercept him before he gets to this house. Please, go somewhere safe."

Then Troy's growly voice.

"Thanks for..." A pause. "Your time."

The sound of footsteps.

Pike glanced at the blue house in the distance. All was still for a moment, then Detectives Gibbs and Troy left the house, stepping into a pool of light on the front porch. They said their goodbyes to Diane Horn, then headed for the black Mercedes parked on the street.

Yes, these two were tenacious.

Pike would have to work extra hard to beat them at their own game.

In order to eliminate the next Hard Sprint survivor.

CHAPTER SIXTEEN

IT WAS a damn nice hotel suite. A sprawling two-bedroom, two-bath unit in downtown Louisville.

Silence took a bottle of Evian from the full-sized fridge, gulped half of it down, and glanced to the wall of windows at the far end of the capacious environment, the pleasing cityscape it presented—towers and traffic and the Ohio River glistening in moonlight.

They'd arrived twenty minutes earlier, and Silence had paid in cash, a standard Watchers practice. It kept things clean. When the hotel clerk had asked for a credit card to cover incidental damages—a custom that was becoming more and more common, Silence had observed—Silence slapped five more hundred-dollar bills on the counter and slid them toward the young twenty-something man. That did the trick. It always did.

The suite had an open floor plan, and it occupied a corner of the hotel's twentieth and top floor. Dark gray carpet, low but plush. Polished metal, black accents along the shelves. Vases. Stainless steel tubes, purely ornamental. And by the twin sofas, a geometric work of metal-and-glass art that served as a fireplace.

Gibbs sat on a sofa, stretched at an awkward angle over the long, black cushions. She'd retrieved a wine bottle and a glass from the welcome basket. Silence had declined to join. Mrs. Enfield's withered voice had echoed through his mind, chastising him, her bone-white eyes in a maternal scowl. He'd already had two beers in as many days. If she found out that he'd had a drink three days in a row—and she *would* interrogate him when he returned to Pensacola—there would be hell to pay.

Gibbs, though, was tipsy. Her chin hovered an inch above her chest as she stared at her wine glass. She had the stem pinched between her thighs, and she cupped the bowl with both hands. One fingernail slowly screeched along the crystal.

When they'd arrived in the suite—which was magnificent by anyone's measure—her reaction had been much more subdued than it had been to the opulent Learjet earlier in the day. The illegal investigation she'd embarked on had surely numbed her consciousness. But Silence sensed more from her lack of reaction. His empathic nature whispered to him again.

Another couple of gulps, and he finished the Evian. He crushed the bottle, deposited it in the foot-pedal trash can, then stepped to the edge of the living room, stopped.

"You," he said and pointed to the bedroom door to the right of the living area. He swung his finger to the opposite door and said, "Me."

He headed for the second door he'd indicated.

"Hey," Gibbs said.

He stopped, turned around.

She blinked. "I could run off."

Her tone of voice gave no implication. She wasn't saying she *would* run off. Rather, she'd spoken so matter-of-factly that it came across as a question: *Why are you turning your back on me?*

"Mutual trust," Silence said and swallowed. "Mutual respect."

Like her, he was communicating surreptitiously. He'd meant what he said, but there was also an implied asterisk. He'd chosen a two-bedroom suite, yes, but not two separate rooms. He had to keep her close, within earshot.

She fidgeted with her wine glass, gave another look to the window and the glistening towers surrounding them. Then her attention returned to Silence. Glossed-over eyes, slightly bloodshot. His estimation moments earlier had been correct. There was something more than tipsiness there. There was pain.

"Do I seem crazy to you?" she said with something resembling a smile—tiny, lopsided, almost bashful.

"No."

She scoffed. "That's all you got? God, you're such a man. I mean, I know speaking is physically difficult for you, but aren't you curious what I meant by that? One typically doesn't ask relative strangers' opinions about..." She hiccuped, fist going to her lips. "One's mental state."

Ohhhh... Now Silence got it. Gibbs was more than just tipsy. She was drunk.

Gibbs tried to adjust her position on the couch, nearly toppled over, scowled at him, more quasi-embarrassment.

"Well?" she said.

"Well what?"

"Aren't you at all curious why I'd ask you such a thing?"

Silence shrugged. "No."

"Asshole." She finally stabilized herself, then reached to the side of the sofa, retrieved her bottle of rosé. It was half empty. "Well, indulge me, handsome." Her voice slurred. "If

I'm forced into this partnership with you, you can at least listen to me."

He took a step closer.

"What I was trying—" She stopped abruptly, hand going to her mouth again, then to her chest, back to her mouth. She cleared her throat. "What I was trying to say is, I've risked everything. My future, my career, my safety. You haven't once asked me why I'm doing this."

She was right. He hadn't asked her why she was doing this. In fact, the *why* of her situation hadn't even crossed his mind. Though he was a killer, Silence and every other Watcher were individuals wholly committed to a benevolent cause. Before joining the Watchers, he'd been a cop like Gibbs, and while he'd encountered more than a few bad apples on the force, the number of well-meaning individuals far outweighed the turds.

He had long been surrounded by people who acted out of purity and good intentions, so he'd simply assumed that Gibbs was conducting her investigation in the same manner. What other reason could she have?

The fact that she assumed another person would think she was insane for doing the right thing further fleshed out the psychological profile he was building for Viola Gibbs.

"I guess most people would think I'm crazy," she said to her wine glass, head drooping once more. "And now I'm here in a luxury hotel suite in downtown Louisville with a big monster of a man and no idea what my life will be like a week from now."

Silence considered offering her something, using his wretched voice to lend a few words of support. She was, after all, offering him quite a bit. She was being "vulnerable," as C.C. would have called it. Silence needed to be true to his offer of mutual trust and respect. So he thought back to what he'd seen moments earlier in her eyes.

"There's more," he said.

She looked up from the glass, narrowed her gaze. "What do you mean?"

"Something else..." He swallowed. "On your mind."

Another scoff. The wine glass teetered precariously in her fingers. "Oh, so suddenly you care?"

Silence didn't respond.

She reaffirmed her grip on the glass, examined it, and her head remained lowered as she said, "Yeah, there's more."

A long pause.

"This assignment ... Well, I guess it's not an assignment at all, is it? This *investigation* brings up some old thoughts. Nagging thoughts. Do you ever wish you could go back in time and change something? Just one thing?"

C.C. on the floor of a mansion.

Motionless.

Her blood was still warm.

"Yes," Silence said.

Gibbs looked up. "Me too."

More pain in the eyes.

"Never mind," she said.

She wobbled to her feet, placed the troublesome glass on the table in front of her—the *clink* of crystal-to-glass contact —and took a circuitous path to her room, shutting the door behind her.

CHAPTER SEVENTEEN

LOS ANGELES, CALIFORNIA

LENA HUBER DIDN'T KNOW where her husband was.

Austin had left earlier in the day to meet Otis Watts, his private detective, a key member of Austin's novel-writing support team. When Austin's own research and that of his technical assistants didn't suffice, when there was more information that couldn't be found in books or newspaper articles or the Internet, Austin called on Otis.

They were an odd pair, for sure—Austin with his intelligence and poise and expensive tastes and lean, sexy body; Otis with his wrinkled, 50%-off polyester and avuncular, salt-of-the-earth charm—but they had formed a collaboration that wasn't perhaps a genuine friendship but was certainly warm and friendly.

Still, the two of them had never met for *this* long before. Austin had said they were going to meet for a late lunch at The Blue Corner.

But that was several hours earlier.

The sun had gone down.

Normally, this wouldn't have been much of a concern for Lena. Austin was often a very difficult man—the quintessentially temperamental artist—so he wasn't the best at keeping her informed about what he was doing, nor was he the best at keeping his word.

And despite his prickliness, he was completely true to her. He hardly even looked at other women. She'd never suspected anything of that nature.

No, what concerned Lena that evening wasn't so much her husband's tardiness but the fact that he'd been acting so bizarrely for the last few days.

So, so bizarrely...

While her nerves had already been rattled by his recent demeanor, they'd been completely destroyed by the phone call she'd received earlier in the evening, leaving her in this bizarre, partly numb, almost catatonic state.

Her fingers encapsulated an oversized, mustard-yellow coffee mug, both hands, and as she squeezed it tighter, she felt no residual heat in the stoneware. She took a sip of the chamomile tea. Cold.

The house felt cold too. She hadn't adjusted the thermostat since the sky had faded from blue to pink to black, bringing a quick temperature drop. There was only one light on in the house, a small table lamp in the kitchen several feet away.

She hadn't bothered to turn on any more lights, hadn't moved at all for a couple of hours, just sat there on the long sofa in the long, open, quintessentially California house. Her tastes weren't so chic as Austin's—despite having a more well-off upbringing—and she'd been insistent that their home have a touch of the traditional, not just modernity. So while there were plenty of squares and long, slashing lines and right angles and high ceilings in the house's design, there were also curves in the doorways, a bit of warmth to the paints and some homey Americana furnishings, including the handmade quilt that was draped over her legs.

A sound jolted her—the garage door opening. Her fingers tensed on the mug.

A moment later, the creak of a door opening, the jingling of keys, and Austin's voice. "Honey?"

"In here," she said.

Footsteps. Austin appeared in the minuscule glow of the kitchen lamp. "Why are you in here in the dark?"

He flipped on the overhead light and squinted in her direction. His dark hair was parted and as perfectly tussled as when he'd left. There was a confused expression on his face that, even with her concerns, made her melt a bit. Austin was certainly L.A.-level attractive.

She answered his question with one of her own. "Where have you been?"

"You know I was with Otis Watts," he said as he sifted through the stack of mail next to the fruit basket on the marble island.

Lena pulled back the quilt and stood. Her thighs were sore and tight after sitting so long on the same day as an intense yoga session. A momentary stretch, and she approached the kitchen.

"That was hours ago," she said.

Satisfied with the mail, Austin stepped to the black French door refrigerator. "It ran long."

She hesitated, and it was a moment before she could steel herself to say what had been going through her mind for the last two hours. "Otis called, and we spoke. *After* your meeting. That was over an hour ago."

Austin stopped chewing the leftover avocado egg salad sandwich he'd grabbed from the fridge. He had been avoiding eye contact, but now he looked right at her, eyes slightly wide. He swallowed his bite and said, "What did he want?"

"He didn't give me specifics, said he's not allowed to. Confidentiality and all that. He just said he's concerned about you." She paused. "I'm worried too, Austin."

Austin groaned, rolled his eyes, returned to the fridge.

"Where were you the rest of the afternoon after you met Otis?"

Austin took another bite and opened the fridge door. There was the crinkling of aluminum foil, and then he stepped out of the kitchen, going for the back of the house.

"I worked in a coffee shop for a while. So what? Should I keep a minute-by-minute log for you?"

Lena followed him. "Is everything okay with you?"

Austin stopped and gave her a smile, one that was very clearly forced. "I'm on deadline. You know how it is, honey."

It wasn't like Austin to be so cryptic, so guarded. For the last three days he'd spent long hours away from the house, and when he was home, he kept his office door shut at times he normally wouldn't, always on the phone, using a hushed voice.

Lena wavered as she responded. "Don't shut me out, Austin." She placed a hand on his forearm. "We're partners in this thing, remember?"

Austin wiped a fleck of avocado from the corner of his mouth, glanced at it, then rubbed it away between his thumb and forefinger. His attention returned to her, another forced smile. "I have more work to do before bed." He looked at her for a moment. "You worry too much."

He kissed her check and turned, heading for the office. Lena remained, watched him close the door behind her. A moment of silence and then soft, muffled noise. But it wasn't the *clack-clack-clack* of his vintage Royal typewriter.

It was his voice. He was back on the phone again, immediately, using that hushed voice she'd become accustomed to the last few days.

Something was very, very wrong about the way her husband was acting.

CHAPTER EIGHTEEN

LOUISVILLE, KENTUCKY

Silence found the secretary, Clarice, looking in his direction, and when his eyes met hers, the woman's attention went to Gibbs. Then back to Silence. Then back to Gibbs. There was a bashful, almost awestruck look on the fifty-something lady's cherubic face, which bore too-thick makeup and a pair of dated glasses.

"I'm sorry," Clarice said, caught in the act, waving a hand like a white flag. "Ya'll just look so nice together. Prettier people I've never seen."

Silence turned to Gibbs. She wore the biggest grin he'd seen since he'd met her.

He gave Clarice a grunt and a nod and returned his attention to a set of blueprints tacked to the trailer's wood-paneled wall. The construction site outside was massive, but so far it was little more than jagged earth, felled trees, machinery, and piles of materials. It was to be a museum, and from the looks of the prints, the place would be magnificent.

Gibbs's footsteps made the trailer's floor squeak as she

slid past Clarice's desk, where the secretary was now furiously one-finger typing on a yellowed computer keyboard.

"You really have a way with words, you know that?" Gibbs said as she stepped beside Silence.

He turned to her, blinked.

Gibbs made a backward motion of her head, indicating Clarice behind them. "She paid you a compliment, and all you gave the poor woman was a grunt."

Silence stared at Gibbs. Thought it through. And grunted.

He returned to his study of the blueprints. A moment passed, and he felt Gibbs's eyes still upon him, turned, found her with a look of trepidation.

"I'm, um, sorry about how I acted last night," she said.

Discomfort swept over Silence.

He was trapped in the tiny central area of a two-office trailer, which was cramped with filing cabinets and boxes and dollies, standing side by side with this individual who only the previous evening had bombarded him with her emotions.

It was way too soon to be touchy-feely again.

"It's fine," he said, even more curtly than he normally would.

But before he could flee into the blueprints again, she said, "It's my brother. That's what I was alluding to last night. He's ... gone."

A wave of guilt struck Silence's gut, a quick one-two combination. He grimaced inwardly.

Shit...

Last night, he thought Gibbs was rattled solely by the nature of this investigation, by the fact that she might well have "forfeited" her future, as she put it. He assumed there was nothing more to it than that.

But clearly he'd misjudged.

Due to his empathic nature, misjudgments like this

happened rarely, and he hated when they did. They almost always ended poorly.

He could see C.C. in his mind, standing before him, shaking her head with disappointment.

"Sorry to hear," he said to Gibbs, imparting as much genuine compassion as he could from his impaired voice.

"No, Dean's not *gone*. Not literally. He's ... just gone from my life. And it's my fault."

There was genuine anguish on her face, and this only emboldened the guilt-boxer in Silence's gut, working him now like a speed bag.

She glanced back at Clarice. Silence did too. The older woman was still pounding away at the keyboard, but she was clearly listening to every word, head angled fractionally in their direction.

Gibbs returned her attention to Silence, gave him a shrug, a little half smile. *I'll tell you more later, if that's okay?* it seemed to say.

Silence was adept at non-verbal communication, so with a nod and solemn eye contact, his response said, *Of course it's okay*.

Gibbs's half smile expanded a bit, to about seventy-five percent, but there was the same look in her eyes that he'd seen the previous night in the hotel suite, the pain.

A sound behind them, and the trailer's thin door swung open, flooding the room with noise, dust, and bright sunlight. A man in a dress shirt, striped tie, and dust-marred slacks entered, holding a clipboard and pinching an orange safety helmet under his arm.

Hubert Tremble.

"Sorry for the wait," Tremble said to Silence and Gibbs as he breezed in. "Please, come with me."

He wiggled past Silence in the tight space and led them to the other office at the opposite end of the trailer, shutting the door behind them and gesturing for Silence and Gibbs to take the two chairs facing the desk, which they did.

Tremble plopped down in the larger chair behind his desk and exhaled as he dropped the clipboard into a tangle of papers and envelopes and other clipboards. His hands went behind his head as the chair leaned back, and he exhaled hard enough to make his lips flop, a man exhausted at only the midway point of his workday.

He was in his early thirties with dark, short-cropped hair, still holding onto his military style. Average height, stocky build. Shirt sleeves rolled up, tie loosened. His glasses were 1950s nerdy, and since the rest of his clothes weren't particularly sharp, Silence wagered that the glasses were worn not with a stylish eye but a blind eye.

"Diane told me Kurt's in trouble," Tremble said as a question, not a statement.

"Yes," Silence said. "Big trouble."

The standard stunned reaction to Silence's bizarre voice was only momentary for Tremble, as the man was clearly more arrested by the notion of his friend's safety. The man's eyebrows drew together.

"You guys cops?" he said.

Gibbs turned to Silence and gave another non-verbal, this one full of hesitancy. *Should we?*

Before the decision was made, Tremble lifted his hands, waved them.

"Wait. Wait! I don't want to know. The pause tells me more than enough. I've been around long enough to know not to ask too many questions. You're here to ask me about Kurt; that's all I need to know."

"Hard Sprint," Silence said and swallowed. "What Kurt tell you?"

Tremble leaned farther back in his chair, interlacing his fingers over his stomach. "Only so much. Understand, we didn't meet until after we were both out of the service. At the VFW. Only two young guys there; the rest are from World War II, Korea, a few from Nam. Kurt and I were both in the Navy, both enlisted, both went to the Gulf, so we had all that in common. But that's about it. I mean, I'm in construction management; he sells stocks. Couldn't be much different."

He chuckled, looking away with fond memories twinkling his eyes. Then an apologetic wave of the hand, and he leaned forward, onto the desk.

"Anyway, I got out right after the war. My tour was up. Kurt had another year left. Starts getting headaches, rashes on his skin. The base docs tell him he's got this Gulf War Syndrome that's been in the news. They say they don't know what to do for him.

"A few months later, his CO gives him TDY orders to Eglin Air Force Base, but even the CO is left in the dark about what's going to happen. It was *that* secretive. So Kurt gets there, meets a handful of other people, all from different branches, almost half of them officers. The only thing they have in common is that they all have GWS symptoms."

He paused, thinking things through.

"All right, the next part is classified. Kurt only told me because they damn near blew him up, killed ten people that night marching them in the murk among unexploded ordnance." Another pause, briefer. "Everyone took an injection before they went out in the bush, an experimental cure for GWS."

Silence and Gibbs exchanged a look.

"Doxycycline?" Silence said to Tremble, referring to an antibiotic that was thought to have efficacy with the syndrome.

The other man shook his head. "That was only part of it. It was some sort of cocktail. The concern was that it would cause immediate fatigue, something that clearly wouldn't do for active-duty service members. So the volunteers took the shot, grabbed their empty M-16s, and followed Captain Pike out into the Florida swamp. A ten-hour hump with hazardous-duty pay. Three hours in, somebody tripped the old bomb."

Tremble looked away, shaking his head slowly, reliving his friend's memories almost as though he'd been there himself.

"Kurt said the blast made everything go white. Pure white, he said. The force threw him twenty feet. He was covered in blood. Everything was silent for a few seconds, and then when his hearing returned, all he heard was screaming. Can you imagine?" He paused. "Kurt was pissed afterward, of course, especially after they hurried things along, hushed everything up. The memories started getting fuzzy for him, so he wrote everything down, including two names he overheard: Kasperson and Noyer. None of the seventeen who went into the field had those names. Kurt never figured out who they were."

He pivoted suddenly, fixing them with a deadly serious stare.

"Understand that I'll never admit I told you any of this, and the only reason I'm doing so is because I'm certain Kurt wouldn't mind."

"What makes you so sure?" Gibbs said.

Tremble raised an eyebrow, looked back and forth between Silence and Gibbs. "Diane didn't tell you Kurt's theory?"

Silence leaned forward, eager for more. He shook his head.

Tremble gave them a grave look. "Because Kurt thinks there was a coverup."

CHAPTER NINETEEN

LOS ANGELES, CALIFORNIA

OTIS SQUASHED his cigarette into the base of the ashtray, one of those ancient ones the size of a salad plate, black plastic, a camelback ridge of peaks and valleys down the center that served as a corral for smoldering cigs. He snaked a hand through the organized chaos of papers and manila file folders on his desk—a heavy metal bitch, just as ancient as his ashtray—and grabbed the audiotape, which he'd put at the far corner, by the window with its mangled Venetian blinds, as far away as possible, as though that would somehow make the thing disappear.

It hadn't.

Otis fidgeted with the tape, tiny in his big hands. A moment of this, and he grabbed the recorder/player sitting on a haphazard stack of invoices, the same device he'd had in his pocket earlier at The Blue Corner.

He'd rewound the tape to the beginning again, so he pressed *FAST-FORWARD* and held a few moments before pressing *STOP*. He'd listened through it enough times now that he had a sense of the length, of the location of the key segment.

He pressed *PLAY*.

Austin's voice came through, scratchy from the small speaker.

"It's a bad coincidence, Otis, my hiring you to look into the incident at the same time as the murders."

A metallic groan. Austin had leaned across the wrought-iron table, getting closer to Otis.

"But if you're implying something horrible, think about this—when we met two nights ago, when I gave you this gig, that was the same night the first person was murdered in Colorado."

"Yeah, man. You're right. I'm sorry," his own voice replied. "Still ... it just seems weird."

A pause. "I want to remind you, that any work you do for me is confidential."

Otis stopped the tape. Exhaled. Then put the player back on the desk beside a stack of newspapers, which he picked up.

The top one was from Colorado—*The Denver Informant*. A flip to the crime section, and he found the article again.

Breckenridge Police: 'No motive' in resort murder; 'senseless tragedy'

The second newspaper was from Panama City, Florida.

City shocked by brazen homicide in parking lot

Otis didn't want to jump to any conclusions, and he didn't want to think that Austin was a sinister person.

But he had to do what was right.

He put the newspapers down and leaned back in his chair, its springs squealing. On the shelf to his right, scattered among other materials, were several of Austin's books. Hard-backs. Too many of them.

Displaying the novels on his weight-warped bookshelves —among his tattered notebooks and texts on forensics and surveillance—was a bit of showiness, if Otis was being honest with himself. Bragging rights. A potential client walks in, sees all the books, and says something like, *Wow, you must be a huge Austin Huber fan*, to which Otis could say, *Oh, those? He just gives them to me. Best-selling author Austin Huber is a client of mine.*

But it was more than braggadocio. No one had ever asked about the novels on his shelves. Otis kept them there because Austin was not only a famous client—his *only* famous client— but Otis also considered him a friend, insomuch as their professional connection allowed.

That word hit Otis hard now.

Friend.

"Oh, shit…" Otis muttered quietly on an exhale.

He leaned across his desk, dragged the phone closer, and before he could talk himself out of it, he pressed the receiver to his ear, and dialed another professional friend.

Two rings, then a response. "LA Field Office, Agent Doyle."

Hearing the deep, familiar voice lightened Otis's somber mood ever so slightly. "Agent Doyle?" he said with a small grin. "Private detective Watts."

"Well, well, well. It's been a while, private detective Watts." Past the background noise of a busy law enforcement office, Otis could hear a reciprocal smile through Doyle's voice. "What can I do for you today? Backstabbing spouse? Runaway teen?"

"Not quite. This time I'm not calling as a colleague; I'm calling as a citizen. What would you say if I told you two murders on either side of the country seem to be connected?"

Doyle didn't immediately respond. There was the staticky

sound of another phone ringing in the distance, urgent conversations. "Different states?"

"Colorado and Florida."

"Well, I'd say you've done the right thing contacting the FBI, but you're being a little light on the details."

"Yeah..."

When Otis offered nothing else, Doyle said, "What do you want to tell me, Watts?"

Otis sat up taller in the chair, preparing himself. "I think one of my clients might be involved in the murders."

CHAPTER TWENTY

LOUISVILLE, KENTUCKY

THE SUNSET WAS EVEN MORE magnificent than the previous evening, further idealizing Lake Heights in Pike's mind, elevating it to fairytale status. The sun teetered on the horizon, just about to disappear, and its light had taken on a magical, golden quality, drifting in beams from behind deep purple clouds in a blazing orange-yellow sky.

Pike had parked in a different area of the community, at the top of the hill, from which he could see Fontaine Street, all the way from the community gates to the intersection at Maisel Court and the house that sat two spots from the stop sign—the Horns' house.

As he waited for Kurt Horn's blue Ford Taurus, he had an unobstructed view of the man's impending route into the community.

He watched through a pair of binoculars—which were another item gifted by his from-a-distance partner, the Benefactor—for a blue Ford Taurus, but his attention kept diverting to another vehicle, parked on the side of Fontaine, right where the street entered the Lake Heights neighborhood.

A black Mercedes.

He wasn't interested in the car itself, rather the two people he knew were inside.

The detectives.

As per their conversation with Diane Horn the previous evening, which Pike had listened to through electronic surveillance, this pair was also waiting for the blue Taurus. Unlike Pike, they had the advantage of knowing the car's license plate number.

A vehicle rounded a curve in the distance. Dark. Sedan. It could be...

Yes! It was. A blue Ford Taurus.

But since Pike didn't have the plate number, he'd only know for sure that it was the *right* blue Taurus if the Mercedes followed it.

A block into Lake Heights, and the Taurus crept past the Mercedes.

The Mercedes remained stationary.

Pike's shoulders dropped. He sighed.

"Damn it."

But then the Mercedes' headlights illuminated, and it pulled onto the street behind the Taurus. It flashed its brights on and off, on and off. Over the distance, Pike could hear a horn blaring.

The Taurus pulled to the side of the road.

And as the Mercedes slowed to a stop behind it, Pike put his vehicle in gear and took off. No time left to observe. Seconds mattered now, every single one.

He smashed the gas pedal.

CHAPTER TWENTY-ONE

GIBBS OPENED THE DOOR, climbed out of the Mercedes, and followed Troy as he slowly approached the Ford Taurus. The air had chilled a bit at this early stage of dusk. Crickets chirped. Quiet neighborhood sounds carried out of windows —television sets, dinner conversations, laughing children.

Troy had parked several car lengths back, giving Kurt Horn space, and as they crept toward the Taurus, the driver-side door swung open, and Horn stepped out, looking as confused as he did pissed off.

"What the hell is this all about?"

A dead-ringer for the man in the file photos. Black, medium complexion, squinty eyes on a round head shaved perfectly clean. Athletic physique. He wore well-made dress clothes—a form fitting shirt with sleeves rolled up, tie loosened, blue pants.

It was him.

Gibbs exhaled. Tension melted from the muscles in her face. For the first time, this self-prescribed mission of hers made sense. She was about to save this man's life. It had all been worth it. Her massive gamble had paid off.

Troy held up a hand in a mediating motion as he continued toward Horn.

"Sir," he said with his monstrous voice. "We need to—"

The roar of an engine.

A streaking blur of movement.

And a vehicle flew in from the side and smashed Kurt Horn against the Taurus.

CHAPTER TWENTY-TWO

AN EXPLOSION OF SOUND. Metal bent. Glass crackled and snapped.

Pike flew forward, slammed into the seatbelt. His chin snapped down, and his arms flailed in front of him, one of them skirting off the side of the dash, kissing the windshield, tearing his knuckles. Something both soft and hard enveloped him—the airbag. The car's mass jolted to the side, wailing, tires screeching. Pike crashed against the door panel.

And the chaos stopped.

Ringing in his ears. He put a hand to his head. Sharp pain in his neck. He groaned. A hissing sound from somewhere under his car's hood. An acrid smell, something chemical and raw.

He squinted through the spiderwebbed remains of his windshield, past the airbag, to the Taurus. Its driver-side door was a tangled mess. Kurt Horn lay halfway inside the car, halfway outside, straddling the door sill, motionless.

Pike yanked the door handle. A metallic whine. It didn't budge. Keeping pressure on the handle, he drove his shoulder into the plastic trim panel, and this time the door creaked open.

He poured out of the car, onto to the pavement, pushed himself to his knees.

And immediately saw someone rushing in his direction. Someone tall and fast. One of the detectives, the giant, cold-faced man.

Shit!

Neighbors emerged from the houses. Some ran toward the accident.

"Everyone all right?" a voice asked.

Pike's shoes scraped at the asphalt as he tried to pull himself to his feet, and as he flailed, he glanced again at the Taurus. The mangled door. And Kurt Horn.

Alive!

The man was unconscious, but somehow the son of a bitch was still breathing, his chest rising and lowering rapidly.

Pike got one foot beneath him, put a little weight on it. It was unsteady, but it held. Both feet now. He stood, stumbled to his left.

He went for his gun to finish Horn off but felt the detective's presence.

He looked.

The big man was even closer. And now he held a Beretta.

A quick glance back to Horn. The twisted metal of the door hid most angles. The only fully exposed part of Horn's body were his two muscular legs, crammed into blue dress pants, splayed at awkward angles on the street

Pike didn't have a shot.

And he could feel the big man right behind him.

Pike dashed toward the nearest house, crossing onto the lawn.

CHAPTER TWENTY-THREE

SILENCE LEVELED his Beretta and shouted, "*Hold, Pike!*"

Instantly, a horrible tearing sensation tore through the mangled scar tissue of his neck. He often raised his voice, but he rarely yelled. Every time he did, he received a wave of agony for his efforts.

Pike came to a quick stop in the front lawn of one of Lake Height's many picture-perfect suburban homes. He put his hands in the air, slowly turned around, and looked right at Silence.

One blue eye. One brown.

Both of them locked in on Silence.

Pike was about five-foot-nine, average proportions with a trim but athletic build. A strong, square jaw on an otherwise plain face. Nothing about his appearance was particularly arresting.

Except those eyes...

Pike wobbled to the side, his feet shuffling, and there was a tiny line of blood on his left temple. Otherwise, he'd taken the car wreck like a champ.

Silence continued forward, gun squarely aimed at the

other man. But even though Pike kept his hands in the air, the creep continued inching farther and farther backward into the lawn.

A smirk formed on Pike's lips.

"You gonna fire?" Pike shouted. "Into a crowded residential neighborhood?" He gestured with one of his raised hands toward their surroundings. "All these houses. All these people coming outside to see the car accident." A pause. "I don't think you will."

There was the sound of sirens from behind.

It was a hell of a presumption on Pike's part, which meant that the man must think Silence was law enforcement, which further meant—

Before Silence could give it another moment of consideration, Pike turned and bolted, going for the back lawn.

Silence sprinted after him, holstering the Beretta.

Ahead, Pike scrambled over a short fence.

A moment later, Silence did too, and as his feet reached concrete, not grass, he saw a swimming pool in front of him.

Snap!

The cracking sound coincided with a sudden, searing pain in Silence's shins that sent him lurching forward.

He had just enough time to see that Pike had hidden behind the fence, clenching a pool skimmer, which he'd swung across Silence's legs.

Silence stumbled forward. One step. Two steps. Trying to stop it.

But it was hopeless.

Splash!

Water engulfed him, and for a moment, his limbs thrashed before he righted himself, pulled himself above the waterline and to the edge of the pool. His fingertips gripped the rough concrete surface, and with a surge of energy, he hoisted his giant frame out of the pool.

And found himself alone.

Pike was gone.

Water cascaded down Silence's long body as he ran to the back of the lawn, past a small resin storage shed, and looked over the fence, found his target.

Pike was several houses away now, sprinting across another back lawn.

The coarse wood of the fence dug into Silence's palms as he vaulted over. Ahead was a long, downhill stretch of yards, none of them fenced in, which gave Silence a wide-open path to catch up with the other man. The problem, though, was that Pike had built a sizable lead while Silence took his plunge in the pool.

More neighbors had materialized, these coming from the back doors of their homes, and as the two men sprinted through the yards, there were screams of fear, shouts to leave. The hill's grade grew steep as Silence ran, propelling him faster and faster, his legs flailing wildly.

At the bottom of the hill, a street crossed their path, and Pike stumbled with the change of surface when he hit the sidewalk. He fell over, quickly scrambled back to his feet, stole a glance at Silence, and took off down the street. When Silence barreled down the last few feet of the hill and hit the sidewalk himself, he managed to keep his balance and chased after Pike, closing the gap.

A block ahead of them was a small, upscale shopping area —an outdoor mall lined with wide pedestrian paths and a large metal sculpture of a race horse, which was surrounded by lush landscaping and illuminated from below. Restaurants. Boutiques. A local knock-off Starbucks. Tables with umbrellas.

Pike ran into the crowd. People screamed, made way. Silence was right behind him.

Pike looked over his shoulder, the mismatched eyes registering fear at the close proximity of his pursuer. He grabbed an elderly man who was pushing a walker and threw the man to the ground, right into Silence's path.

Silence leapt over the man and his metal contraption, toes narrowly missing a steel pole. He landed safely on the other side, but he lost momentum. Pike now had a lead again, and he turned a corner, disappearing past another throng of people.

As Silence rounded the corner, he came to a sudden stop, chest heaving, and he hesitated for a half moment at the new obstacle that had been revealed.

A massive crowd of people.

It was an outdoor theater, and a performance was about to begin. A large field of lush Kentucky bluegrass strewn with blankets and lawn chairs. At the back was a permanent stage with a canopy, massive speakers, and high-end set dressing. A sign to Silence's right read: *SHAKESPEARE UNDER THE STARS.*

Silence scanned the crowd. Picnic baskets and wine bottles. Laughing, relaxed people. Playbills. Cheese trays.

But no murderer with mismatched eyes.

Silence stepped into the field, and immediately there was a voice behind him.

"Sir. *Sir!*"

He turned. An acne-riddled teenager wearing ill-fitting black dress pants, a white shirt, and a red tie approached.

"Sir, do you have a ticket?"

Silence grabbed his soaked wallet, peeled off the first dripping bill he could grab—a fifty—thrust it at the kid, and turned back around.

The kid called out behind him. "Let me get your change, sir. Sir?"

Silence moved through the crowd. The smell of food and

wine and bug spray. People stared at him, made whispered comments about his dripping clothing.

He squinted at the encroaching darkness. So many people. Hundreds. Pike could be sitting by the stage. Or at the back. Or he could have slipped into the restrooms.

A woman giggled until Silence's attention snapped to her, and they made eye contact. Her laughter immediately ceased, and she turned away.

A child's voice behind him. "Daddy, why's that man all wet?"

Silence exhaled and gave a final, futile scan of the crowd. He wiped wet bangs from his forehead.

Then a whistle.

He turned.

Way on the opposite side of the theatre, a golf cart rumbled down the concrete path. Stenciled letters labeled the cart as: *COMPLIMENTARY SHUTTLE.*

On the backward-facing seats at the rear of the cart were three people squeezed in against each other. One of them was Pike. Waving at Silence. Smiling.

The cart rounded a corner.

And Pike disappeared.

CHAPTER TWENTY-FOUR

LOS ANGELES, CALIFORNIA

AUSTIN PUT the phone's receiver back in its cradle.

"Shit," he muttered.

Another wrong identity. And so he crossed another name off the list, removing another potential.

He swiveled the desk chair past his antique Royal type-writer to his IBM, which was connected to the Internet via AOL. He opened the World Wide Web feature and returned to the Louisville, Kentucky, newspaper website he'd been frequenting. He opened the crime section and found the minute-by-minute headlines, clicking on the one that hadn't been there the last time he'd checked:

BREAKING: Man in critical condition after brutal hit-and-run incident

The photo showed a dark blue Ford Taurus sitting askew on the side of a street in what looked to be an upscale, upstart suburb. The driver-side door mangled. Emergency personnel and vehicles. Crime scene tape. A stretcher.

Austin quickly read through the short article.

A man had been standing by his Taurus when he was struck by another vehicle, a rental. The assailant—who was not identified, as the Crown Vic had been rented with a fraudulent driver's license—abandoned the scene on foot. The victim was in critical condition but alive. Austin read the man's name aloud.

"Kurt Horn..."

He leaned back in his chair, looked away from the computer to the window, where, beyond white horizontal blinds, a palm tree moving gently in the breeze, illuminated by the bright exterior lighting Austin had installed a few months after purchasing the house.

Kurt Horn had been attacked.

And had *survived*.

Austin's fingers clenched into fists.

The article on the screen in front of him made his mind flash on Otis Watts, the quasi-implication that the detective had made at The Blue Corner. With his suspicions aroused, Otis had surely searched through the national papers along with whatever crime databases afforded to him as a private investigator.

Which meant he would soon find out about Kurt Horn as well. If he hadn't already.

Austin never should have trusted Otis Watts. On the surface, he looked like a shyster—a slimy used car salesman, a greedy insurance agent, a discount carpet dealer with a gambling debt he was itching to pay off. A weasel. But the reality was, there was a damn honorable core to the old slob. Austin hadn't fully recognized this quality until yesterday's lunch meeting.

Which might have been too late. The old fool's scruples were going to be problematic for Austin's plan.

Otis had a contact at the FBI.

What if.

What if, what if, what if.

Yes, Otis Watts was a problem.

A tap at his door, and he turned to see it inch open, a slight squeal from the hinges. Lena. In her hand was a small dish with a muffin and an apple. And on her face was that look of concern she'd worn when he'd last seen her.

Her medium-brown hair was tinted by the hallway light she'd turned on, giving it a warm glow that was at odds with her eyes, which were bloodshot, eyelashes damp. Her cheeks, too, were moist, including the prominent beauty mark on her left cheek. By conventional standards, it was almost too large, but someone as beautiful as Lena could pull it off. A latter day Marilyn Monroe.

She stayed in the doorway, and extended the snack plate toward him a few inches, a sweet gesture and almost pitiful.

"Thought you might be hungry."

Austin clicked the Louisville website away, then turned to her with a smile that was at the same time appreciative and frustrated.

He crossed the room and took the plate.

"Thanks."

Lena's eyes flicked to the computer and back to him. "Austin, what are you doing?"

"I told you. I'm writing. You know I can't have distractions, babe. Please."

"I didn't hear the typewriter."

He examined the muffin. Banana nut. Not his favorite, but it would do. "Research. The Internet. Wave of the future, ya know?"

"But I heard you on the phone again."

His jaw clenched, and he set the plate down on the desk too hard. The stoneware clanked loudly against the designer concrete surface.

"Is this an interrogation, Lena?"

She stared at him for a moment. Fresh tears welled in her eyes, making her squint, revealing the delicate crow's feet that had developed over the last few years.

"You're scaring me."

She walked away.

He watched as she disappeared around the corner, into the darkness of the living room. She still hadn't turned any lights on.

He shut the door.

Had she seen the article on the computer screen? Probably so. She might not have read the headline, but she definitely would have seen the image of the mangled vehicle.

And since she and Otis had spoken on the phone, Austin would have to assume she would tell him what she'd seen.

So now Austin needed to be wary not only of the private detective, but his wife as well.

Yes, Lena was becoming a problem, something that could derail his mission.

Complications were multiplying, threads of control disintegrating.

And Austin hated not being in control.

No time to worry about any of that now, though. He had to stay focused on his task.

Another look at the banana-nut muffin, and he skipped over it in favor of the apple. He dropped back into his desk chair, took a bite, and looked at the list of names and numbers on his notepad.

Then he picked up the phone.

CHAPTER TWENTY-FIVE

LOUISVILLE, KENTUCKY

PIKE COULDN'T BELIEVE he was back at this horrid place, but at least the nighttime darkness hid some of the nastiness, blurring the edges.

When he stepped through the doors of Kendrick Horn's shithole shack of a home, the red-haired crackhead was there, in the same position he'd last found her, curled in a ball on the threadbare plaid armchair, surrounded by debris.

She was, however, much more cogent than the last time, and as she locked eyes with him and the color drained from her face, it was clear that she was even more shocked than Pike about his return.

He moved toward her, stepping over an upturned and ruined baby walker. The implications of this discarded item were sickening.

Christ, the smell of the place. Urine and cigarettes and sour beer and hopelessness.

"What do you want?" the woman said, shielding her face and crawling up the back of the chair.

Pike stopped a yard away from her. "Just an offer."

"You ... you killed my friend Ken. He was a good man."

Among the patchwork of skin lesions on her face and forearms, one sore pulled his attention. On her left cheekbone. Bigger than the others. Angry red and open.

He forced himself to focus.

"No, Ken was not a good man. Did you know he beat a girl up so bad she spent a month in the hospital? This was years back."

"Ken?"

Pike nodded. He continued with the lie, breaking whatever bonds she had to the place, flimsy though he suspected them to be.

"That's right. And another two years before that. She was..." He paused, took in a dramatic breath deep enough to flair his nostrils. "A friend of mine. A very special friend of mine."

"Ohhh. So that's why you...?" She trailed off and made a pistol with her fingers.

"That's right."

"Damn..."

She scratched at the mottling on her left forearm, hard enough to make an audible sound. This made Pike's own skin crawl, but again he forced himself to continue with the performance unfazed.

The woman looked away from him as she continued to scratch. "You're a good man, mister, to come back after all these years and make things right. I always knew there was something off about Ken. I didn't fully trust him, understand. You believe me, right? He just gets me crumbs. And ... well, you know."

She looked away with an embarrassed, sheepish smile.

Pike took "crumbs" to mean crack rocks.

As far as the "you know"...

He glanced around the filth, wondering where in the hell they'd committed "you know," pictured them banging away on the tattered recliner.

"But why are you back?" the woman said.

Pike just smiled. "What's your name?"

"Ruby."

"Ruby. That's a pretty name. I'm Tristan." He got closer to her. "I'm here because I have a job that needs doing. You seem like the right person for the job."

An incredulous snort. "Me?

"It's five thousand dollars. Do you really want to ask questions?"

Her eyes lit up. Pike knew it would be an astronomical sum to a druggie. That's why he'd started with a relatively high amount. Really, though, it was nothing. His unknown partner, the Benefactor, was giving him an endless pool of funds for his venture.

Ruby hopped out of her chair. "Yes! God, yes. Of course!"

"Good. Then gather your stuff," he said. "We're headed across the country. Ever been to California?"

CHAPTER TWENTY-SIX

SILENCE WAS STILL SOAKED by the time he returned to the scene of the accident. The foot chase had done little to dry him, nor had the cool, pleasant nighttime air, which now felt frigid.

He'd draped his sport coat over his arm, and it flopped limply like something he'd just hunted down, bleeding water onto the concrete, a steady drip. He'd have the jacket—and the rest of his clothing—professionally cleaned back at the hotel.

It was now completely dark, and the houses ahead pulsed blue. Cop cars and an ambulance. Police tape glowing in the gentle breeze. Gawkers. His Mercedes. He slowed as he approached the scene, hovering a couple of blocks back. Lights.

He squinted as he studied the crowd. No Gibbs. Good. But where had she—

Psst!

Silence turned, and Gibbs approached stepping out of the shadows and into the streetlight.

"Hey," she said.

Silence pointed to the scene ahead. "You tell them anything?"

She shook her head. "I lied. I stabilized Horn until they arrived, told them I was walking the neighborhood, that I didn't know about the Mercedes, then disappeared before they could get my name."

"Good."

Gibbs was catching on, learning how to play the clandestine game. He liked it.

"Back to hotel," he said and turned away.

Gibbs stayed put, pointing back to the accident. "But your car..."

"We take cab."

"You're just going to leave it?"

Yes, he was just going to leave it.

Eventually, someone in a position of authority would investigate the abandoned vehicle. And they would find the brand-new Mercedes was registered to a non-existent Louisville citizen at a non-existent address. It would be a real head-scratcher, an administrative nightmare, but soon enough the vehicle would go to auction, and the authorities would move on to more important matters, and the bizarre Mercedes would be forgotten.

"It's a burner," Silence said.

———

Back at the hotel, Silence's clothes had gone to the laundry service with an extra tip for quick turnaround. He'd switched into pajamas—gray T-shirt, cotton-poly blend, V-neck, loose fit, and black modal pants, Calvin Klein.

Gibbs was at the wine again, and after Silence unplugged his laptop from the phone jack, wound the cords, and collapsed the computer, he dropped into the sofa across from her.

"Drink with me," she said and offered him a glass. Her hand was steady, unlike the previous night.

Again, Silence's mind went to Mrs. Enfield and her monitoring of his drinking. Still, there were times when he needed to do what was most mission-appropriate.

So he would have one drink, even if it was wine. He preferred beer.

He took the glass. She poured.

He placed the computer on the table between them, and spun it around so she could see the email message he'd received.

```
Lynn Davidson
348 Ledbury Street
San Francisco


Proceed immediately to San Francisco.
Transportation: Bowman Field, 0400.
```

Gibbs beamed. "How did you figure this out?"

"We have our ways."

He could have just said, *We have Specialists.* They were the real miracle-workers of the Watchers.

He took a sip. The wine was not without its charm, but he wished it was a good 'ol Heineken. While Silence preferred to surround himself with high-quality furnishings and drape himself in stylish clothing, his tastes in food and drink were quite plain. Burgers, pizza, beer, doughnuts.

C.C. had told him he had an "unrefined palate."

He drained the rest of the glass, stood, and turned for his bedroom. "'Night."

"Mind if I share something with you?"

Silence froze. His immediate reaction was one of resistance, but then he remembered that earlier in the day at Hubert Tremble's construction trailer he'd promised her that she could finish the story she'd started.

He also remembered how he'd unwittingly been curt with Gibbs before finding out about her brother.

He would improve on his earlier mistake. This would make C.C. proud of him. She'd been a self-improvement aficionado and had thrust this hobby onto Silence as well.

So Silence returned to the sofa across from Gibbs and sat.

"Go ahead," he said.

Gibbs tucked a wayward strand of hair behind her ear, ran a finger along the rim of her wine glass.

"I told you about my brother. Dean. How he's out of my life." A pause. "He had an alcohol problem. Landed himself in the ER. On the way to the hospital, his wife hit a patch of black ice, wrapped the car around a telephone pole. My two-year-old nephew was in the vehicle with her. Both dead. They wouldn't have been out on those icy roads if my brother hadn't been so shitfaced he fell down a flight of stairs and broke his bones. I blamed him for their deaths, never forgave him."

She traced a finger along the seam at the edge of the sofa cushion.

"Well, last night I was pretty drunk, as you could tell, and when I woke up this morning, it got me to thinking, maybe people handle addictions in different ways. Maybe it's true that some people are more prone to addiction than others. Do you agree?"

"Yes," Silence said.

She nodded, and her finger continued to explore the cushion seam. "I mean, *he* didn't kill them. Not directly. It's not like he got drunk and drove them into that telephone pole. Maybe I should forgive him."

She looked at him as though her last statement was a question and waited for an answer, blinked.

After a pause, he replied. "I think you..." He swallowed. "Should forgive. And call him."

Her mouth parted.

"You're right," she said and looked away, to her glass. "Who am I to judge him? I mean, I sure can't handle my alcohol. I'm not drunk like last night, but believe me, I'm tipsy."

She giggled, the most feminine and most unguarded he'd yet seen her. And when she looked back to him again, there was the look.

The look.

It can happen in a flash, without warning and certainly without reason. Some sort of telepathic communication between human beings, primordial, not of this realm.

Before he'd become Silence, before the incident that had stolen his voice, his face, and C.C., the man he'd been was handsome enough to turn a few heads, to get the occasional compliment.

But when the Watchers conscripted him as an unconscious, nearly-beaten-to-death individual with a destroyed face, they took the liberty of reconstructing him. The plastic surgeon Specialist who did the work had been a Beverly Hills elite who used Silence's destroyed head as an empty canvas with which he crafted his masterpiece, his magnum opus, turning Silence into an exotic-looking Adonis.

Silence's new appearance was problematic for him, because he was true to C.C.

He often received "the look."

But not in a situation like this.

Alone with the woman.

In a posh hotel suite.

With flowing alcohol.

He pictured C.C.

Curly, dark hair.

Dark eyes, twinkling with life. Warm smile.

A flash of her dead face. Beaten nearly as badly as his had been. One side horribly contused, unrecognizable. The other side torn and mangled, flaps of skin, underlying tissue.

Cold flesh.

And then she was back. Smiling.

I love you.

I love you, too.

Gibbs's eyes were droopy now—either alcohol eyes or bedroom eyes. Or both.

A fraction of a grin on her lips. "Hey, do you think—"

Silence stood and headed for his room. "Goodnight."

CHAPTER TWENTY-SEVEN

SAN MATEO COUNTY, CALIFORNIA

PIKE HAD the Dodge Intrepid's windows rolled down as he blasted north on Highway 101. Fresh California morning air poured through the cab but did little to drown out the stale smell of cigarette smoke ingrained in the seats of this supposedly non-smoking rental vehicle he'd acquired at San Francisco International Airport. But this annoyance barely registered.

The euphoric feeling pulsing from below drowned out any other sensation.

He gave a small moan that turned into an unbridled laugh as he let the crown of his head drop to the headrest. He glanced to the side, out the window to the dark gray, misty morning. In the east, a glow was forming, ready to light the world.

Pike kept one hand on the wheel and the other buried in Ruby's oily red hair as her head moved up and down. When she'd made the proposal—twenty dollars for top-notch work, she'd assured him—it quickly dawned on him that he'd never experienced road head.

What had been even more surprising was how quickly he accepted her offer.

And while the experience was more than he had dreamed of, something felt off.

Wrong.

Almost … immoral.

Kind of like cheating.

Then the logical part of his brain fired again. It was just oral sex.

Just sex.

Sex.

Rita.

He saw a woman with reddish-brown hair, brown eyes.

Laughing.

Asking him about his day.

She smiled a lot.

She loved taking Polaroid photos. And she loved to travel.

Combining the two was the epitome of joy—taking Polaroid pictures while on vacation.

How was your day?

She smiled a lot. A big smile, full of teeth, and joy.

Polaroid photos of her smile.

How was your day?

I … I didn't get the job.

Aww, babe. It's okay.

She smiled a lot. Even during sex.

Naked. Skin moist. Her hands on his sides.

Just sex.

Ruby crashed her head down harder than before, and Pike gasped, grinning like an idiot.

And suddenly frowned.

Who the hell was Rita?

And ... why was he here? Why was he doing this?

It had been years since the incident at Eglin. What had he done in that time?

He just ... couldn't remember.

Years.

He kept reminding himself.

It had been *years*.

What had he done since then?

Think.

He obeyed the command, searching his history. And he immediately landed back at Hard Sprint.

The explosion.

The screams. The copper scent of blood.

They'd been way out in the bush. Way out there. The middle of nowhere. There had been some moonlight, but the trees hid it.

So many had died. And a few hadn't.

Traitors.

Terrorist spies.

Yes! *That's* why he was doing this.

There was a sudden wave of sensation from below, and he returned to Highway 101. He moaned. Ruby had crafted some special magic so powerful that it teleported him back into reality.

At just the right moment. His cellular phone chimed.

He checked the screen and answered.

"Yes, Benefactor?"

The man gave him the address for the correct Lynn Davidson. Pike wouldn't have to search the whole city.

"Well, that's—" He stopped abruptly with a move from below. "Good news."

The Benefactor agreed and hung up.

In the nick of time.

Pike frantically pressed the END button, letting out a

loud noise, fingers clenching.

Rita.

Ruby moved his arm, and she went back to her seat, wiping her lips. After fastening her seatbelt, she held out her hand. Pike produced a twenty from his pocket.

Rita thanked him.

No, Ruby thanked him.

He zipped up and refastened both of his belts—his seat-belt and the one belonging to his pants. He somehow settled even farther back into his seat, smile on his lips.

Because not only had that just happened with Ruby, but a wonderfully ominous sign zipped past on the highway.

WELCOME TO SAN FRANCISCO

CHAPTER TWENTY-EIGHT

SAN FRANCISCO, CALIFORNIA

WHEN THEY'D GOTTEN into the latest Mercedes at the San Francisco airport—this one just like the previous one, only white instead of black—Gibbs told Troy that this was her first visit to the City by the Bay. Though he hadn't responded to her statement, he soon became a tour guide of sorts as he drove them through town, offering short, nominal, low-syllable-count commentary as he pointed through the windshield.

Candlestick Park, he'd said.

Bay Bridge.

Ferry Building.

Chinatown.

His face had remained as blank and inscrutable as always —like a fully automated, robotic docent—but the gesture made Gibbs smile.

So adorable.

She surprised herself with the smile, and realized that it wasn't just because of Troy's sudden and perplexing act of kindness, but also because of the city itself. She'd only been there a few minutes, and she was already understanding the fascination people had with it, the reason Tony Bennett had left his heart in the city. Aside from the beautiful blue sky, the pristine surroundings, and the cheerful palm trees, there was an energy in the air that was unmistakable. It felt like hope.

And, for a moment, it made her forget her troubles, the uncertainty of her future.

She also lost track of what she was doing; she didn't even know their objective.

"Where are we going?"

"We eat," Troy said.

"Alrighty," she said and shrugged. "We eat."

She looked out the window again as they rolled down the Embarcadero, a major thoroughfare that ran along the eastern waterfront, lined by long piers jutting into the bay—some of them serving their original purpose and lined with boats, others repurposed into shopping centers.

Gorgeous. All of it.

Maybe I'm only visiting for a few hours, Tony, she thought, *but I'll be leaving some heart here too.*

———

A few minutes later, they were at Fisherman's Wharf, a tourist destination on the waterfront loaded with souvenir shops and places selling sour dough and chowder. Though they hadn't gone to the water's edge, she could see a magnificent view of the bay with Golden Gate Bridge in the distance.

She ate a sourdough bread sandwich. Troy, surprisingly, munched a salad.

"Lynn Davidson's not home," he said and swallowed. He glanced at his watch. "Half an hour."

"How do you know she's not home?"

"We have—"

"Your organization has it ways, yes."

She rolled her eyes.

Troy's cellular phone rang.

"Speak of the devil," Gibbs said.

Troy flipped the phone open. "Yes?"

She heard a muffled voice from the other end of the line.

"Yes, sir." He snapped the phone shut, turned to Gibbs. "TV."

She cocked her head. "Huh?"

"We need TV."

It took her a moment to comprehend his latest abbreviated sentence, then she turned around and scanned the smattering of shops and restaurants for a television set.

"There," she said, pointing to a chowder stand with a small set affixed to its stainless steel roof.

As she and Troy started toward it, she noticed that a small crowd had formed around the image. Hushed voices became audible as they approached.

Oh my god! I know where that is!

Are they going to show it if it happens?

A long line of block letters at the bottom of the screen read:

EMERGENCY CREWS ADDRESSING SUICIDE SITUATION IN FINANCIAL DISTRICT

Above the text was an image of a tall building with a lone figure plastered to its side, standing on a ledge. A woman. Screaming.

A jumper.

"And it appears the woman has been at the Thatcher Tower for over two hours now, Dan," a female voice said from the television set. "For those of you just tuning in to this unfolding story, a woman calling herself Lynn Davidson is perched on a high-rise ledge, threatening to jump. While her demands are unclear..."

A scratching noise to Gibbs's left. She turned.

It had been Troy's shoes on the brickwork. He was dashing away, shouldering his way through the crowd.

She took off after him.

CHAPTER TWENTY-NINE

AFTER BRINGING THE NEW, white Mercedes to a screeching stop a few blocks away from the action—behind a police barricade—Silence and Gibbs sprinted to the Thatcher Tower.

Silence craned his neck and readied the binoculars that he'd grabbed from the Watchers' kit in the Mercedes' trunk. The magnified view was dizzying as he traced up, up, up the brick facade of the tower, an old, turn-of-the-century job, maybe twelve stories tall. Pink-orange dawn light glinted off the windows, making him squint. He found the dark spot he'd seen moments earlier, the focus of everyone's attention on the ground, the screaming woman, the jumper.

She looked nothing like the photo of Lynn Davidson he'd seen in the materials the Watchers supplied...

Even with the distance-amplified wobble and the small image presented by the binoculars, he recognized the signs of a junkie. The woman was thin with overly prominent cheekbones. Sores all over her skin. She screamed and gestured wildly with one arm as she held on tightly to the window frame with her other. The wind tossed her red hair, and—

Red hair...

Silence focused on her face, and a recent memory flashed through his mind—visiting Kendrick Horn's house when he and Gibbs had first arrived in Louisville, the news channel outside the house, the cop interviewing a woman on the porch.

Silence didn't just recognize a crackhead when he saw one. He recognized *that* crackhead. He'd seen the woman before.

He lowered the binoculars.

"What is it?" Gibbs said, stepping closer.

"Pike... Diversion..."

"Huh?"

"Pike know's he's getting..." He swallowed. "Police attention now." He pointed to the building. "Woman from Louisville." Another swallow. "We've been had."

He pulled out his PenPal, flipped it open to the last marked page, the most recent note, the address he needed.

Lynn Davidson
348 Ledbury Street
San Francisco

"Come on!" he said and sprinted back toward the car.

———

Silence had already slowed the Mercedes from its roaring, feverish pace long before he got to Lynn Davidson's house.

Because he'd seen police tape and emergency lights from blocks away.

The house was in a wooded neighborhood of two-story, cozy-looking homes. Classical American architecture, much less stately and attention-grabbing than the city's famous Victorian homes, with a stolid, dependable beauty. Full-grown trees, age-kissed sidewalks—what a real estate agent would call an "established" community. The sounds of insects echoed among the giant tree trunks.

Police squad cars with flashing blue lights surrounded 348 Ledbury. An ambulance was parked at the corner of the lot—also with flashing lights, red—and a group of medical personnel were slowly guiding a cloth-draped stretcher toward it.

"Shit..." Silence uttered.

He exhaled. And for a moment, he just sat there with his hands on top of the steering wheel. Gibbs said nothing.

Then Silence stepped out of the car, leaving the door open and leaning against it. He watched the stretcher being loaded into the back of the ambulance.

Lynn Davidson. Dead. And only because Pike had been able to fool them.

Silence allowed self-loathing to roll through him, a technique that C.C. had taught him. She had said that instead of trying to reject or deny negative emotions, a person should acknowledge the emotions' existence and simply permit them to pass through, not giving them power.

He closed his eyes. Let his body slacken. Felt his touch points—his feet on the ground, a bit more of his weight on the left foot than the right; his forearm pressed against the Mercedes' door, the weatherstripping pressed to his skin, sticking with a slight bit of sweat; his other hand on the car's roof. He felt the air around him. Quiet voices from a block up, the emergency personnel.

He opened his eyes.

A five-second meditation. Another of C.C.'s techniques.

Refocused, he pulled his mind back to rationality, away from foolish emotions, from negativity, and zeroed in on the upcoming tasks.

There were two more Hard Sprint survivors unaccounted

for: Milano and Langstaff. Pike's next two targets. Of course, Kurt Horn had survived Pike's attack, which meant that Pike might go back to finish him off, and—

Silence's thought process stopped abruptly. While his mind had been processing computations, his eyes had been working subconsciously, and they found something peculiar— a man with his hands in his pockets, on the civilian side of the police tape, the opposite corner of the property as the ambulance.

It was the same man Silence had seen in Florida and Kentucky.

He was dressed entirely differently from before. Not his beach-going vacation clothes or his T-shirt and jeans. Now he wore a black suit, white shirt, sensible blue tie. The man watched the proceedings on Ledbury, then turned in Silence's direction.

And made eye contact.

A few moments of this, then the man started walking in Silence's direction.

Silence's skin prickled, and he sensed the weight of the Beretta pressed against his ribs in its shoulder holster.

"Should we leave?" Gibbs said, her voice tinged with panic.

"No."

The man drew closer, his hands remaining in his pockets. The earlier glimpses at the Pensacola airport and outside the Horn house in Louisville had been fleeting. Now Silence could study the guy.

Early thirties or so. About five-foot-nine. Muscular build. Squinting eyes. Dark blond hair, parted and styled. A patch of I'm-so-cool hair growing from his chin. One hand remained in his pocket; the other came out and swung at his side with the a slow, lazy energy. Just taking a casual stroll.

Ten feet away.

Silence tensed.

The man stopped right in front of the Mercedes' grill. He looked back and forth between Silence and Gibbs.

"I was wondering when you two would arrive," the man said.

"The hell are you?" Silence said.

On the surface, this would seem like a situation in which a Specialist would be there. But the Specialist he'd been dealing with through email and over the phone since the previous night had mentioned nothing of the sort. And if this man was a Specialist, he would have made some sort of attempt at confirmation already, like the Specialist in Mendocino had two days earlier.

The man kept his eyes locked on Silence for a moment before turning to Gibbs.

"Agent Gibbs, I presume, from the Florida Department of Law Enforcement, recently placed on administrative leave. I'll also presume you came here to stop another murder, to save Lynn Davidson."

Gibbs just stared back at him for a moment before she gave a small nod.

The suited man pivoted to look at the ambulance before returning his attention to them, first to Silence, then back to Gibbs.

"I'm afraid you're a little too late," the man continued. "Lynn Davidson ate a few bullets half an hour ago while some strung-out chick from Kentucky was threatening to kill herself, calling herself Lynn Davidson, giving our assailant time to get away. So whatever it is you're doing running all over the country, playing rogue detective, the killer's caught onto you, and he fooled you bad. You've failed, Gibbs."

"*Who are you?*" Silence said louder, growling.

The man reached into his pocket, retrieved credentials, and handed them to Gibbs before facing Silence again.

"I'm Special Agent Clive Booker, FBI. And I'm taking over your investigation."

CHAPTER THIRTY

THE WALLET SHOOK in Gibbs's trembling fingers.

The bottom half held a badge, and filling the top half was an ID card behind clear plastic. *DEPARTMENT OF JUSTICE* spanned the top of the card. In big, bold, blue letters beneath that was *FBI*, sitting adjacent to a photo of the man before her—head-and-shoulders, dark jacket, white shirt, tie, grim expression. And at the bottom of the card, a signature—*Clive Booker*.

The credentials were genuine.

Gibbs had seen plenty of similar credentials throughout the years, having worked directly with her fair share of FBI agents. For a moment, she'd actually hoped that his ID was a forgery, because if it was fake, this would mean the man in front of her wasn't a real government man.

But since he was a government man, her phobia had been realized. Her greatest fear had come to life.

Initially, she had thought that Troy was a man in black, come to get her. That fear had subsided over time with the trust they'd forged. Whatever Troy was, whatever "organization" he belonged to, he wasn't the dark suited mystery figure lurking in her nightmares.

But Clive Booker was, this man who had somehow been following them the entire time and had now presented himself as an all-powerful figure threatening to take over her investigation.

She'd known there were people after her. She should've listened to her gut.

She reached the badge to Troy, who studied it for a moment before handing it back to Booker and saying, "What is this?"

Booker gave Troy a smug grin, but turned to Gibbs when he answered the question.

"*This* is our commandeering of your investigation, Agent Gibbs." Booker didn't have the clear, precise, no-nonsense way of speaking that Gibbs had been accustomed to from federal agents. His voice wasn't unprofessional per se, but it was laid-back, slightly nonchalant. "The FBI has been monitoring your work."

"We know," Troy growled beside her.

Another wave of panic flushed over Gibbs's skin. If Troy knew the FBI was monitoring them, why hadn't he told her? Maybe he wasn't to be trusted after all. Maybe he *was* another man in black.

Yet he and Booker clearly weren't on the same team...

Her head was spinning.

Booker glanced at Troy, another smug grin, then back to Gibbs. He hooked a thumb toward her companion. "Who the hell's your buddy here?"

Gibbs needed a moment to formulate a response. "This is Troy. Um, personal security."

"Mmm-hmm..." Booker said, raising an eyebrow. "Well, you and your bodyguard will be consultants assisting me as I continue my investigation. Any materials, contacts, or other resources you've obtained will be handed over."

"Oh, really?" Gibbs spat. "What makes you think you can—"

Booker stepped toward her, grin leaving his face, and as he did, Troy swooped over, his broad frame blocking the other man's path. Booker glared at him before turning back to Gibbs, his expression still dark, eyes penetrating.

"I *can*, FDLE Special Agent Gibbs, because your investigation is illegal. The FBI is gracious enough to allow you and your friend to continue with me as consultants. Unless, of course, you'd rather wear a pair of handcuffs."

Gibbs couldn't form a response. She turned to Troy, and he looked at her intently. His facial expression was flat yet resolute. Somehow this steadied her.

Booker smiled.

"Very good," he said in response to her non-response. "You can be reasonable, I see." He gestured toward a black SUV idling at the end of the block. "After you."

Gibbs was stunned by how quickly Troy complied. After only a half moment of hesitation, he headed up the sidewalk toward the vehicle that Booker had indicated. Gibbs, on the other hand, felt cemented to the ground, but when she looked at Troy, his eyes gave her the indication to follow him.

That was twice in less than a minute that Troy had allayed her nerves with a simple look. The guy was quite talented at non-verbal communication, which made sense given his condition.

Booker fell into step behind them, and after they'd crossed through the mottled shade of the old trees—through beams of warm early-morning light poking between the branches and palm fronds—the agent opened one of the SUV's rear doors, motioning for Troy and Gibbs to slide across the bench seat. Gibbs went in first, then Troy folded his big body through the doorway. The door was shut, and there was a *clunk* as they were locked in. Booker's silhouette moved across the windows toward the driver door.

She and Troy would have only a second alone together in the backseat. She spun on him. "What—"

Troy brought a finger to his lips, a *shush* gesture, cutting her off mid sentence. He took his notebook from his pocket, and with amazing speed, scribbled out a note, placed it on his knee for her to read.

Don't worry. I have a plan.

The driver-side door opened, and Booker dropped into the seat, looked in the rearview, met Gibbs's gaze. She turned away, stole a glance at Troy's knee.

The notebook was gone.

Like it had never been there.

Troy's hands were already folded on his lap.

"Let's roll," Booker said, and he pulled the SUV away from the curb.

CHAPTER THIRTY-ONE

LOS ANGELES, CALIFORNIA

LENA HUBER GRABBED the back of her husband's shirt before he stepped through the front door and into the golden early morning light flooding their front porch. She brought him to a halt, pulled him around to face her, then reached behind him and yanked the folded piece of paper she'd seen in his back pocket.

In the moment before he stole it back from her, she saw that it was a list of printed driving directions from the map software he had on his Macintosh computer. At the top, centered, was the destination:

348 Ledbury Street, San Francisco

Austin swiped at her with two hands—one grabbing the stapled stack of papers, the other taking hold of her wrist, twisting hard enough to make her gasp.

She stared at him for a moment in bewilderment. He

stared back. With just as much bewilderment in his eyes. He'd never touch her like this. Ever.

Her eyes went to the papers in his hand. "San Francisco? Why are you leaving our house to go to San Francisco at the break of dawn?"

"Research, honey. I'm on deadline. I don't have time to tell you every detail about my days. I have one more stop to make in L.A., then I'll be up there for the day. I'll be back."

"When's your flight?"

"Driving," he said on an exhale, frustrated, as though every second mattered and he couldn't be bothered by nonsense.

"That's a *six-hour drive*. Are you staying overnight?"

"Yes."

"And you … you weren't going to tell me?" Her words came out small, pathetic, sad.

Austin didn't reply.

"What's going on, Austin?"

Her voice was unsteady, and the fear in her eyes must have been palpable to him. But he just met her gaze blankly, no expression on his face.

"Research," Austin said. "That's all I'm telling you for now. This will all make sense later."

She inched closer, reached for the papers in his hand. "Where is that, the address?"

He said nothing, only stepped away from her hand.

"Austin, *please*, what is going on?" She put her hands on his shoulders and looked up at him, into his eyes.

Still no expression on his face as he stared down at her. He turned back around and rushed out the door, shutting it behind him.

Lena heard something. Her own breath. Wheezing from her lips. She looked down at her wrist where he'd twisted it.

The flesh was slightly pinked, and when she wrapped her hand around it, she felt warmth.

Austin was a difficult man—fussy, demanding, and often self-centered. But he loved Lena, and he'd never touched her like that.

And while this notion hurt her to the core, her presiding thought at the moment was of the mysterious address on the computer printout.

For the first time ever, she felt frightened of her husband.

CHAPTER THIRTY-TWO

SAN FRANCISCO, CALIFORNIA

IT WAS A TINY, rentable conference space in a cheap motel off Geary Boulevard, but to Gibbs, it felt like an interrogation room, like a cramped, dark space with a single door and no windows, concrete walls, several stories underground, somewhere ominous like Langley or Quantico.

And this sensation was elicited by the man in black standing beside her, glancing up at the water-stained drop tile ceiling with a smirk.

"I guess this will have to do," Booker said.

The fed had told Gibbs and Troy that they needed somewhere private to talk, and in a massive city like San Francisco, the options were either an empty park or a conference room. When the prior option proved unattainable after several circuitous miles of searching, Booker conceded to the Sleepy San Fran Motel when they drove past its faded sign that proclaimed, *Conference Space Available*.

The room smelled like bulk-discount cleaners and old cigarette smoke. Though the carpet bore fresh vacuum tracks, it also had a number of deeply embedded stains. A rattling wall unit air conditioner under the draped window spat out a stale, overly cold breeze.

Booker motioned for Gibbs and Troy to have a seat, and Troy did so with the same unhesitating compliance with which he'd gotten into the back of the SUV outside Lynn Davidson's house.

But as he pulled out the squeaky office chair and it accepted his mass with a groan, Troy shot a slight glare across the table at the FBI agent, more of those highly tuned non-verbal skills. It was as though Troy's pride was wounded but he wanted to make sure that Gibbs was comfortable.

Not only was she amazed by his nonverbal skills, but she was growing more and more fond of the way he seemed to shield her. Somehow he had ascertained her hesitance toward the man in black, which must have been perplexing to him, given he didn't know about her phobia but *did* know that she was a highly trained state law enforcement official. The protective quality—and, of course, the uber-cute tour guide routine he pulled when they arrived in the city—did make her feel more at ease facing her greatest of fears.

It took the edge off.

If only ever so slightly.

Across the table, Booker pulled out another one of the wheeled office chairs, dropped his attaché case on the table, and took a seat across from Troy and Gibbs. He fished a micro cassette recorder from his pocket, set it in the center of the table, and said, "For the record."

A press of the top, red button, and tiny motors inside the device began to hum as the tape wound. Booker then clicked open the latches of his attaché case and retrieved a folder, which he handed to Troy, who flipped it open, quickly thumbed through the contents, then passed it on to Gibbs.

She perused the materials. Names and lists. Biographical

information. Phone numbers and addresses and service records. Most of it was duplicate information of what she and Troy had already procured, except for a military report at the bottom of the stack.

She felt eyes upon her, looked up. Booker had folded his arms across the heavily scuffed laminate surface of the table, leaning across its depth, getting as far into Troy and Gibbs's space as he could.

With that stupid smirk.

"What we're dealing with is a person who was involved in a military exercise at Eglin Air Force Base shortly after Desert Storm. I'm sure you've uncovered that much in your investigation to this point."

Both Gibbs and Troy nodded.

"What you probably haven't uncovered is that the killer, Tristan Pike, not only the officer who led the group into the field that night, but he was also the first to separate from the service after the incident. Only weeks later. Medical discharge."

Gibbs turned to Troy, found his eyes waiting for her. Though his countenance was as steely as ever, there was undeniable amazement in his eyes.

The feeling was mutual. After glancing at the military report and then receiving this bit of information, Gibbs felt her trepidation slacken. Considerably. Booker was the real deal, and to this point, she'd let her imagination run wild with her, thoughts of him torturing her, locking her away for all eternity.

But he'd already supplied some real and entirely conse-quential intel. Since Gibbs's self-prescribed mission was to save the remaining Hard Sprint survivors, maybe teaming with a fed wasn't such a bad idea after all. It would seem that Booker—as smug and dictatorial as he'd been in comman-deering the investigation—actually was on the right side.

Booker looked back and forth between them, grinning, studying their reactions. "And have you heard about the drug?"

"Yes," Troy said.

Booker nodded, stroked the blond growth coming from his chin.

"EX391. The experimental drug administered to the Hard Sprint participants, something to quell the effects of their Gulf War syndrome. All evidence and all earlier trials had suggested it would be harmless. No one anticipated the side effects."

"Side effects?" Gibbs said.

"We'll get to that." Booker closed his attaché case. "The man you've been hunting, ma'am and sir, based on your description and all the others, is Tristan Pike. Multicolored eyes are pretty damning. As far as the potential victims, we have leads on all the Hard Sprint survivors excepts Donnie Langstaff. I'm guessing you have no leads on him either."

Gibbs and Troy shook their heads.

Booker gave another one of his little smirks. "Okay, then. I've given you what we have, so play nice and tell me, what have *you* found?"

Gibbs just shifted in her seat, considered what she should say, and in that moment of hesitation, Troy jumped in.

"Two names," he said and swallowed. "Kasperson and Noyer."

Booker's eyes widened.

"Noyer, huh?" He drummed his fingers on the table. "That's interesting." He paused. "In terms of Kasperson, you're certainly on the right track there. That's the pharmaceutical company that produced EX391.

"And Noyer—he was an Army colonel at Eglin. I have no clue why his name would have come up in connection to Hard Sprint." He looked away for a moment, squinting with concentration. "He's a one-star now. At Meade. Ostensibly with Defense Information, DISA, but he spends just as much time at the NSA."

Gibbs bristled at the final acronym. NSA—the National Security Agency, the United States' organization that monitored and collected information from around the world for intelligence and counterintelligence purposes. The organization most whispered about among conspiracy theorists.

And the one that triggered her phobia the most.

Paranoia returned once more after its brief departure, crashing down. Her skin prickled. Cold sweat broke out on her forehead.

"As to why Pike is seeking revenge," Booker continued, "After some more digging, we found that Bell and Artiga, the first two victims, actually knew each other prior to Hard Sprint, unlike the other service members. Bell was a JAG. Artiga was a logistics officer or something of the sort. They met at a hoops league at a post gym, linked up again in the desert ... and once more at Hard Sprint, of course.

"Both separated honorably shortly after the incident. Stayed in touch off and on. And then suddenly, shortly before they both got killed, they had a flurry of communications. We got it all in the phone records."

He pointed to the folder, lying on the table in front of Gibbs.

"Seems that Artiga was suffering bizarre symptoms, figured it had something to do with the shit they pumped in his arm at Hard Sprint, goes to his old buddy Bell, and the lawyer starts investigating, finds out about Kasperson, goes down the rabbit hole on EX391. A few days later, Pike slaughters both of them."

"How did Pike know they were investigating?" Gibbs said.

"Unclear," Booker said with a shrug and finally retreated from his encroachment on the table, leaning back into the squealing chair, putting his hands behind his head. "What we're looking at is a massive coverup. The name 'Hard Sprint' exists nowhere in the paper trail. No one even remembers there was an incident beyond a few select emergency personnel from Eglin Air Force Base and Okaloosa County, Florida. The explosion was deep in the bush, way too far to draw attention from the local press.

"If you go looking for Kasperson, Incorporated, you'll have a hell of a time finding anything there either. The company shut down only six months after Hard Sprint. Board members, scientists, lab grunts—all the names lead nowhere. It's all one big dead-end.

"The biggest mystery about Pike himself is why he's doing this. Medically discharged after Hard Sprint. Never got back on his feet. Emotional issues. A divorce. A slew of bullshit jobs. It just doesn't make sense how he'd have learned that Bell and Artiga were investigating EX391. Nor why he'd continue attacking the other survivors."

Booker stopped then, brought his hands from behind his head and placed them on his stomach, interlacing his fingers, signaling a break. He studied Gibbs and Troy again, and after a few long moments where the only sound was the rattling air conditioner behind them, he said, "So ... you got anything else?"

Troy nodded. "Pike has partner." He swallowed. "Someone supplying..." Another swallow. "Intel, resources."

"Oh, there's no doubt of that," Booker said. "Except you're slightly off. He doesn't have a 'partner.' He has 'partners.' We've worked out the timeline, and we're confident that it's a trio of individuals."

He pulled a pack of gum from his pocket, waved it toward Gibbs and Troy, who both declined, and then popped a stick in his mouth.

"Two guys on the outside," he continued, balling up his

gum wrapper and tossing it toward the waste basket in the corner. "Individuals with means, supplying Pike with information and most certainly with funding. We've found one of them, through a private detective in LA, of all people. The detective reached out to an FBI contact, said he suspects a client of his is involved in the murders—Austin Huber."

"Austin Huber the author?" Gibbs said.

Booker nodded. "Evidently Huber sent the detective digging into not only the victims but the rest of the Hard Sprint survivors, claiming to be researching a new book, *An Abuse of Power*. This was just *before* the murders began."

"Which means?" Troy said.

Booker shrugged. "It means now that we've exchanged notes and with no leads on Milano or Langstaff, we need to get down to L.A. and find this Austin Huber guy."

Gibbs scooted forward in her chair. "You mentioned side effects of EX391. What are they?"

Booker chomped his gum a couple of times before replying. "It's a long list. At the top, you've got the usual—drowsiness, dizziness, nausea, sexual complications, fatigue. You know, the same issues they rattle off at the end of any drug commercial. But there's also insomnia, anxiety, panic attacks, suicidal thoughts." He paused momentarily, and his gum-chomping slowed. "And memory loss."

Gibbs's mind went into overdrive. The implications that memory loss could have on the investigation were staggering. If the victims had faulty memories, that would undoubtedly have affected the circumstances that led to their individual fates.

But even more tantalizing—and terrifying—was that the very person who was committing the murders had also taken the drug in question.

If Pike had memory loss...

She turned to Troy.

It was clear that this latest bit of intel had had the same effect on his line of thinking. He gave her a small nod.

Booker's grin returned, as did his obnoxious gum-chomping. He leaned across the table as he had earlier and let his open palms fall to the surface with a loud double smack.

"And now, lady and gentleman, we need to get to L.A.," he said. "If there are no flights that—"

A cellular phone chimed. Booker's. He pulled it from his pocket, looked at the multiplex LCD screen, grinned.

"Excuse me." He pushed away from the table and headed for the door in the back of the room as he answered the phone. "Yes?"

He closed the door behind him. His figure and voice cut back and forth across the door's small window as he paced a tight circle in the hallway. Gibbs couldn't discern what he was saying. For as cheap as the motel was, the contractors had evidently not skimped on the doors and sheetrock.

She glanced at the micro cassette recorder a few inches in front of her, its tiny wheels spinning behind the piece of clear plastic on the front, then faced Troy.

She pointed at his jacket and mouthed, *Notebook.*

Troy took her meaning, pulled his PenPal from his pocket, opened it, and handed her the pencil.

She scratched out: *So what's this plan of yours?*

Maybe she was trusting Booker more than she had been— a whole lot more, as a matter of fact—but that still didn't change the fact that he had essentially taken her and Troy hostage. Troy was her partner in this, and she needed to see where they were standing.

She slid the notebook back to him, and his gaze went from the notebook to the recorder before he took the pencil from her.

TAP! TAP!

Gibbs jolted in her seat as the sharp noise cut through the

room. Booker was looking through the window, phone to his ear, grinning darkly. He waved a *no-no-no* finger at them.

Troy put the notebook back in his pocket.

At the door, Booker stopped pacing. As his muffled conversation continued, he didn't take his attention off Gibbs and Troy, his lips moving with his indiscernible words, still grinning.

Troy glanced at Gibbs and gave a tiny, almost imperceptible wink.

CHAPTER THIRTY-THREE

LOS ANGELES, CALIFORNIA

SHE FELT strange sitting at Austin's writing desk. Wrong. This was his sacred space—the author's shrine to the muse; the artist's hallowed territory—and while Austin had never outright told Lena she couldn't sit there, the unspoken agreement between them was an ironclad contract.

She'd closed the blinds and shut the door, locked it, just in case he doubled back, and this not only threw the room into darkness but also amplified her feeling of *shouldn't-be-here*ness. Bright sunlight slipped in through the gaps of the closed blinds, penetrating the relative darkness. Outside, a bird chirped, and palm fronds scraped quietly at the glass.

Shallow breaths shuddered from her mouth, and her stomach roiled. The word *betrayal* kept flashing though her mind, electric and red and sinister. Austin had betrayed her—leaving without explanation, grabbing her wrist. And now she was betraying him, violating his most treasured of spaces.

What was she doing? What the *hell* was she doing? Austin's erratic behavior would have frightened her no matter what, but coupled with her phone conversation with Otis Watts—where the old detective told her that he too had worries about Austin—she was beginning to feel terrified of her husband. Dark, unthinkable thoughts had been tormenting her.

Saliva flooded the back of her mouth, and she sensed her stomach again. She put a fist to her mouth. Another deep breath. She sure as hell wasn't going to allow herself to be sick. Mind over matter. Push through this.

The desktop before her was immaculately clean. The Macintosh was on the right side, a small clock on the other— matte black metal frame; minimal, modern design. Otherwise the glass surface of the desk was completely empty. She pulled open the top right drawer. A stapler. Boxes of paper-clips and pens. And a notebook. With a green cover. The one she'd seen him writing in the previous evening.

As she picked it up, the notebook felt clean and fresh, brand-new. That's how Austin liked things. Perfect and nascent and spotless. This brand-new notebook was so Austin Huber that it made her smile in spite of the devious, gut-wrenching task she was on, despite the dark suspicions in her mind. Whatever Austin was up to, he'd decided to start with a clean notebook. She knew her husband too well.

She flipped it open. The first page was covered with phone numbers, written in Austin's tiny print, all of them crossed off. Most of the area codes were out-of-state, and she didn't recognized them. They were grouped together, and each group was headed by a single word that appeared to be a name: *PIKE, LANGSTAFF, BELL, ARTIGA, HORN, DAVIDSON.*

Something flickered through her consciousness, some-thing about the names...

She bolted out of the chair, threw open the door, blinded by the bright early-morning light flooding through the house, then ran to the kitchen, to the island, and grabbed the copy of *USA Today* she'd been reading only minutes earlier, just before Austin's dramatic exit. She opened it, turned to the article, which was buried in the national news section.

Recent murders across the country appear to be linked

She scanned the article, found the names. In the second paragraph was *Elliott Bell*. The following paragraph showed the name *Derek Artiga*.

Clutching the paper, she sprinted back across the house, into the office, shutting and locking the door, throwing the room back into shadow. She fell into the chair, spread the newspaper out beside the open notebook. The palm fronds scratched at the window.

Her finger trembled as she turned to the next page of the notebook. Unlike the previous page, Austin had only written a small amount—a single, short list centered toward the top of the page. A list of names, the same ones that had been on the previous page with the phone numbers, now addended by given names and locations.

> *TRISTAN PIKE - N/A*
> *DONNIE LANGSTAFF - ???*
> *ELLIOTT BELL - Breckenridge, Colorado*
> *DEREK ARTIGA - Panama City, Florida*
> *KURT HORN - Louisville, Kentucky*
> *LYNN DAVIDSON - San Francisco, California*

She found the names in the newspaper article again. *Elliott Bell* in the second paragraph:

Officials in Breckenridge, Colorado, say that Elliott Bell—an area lawyer and former Army Judge Advocate General—was murdered in his home late Tuesday evening.

And *Derek Artiga* in the next paragraph:

The following afternoon, another Army veteran, Derek Artiga, was murdered in a similar fashion in Panama City, Florida. Though Bell and Artiga never served together, sources indicate that they had maintained communication with each other for years since they both separated from military service. Officials are baffled at the connection.

Murders...
She shuddered as she looked back at her husband's list of names.

Six names—four with addresses, two belonging to recently murdered individuals.

Her eyes fell to the last entry on the list.

LYNN DAVIDSON - *San Francisco, California*

San Francisco...

Her mind flashed to the printed directions she'd pulled from Austin's pocket, the address, in San Francisco, his anger when she pressed him for why he was going to drive six hours to get to that city in the middle of the morning.

She gasped and dropped the notebook onto the desktop, her stomach roiling, mouth salivating again. The page flipped back, revealing the list of phone numbers and names. Under the *DAVIDSON* section, all the phone numbers had the 628 San Francisco area code.

A tumult of thoughts surged through her mind.

Austin had been on the phone constantly the last few days.

Two people murdered.

Lynn Davidson in San Francisco.

She took a couple of short, choppy breaths. Her body quivered. Then she looked at the phone, and without willing it to do so, her hand went to the receiver, fingers shaking so badly she could hardly dial.

Otis Watts's three-pack-a-day voice replied. "Hello?"

"Otis? Did I wake you?"

"Yeah, but ... What's wrong, Lena?" Deep concern in his tone, overpowering his disoriented lilt.

"I'm sorry to call you at home. It's Austin. I think something horrible is going on."

The receiver hissed as Otis let out a long sigh. "I ... have a few concerns about him as well."

"He just left the house, headed to San Francisco. And I ..." She could barely make herself say it. "I think he's involved in something terrible."

"Murders in Colorado and Florida?"

Her lips parted, and it was a half beat before she could reply. "Yes. How do you—"

"That's why we've been meeting lately. He's had me look into the people who were murdered. He gave me the job a day before the first murder."

She couldn't respond.

"Lena...?"

"I'm here, Otis. I found a list on his desk. An he just left for San Francisco. There's a name that—"

"Lynn Davidson. In San Francisco."

"Right."

"Listen carefully, Lena." Otis always had a commanding voice, and now, at the darkest moment she could imagine, he spoke in a tone that calmed her frantic heart ever so slightly. "It's not safe for you there. Get out of that house immediately."

"I will."

Yes, she would follow Otis's advice and get out of the house.

But as she drummed her fingers on the receiver, she knew she wasn't going to a hotel. Lena was the take-command type.

And she was going to get to the bottom of this situation.

CHAPTER THIRTY-FOUR

SAN FRANCISCO, CALIFORNIA

AFTER KILLING THREE PEOPLE, Pike felt bizarrely out of place in a trendy San Francisco coffeeshop. A murderer surrounded by yuppies and hippies.

In the back was a long counter lined with chrome espresso machines and grumbling bean-grinders. Ferns everywhere—on shelves and stands in the corners and dangling from chains. The warm scent of coffee intertwined with hints of fresh-baked cookies and muffins.

Tristan's purpose for being there wasn't the chai latte sitting by his hand. It was the computer in front of him, one of four set up on brightly colored round tables in the back corner. He picked up the laminated piece of copy paper by the keyboard, which was labeled, *INTERNET SEARCH TIPS*. It might have been a trendy place, but at least it catered to the less technologically inclined like Tristan.

One of the guidelines suggested containing search terms within quotation marks for more relevant results. Following the directive, he slowly pecked at the keyboard, entering a slew of symbols in the Yahoo! search engine field.

"remo milano"

Immediately, Yahoo! gave him a response.

No results found

Pike exhaled. He tried again with the other name.

"donnie langstaff"

A short list of results populated the screen.

A college athlete in New Hampshire.

A realtor in Scotland.

But no former U.S. Army officer Desert Storm vet.

Pike slammed his fist on the table, rattling the mug, spilling chai tea over the lip and onto the saucer.

Gasps from the trendy folks around him. One person quietly uttered, "Shit..."

He grabbed the mug, stood up, and went to the window, looking out onto a bright California suburban scene full of restaurants and boutiques and other trendy coffeeshops.

Something poked at his side. The Polaroids, in his inside jacket pocket. He pulled them out.

All of them.

Including the mysterious envelope.

It was a standard white envelope that had been folded over a stack of Polaroids within and sealed tightly with clear packing tape. On the front, in big letters written with a black marker, was: *DO NOT OPEN UNTIL AFTER THE MISSION*

The handwriting was his own, but he had no recollection of writing it.

So far he'd been good about obeying this command he didn't remember giving himself. But now, with Milano and Langstaff apparently nonexistent, with his mission in shambles, there was no need in continuing his compliance.

Screw it.

He tore the envelope open, his heart pounding with the thrill of intrigue, mystery.

And when he pulled the stack of photos out, he nearly dropped them.

It was the woman he'd seen.

On the highway. In his mind.

The woman who belonged to the name he'd been hearing.

Rita.

Travel photos. Many of them featuring Pike.

He looked fuller, healthier, happier.

They were on a Ferris wheel.

They were in New Orleans.

They were kissing.

They were at a plaza with red brick and a fountain with squarish tubes. He didn't know the name. He didn't remember it.

But somehow he knew it was there, at the city where he was currently located, San Francisco.

There were two photos of this San Francisco plaza. One in which they were all smiles. Another with goofy faces—crossed eyes, stuck-out tongues.

He shoved the photos back in his pocket, his hands shaking.

And he caught a hint of his reflection in the window, enough to see the thick stubble on his cheeks. He brought a hand to his face, whiskers tickling his palm. Tender spots pulsed with subtle pain as his hand explored—bruises and scratches and cuts, the combined effects of three days of hunting humans under formidable circumstances.

He felt more cuts, more scabs crusting in his unkempt scruff. There was a large bruise on his right cheekbone, compliments of the airbag back in Kentucky. He moved his jaw side to side. His entire face ached. In fact, his whole body was hurting. The mission was taking its toll.

And he was beginning to wonder if the mission was all for naught. Because if even one of the Hard Sprint survivors remained out there, he would have failed.

And there were *two*.

Milano and Langstaff.

Who both seemed to have disappeared from the face of the earth.

Then, as if in answer to a prayer, his cellular phone rang. He pulled it from his pocket, checked the number on the screen.

And exhaled.

Smiled.

The Benefactor had yet to let him down. This call would be the answer he needed, the guiding light pointing him toward the end of his mission.

He flipped the phone open. "Yes, Benefactor?"

CHAPTER THIRTY-FIVE

GIBBS MADE no more attempts at non-verbal communication with Troy. She just tried to avoid the stare of the face looking in through the rectangle of glass on the door. Smiling. Speaking muffled, inaudible words. Cellular phone pressed to his ear.

After several more moments, Booker reentered the room, collapsing his phone. He approached the table and stopped by his chair but didn't sit. Instead he plunged his hands into his pockets, tucking the sides of his jacket behind his forearms.

"Well, that was an interesting call. Guess who used his credit card today to purchase an airline ticket to right here in San Francisco. Looks like Austin Huber isn't relying on his private detective anymore. The guy's taking matters into his own hands. His flight lands in…"

He trailed off and checked his watch.

"An hour." He gave a two-handed upward swipe, waving Gibbs and Troy out of their seats. "Up and at 'em. We'll give the bastard a warm welcome at the airport."

———

The backseat of Booker's SUV was becoming increasingly familiar, and it was providing Gibbs a different type of San Francisco city tour than the one Troy had given her when they first arrived in the city, when he'd pointed out many of the famous San Francisco landmarks.

From the SUV, she'd gotten to see a more normal, everyday side of the city, and as they left the cheap motel behind them, they rushed down Geary Boulevard, a broad thoroughfare that cut through the Richmond area—lots of two-story buildings, gas stations, coffee shops, restaurants, all of it with a very Californian flare.

Beside her on the bench seat, Troy had gone quiet.

...well, he was always quiet.

But now his eyes were glossed over with deep concentration. She imagined he was processing the intel they'd just gotten from the strange impromptu briefing with Booker.

As she studied him, he suddenly leaned toward the driver's seat in front of him and said, "We eat."

He pointed through the window, and Gibbs followed his finger to a diner on the corner of 16th Avenue—an all-American place with highly decorated walls proclaiming things like: *BURGERS, MILKSHAKES, OPEN ALL NIGHT.*

Booker glanced in the rearview, grinning. "You're hungry, big dude?"

Troy didn't respond.

The turn signal started to click, and Booker slowed the SUV. When they pulled into a slot at the side of the street and came to a stop, Booker threw the gear selector into park and then turned around, leaning through the gap between the two front seats like a parent tending to his children, still wearing that stupid grin.

"Okay, let's—"

Troy's fist shot forward, so fast it didn't even blur, snapping Booker's nose with a spray of blood.

The agent gave a wet grunt.

Gibbs screamed.

And Troy's fist pistoned forward again, twice, racking the other man's face.

Whack! Whack!

Booker collapsed into the hammock of his seatbelt, limbs drooping, chin to his chest, blood dripping from the end of his nose. Out cold.

"What the hell are you doing?" Gibbs shouted.

Troy turned to her, briefly glancing down to examine his fist, squeezing ache from his knuckles before looking back up to her.

"That man's no FBI agent," he said.

CHAPTER THIRTY-SIX

LOS ANGELES, CALIFORNIA

OTIS LEANED FORWARD on his desk, one elbow resting on the surface, propping up his head. With his other hand, he held the receiver to his ear. He sensed that he was squeezing it too hard. Tension had built. He loosened his grip, felt a cool breeze on his palm; his hand was sweating.

"Okay, Lena," he said. "Call me when you make it there, all right? Be safe."

He hung up and slowly leaned back in his chair, the cracked cushion wheezing, springs squeaking. He took a deep breath, held it for a moment, and let it gradually escape his nose.

People turned to Otis for personal matters—*find out if my wife's cheating; find out if my employee's lying*—but they did so with the promise of payment. In the real world, no one relied on Otis. He had no wife, no kids, and one brother he never spoke to. Otis was the type who ate microwave dinners on his sofa, wondering how he could have prevented his divorce twenty years ago, wishing that sweet death would come sooner than statistically predicted.

He wasn't the type to help the beautiful wife of a minor celebrity in a horrible situation. And this situation with Austin was beyond horrible. Otis couldn't imagine how he was going to help.

But he knew he was damn well going to try.

Even a screwup gets a few chances to do the right thing.

His office door rattled, opened.

And in walked Austin.

After the phone call with Lena, a thought flashed through Otis's mind. *There's a potential murderer in my office.*

His heart pounded.

Austin wore a pair of slacks, short-sleeved shirt, untucked. His hair was neatly styled, but he needed a shave, and his eyes were bloodshot. Even if Otis didn't suspect that Austin was involved in multiple murders around the country, he would have still been frightened by his friend's appearance. He looked like different—different, even, from the man who sat across from Otis at the posh restaurant in Santa Monica the previous day.

And anyone would have been frightened by what Austin was carrying.

A pistol. Aimed at Otis.

In his other hand was a bicycle U-lock. Somehow Austin's bewilderment over this item only amplified his fear.

"The little revolver," Austin said. "Let me have it. Slowly."

Otis's fingers trembled as he pulled out the right desk drawer and retrieved his holstered Colt Detective Special. He carefully reached it to Austin, who shoved the tiny weapon in his back pocket.

"What is this, Austin?" Otis said, and his voice came out so pathetically that it instantly embarrassed him. Only moments earlier he was so proud of himself for being brave on Lena's behalf, and already he was showing his true colors again.

"I'm not here to hurt you, Otis," Austin said as he stepped toward him. "My business isn't with you."

Otis inched back in the old chair.

Austin leaned toward him, but instead of striking him—an image that had flashed across Otis's mind—he grabbed the telephone from his desk and unplugged it. He tucked it under his arm, shoved his hand through the bicycle lock's loop, and held it open in front of Otis.

"Cellular," he said.

Otis slowly reached into his pocket and retrieved his cellular phone and placed it in Austin's outstretched hand.

"I'm doing something tonight," Austin said. "And I can't have you interfering. That's why I'm locking you in."

He displayed the bicycle lock, then reached behind his back and produced a greasy McDonald's sack, which he dropped on the desk with a thud.

"Best I could do on short notice. It should hold you for a while."

Austin looked at him for a moment, and Otis wasn't sure if he wanted Otis to say something or if he was processing his next words. Finally, Austin pointed to the small television set on the corner of Otis's desk.

"Watch the news. You'll see. And later, when someone comes to visit you...."

He trailed off, looked to the side.

"Just remember that friends take care of friends."

Austin watched him for another moment, then turned for the door and left. There was a series of loud rattles as he put the bike lock into place.

And then he was gone.

Otis went to the door, tested it.

Austin hadn't lied.

Otis was locked in.

CHAPTER THIRTY-SEVEN

SAN FRANCISCO, CALIFORNIA

"THEN WHO THE HELL *IS HE?*"

Silence winced as Gibbs's exasperated scream ricocheted off the close quarters of the SUV.

Gibbs's arm was so rigid it quivered, finger pointing to the man dangling from the seatbelt with blood dripping from the tip of his nose. She stared at Silence with eyes that, perplexingly enough, burned with both red-hot rage and something resembling fear.

Silence was so taken aback that he didn't immediately answer her question. She was a state-level agent and a professional, and yet there seemed to be genuine dread in her eyes, more panicked than he would have expected from a person in her position. And he suspected it was because of some underlying issue he wasn't understanding.

Gibbs jabbed her still-pointing finger toward Booker again, and she repeated herself vehemently. "If that man is not an FBI agent, then what is he? And why is he posing as one?"

"Don't know yet," Silence said.

This seemed to perturb her, another almost nonsensical response, and she exhaled through flared nostrils.

"I saw his credentials," she said. "They were genuine."

Silence shook his head. "They weren't. Trust me."

Booker's credentials were an excellent forgery. World-class, even. But a forgery nonetheless. Tiny, almost unde-tectable fallacies in the font; microscopic mistakes in the badge's curvature.

"The note you showed me earlier," Gibbs said, and when she continued, she used a gravelly tone, her impersonation of him. "*Don't worry. I have a plan.*" She pointed at Booker's unconscious form again. "Is *this* part of your plan?"

She was still in near hysterics, but Silence couldn't help but snicker. Her impression of him had been pretty damn good.

"Is something funny, asshole?" Gibbs said. Her tone was angry, but by the end of her sentence, her lips had started a smile of her own, in spite of herself and in spite of the deadly tension of the moment. She gave a little sigh-laugh, shook her head, and said, "So what are we going to do now?"

Silence pointed through the windshield at a small neigh-borhood greenhouse at the corner of the block on which the restaurant sat.

"I stay with him," Silence said and swallowed. "You go greenhouse. Buy hose."

———

Ten minutes later, Gibbs had returned with a spool of garden hose, and Silence had put it to use.

While 16th Avenue wasn't, apparently, a terribly busy street, there were enough pedestrians to make it impossible to move a bloodied, unconscious man out of a vehicle's driver's seat without being noticed. So Silence had retracted the driver-side visor—a fraction of privacy—and restrained Booker by looping the garden hose around the man's torso at the elbows. Gibbs was behind the driver's seat, holding the hose tight, and Silence had moved to the passenger seat.

Now Silence just had to wake the bastard up.

He snapped twice in front of Booker's slouched face. Nothing.

Plan B, then.

He placed a thumb and a finger on the edges of Booker's nose, one on either side of the bridge.

Gibbs shuffled in the back seat. "Oh, God, what are you gonna—"

Before she could finish, Silence gave a quick pinch of his fingers.

Booker roused with a scream, jolting in his binds, head twisting left then right, eyes scanning, instantly going into defense and situational analysis. Only one second of this before he realized the predicament he was in. His eyes burned at Silence, a caged but defiant beast.

"Are you out of your goddamned mind?" Booker said. "I'm a federal agent, and—"

"You're not."

Booker's lips froze mid-speech, eyes slightly widening before they narrowed, and a darker version of his standard grin came to the corners of his lips.

"You think not?"

Silence nodded.

"Well, that's interesting, because from the first moment I saw you, I knew you were something more than a bodyguard. A lot more. Now the question is, who are you?"

"*I'm* asking questions." Silence swallowed. "Who are you?"

"Piss off."

Silence brought his hand back to Booker's face, squeezed

the bridge of his nose again, the man's blood sticky-slippery between his fingertips.

Booker screamed until Silence released.

Panting, Booker said, "You think you can break me? You don't know my training."

"You don't know mine."

Booker smirked. "What are you? SAD?"

"Worse," Silence said.

That was the second time in two days someone had thought Silence was part of the CIA's Special Activities Division. The first person to think so was sitting behind him in the SUV's backseat.

He turned to Gibbs.

She'd been quiet through the first moments of this interrogation, and as he looked at her now, he again found a countenance that was at odds with Gibbs's position as an investigator. Way beyond uncomfortable. Practically inconsolable.

And for a moment, this made Silence wonder if Booker wasn't a federal agent, then maybe Gibbs wasn't a *state* agent. Then he remembered all the intel the Watchers had gathered about Gibbs. Ironclad intel.

Silence admonished himself. There was no time to slip into paranoia.

He turned back to the front seat, to the bloodied, constrained man scowling at him.

"Who's Noyer?"

Again, no response, just a grim line of a mouth and narrowed eyes, blood dripping off his nose.

Silence grabbed the bridge of his nose between his fingers again, clamped down with machine strength, squeezing the beefy parts of his fingers together so hard that they slipped off, lubricated by the blood.

The man howled.

"*Talk!*" Silence said, loud enough to send a jolt of pain through his ruined throat.

Booker just stared at him, teeth bared now, panting.

Evidently this guy, whoever he was, didn't think that Silence would go the full mile.

Evidently the man wasn't going to give up the information.

So, evidently, he was useless to Silence.

He put his hands on either side of Booker's head, brought the energy into his shoulders for a quick snap, and—

"*Okay!* Okay!" Booker said, chest heaving, genuine fear in his eyes.

Well, well, well. Booker could be reasoned with after all.

Silence wasn't really going to kill him.

But he'd sure made it seem that way.

"Stuart Noyer was the officer in charge of Hard Sprint. Pike was the company-grade officer who led the team into the field, but Noyer was in command. Completely off the record. That's why you haven't found his name yet; the whole thing was a big coverup. That's all I know about him. I swear."

Silence considered this. If Kurt Horn had overheard the names Noyer and Kasperson, then—

A shout from outside the vehicle. "*Hey!*"

Two men approaching. Both wearing jeans—one in a T-shirt, the other in a polo. Both with gym-hardened physiques and squared-away demeanors.

And both brandishing pistols in low-ready position.

Cops.

Either off-duty or plain-clothes.

A chance run-in with people who took their job seriously. Right place at the right time.

Everyone froze. Silence, Gibbs, and even Booker. Then Booker suddenly jolted forward, pulling himself out of his binds. He slapped the door handle and tumbled out of the vehicle onto the pavement.

Silence and Gibbs stayed put, as the cops now had their weapons aimed, one at Booker, the other at Silence.

The one to the rear left—the one in a polo shirt, black, forties—shouted.

"Step out of the vehicle!"

Silence and Gibbs complied, hands up, stepping onto the street.

Booker stumbled to his feet, started toward the cops. "Officers, thank God you're here!"

"Sir!" the white guy shouted, keeping his gun leveled at Booker. "We need to see your hands too."

Booker didn't put his hands up. "I was just walking down, the street, and these two—"

"*Sir!* Show us your hands!"

Booker nodded fervently. "Okay. Okay. My hands."

And then a blur of movement.

Booker's arm disappeared beneath his suit jacket, returned with a pistol—what appeared to be a Smith & Wesson 5900 series from the flash that Silence saw of it—and fired twice.

First into the white guy's chest. A fractional, split-second adjustment, then a second shot struck the black guy below the throat.

The blasts boomed off the surrounding walls. Screams. People sprinting away.

Silence's hand went to his shoulder holster, retrieved his Beretta just as quickly as Booker had pulled his own weapon.

But he didn't fire. He had only a fraction of a second.

And he used that moment to throw his shoulder into Gibbs, shoving her through the passenger side of the SUV, using the open door as a shield, jumping in behind her.

THWACK! THWACK! THWACK!

Rounds struck the sheet metal.

Silence scrambled over the center console, staying below the dash.

And with good reason.

Because two more rounds hissed through the windshield, piercing the leather headrest, which instantly mushroomed with foam and stuffing.

Legs in position, torso still low, he threw the gear selector into reverse. The tires screeched, and he immediately yanked the steering wheel to the side.

The SUV shuddered in a screaming arch, palpable force that threw Silence into the door panel. Gibbs collided with his shoulder.

Facing the opposite direction, he pulled the gear selector into drive and smashed the gas pedal.

THWACK! THWACK!

More rounds cutting through the bumper. The rear window shattered.

Ahead was Geary Boulevard. Silence pulled the wheel hard to the right, and the SUV's tires squealed again as Silence pulled into traffic.

The windshield was a distorted latticework of jagged fissures. Visibility almost nil. He gave it a sharp palm strike. And when it didn't move, he gave it two more.

The windshield blew out partially from its seal, and Silence grabbed the edge, yanked down, peeling back enough to create a patch of visibility. Wind rushed into the cab, making him squint.

He turned to Gibbs.

She was clenching either side of the passenger seat, eyes wide, hair speckled with safety glass.

"You hurt?" Silence said.

She shook her head.

Silence glanced to the rearview.

Blue police lights coming from behind, slowing at 16th Avenue.

"Well, what now?" Gibbs said.

"Must ditch car," Silence said as he pulled onto the next side street. "Take cab to airport."

"No, jackass, I mean where the hell do we go from here? Who was that man if he's not an FBI agent? Wait... Who the hell are *you*? I want the truth. How you tortured that man ... The casual way you were about the snap his neck ... You're an assassin, aren't you?"

Silence didn't take his eyes off the road, just nodded. "Yes."

She gasped.

He pulled the SUV into an open spot on the side of the road, put it in park, and turned to her. "But a nice one."

He offered a smile.

At first Gibbs just looked at him perplexed, almost startled. But then a tiny smile of her own appeared, followed by an exasperated laugh identical to the one she'd given minutes earlier after Silence had broken Booker's nose and rendered the man unconscious.

At a certain point, all a person can do is laugh. Just fiddle away while Rome burns to ashes. Gibbs had reached that point.

"But you were never planning on killing me?" Gibbs said.

Silence opened his door.

"Never."

CHAPTER THIRTY-EIGHT

SAN MATEO COUNTY, CALIFORNIA

PIKE HATED AIRPORTS. Too many people. Too much hassle and commotion. Too many free-flowing emotions—joy, sadness, urgency, despair.

He was at a row of seats in SFO's Delta terminal, facing the hallway looking through the swarming mass of luggage-toting people crisscrossing the floor, watching for the target. The overpriced baseball cap he'd bought at one of the airport stores was pulled low over his face, hiding the mismatched eyes. He took the folded sheet of paper from his pocket and flattened it out.

Back at the café, he'd printed off a photo he'd grabbed from the World Wide Web. Though the file was color, the café's printer was black-and-white. In its printed form, the image filled most of the 8.5 x 11 sheet of paper, showing an attractive, sophisticated looking couple smiling in front of a cluster of palms and rolling California hills beyond, the sunset illuminating their perfect faces just so.

Austin Huber and his wife, Lena.

Huber was the reason Pike had come to the airport, the reason he was scanning the crowd, every individual that bustled past him. The Benefactor had told Pike on the phone that Huber had purchased a ticket that morning for San Francisco, though the man hadn't been able to determine the arrival gate.

Being an avid reader, Pike was already familiar with Austin Huber's appearance, so the printed photo was merely a refresher, something to compare against potential targets exiting the L.A. flights.

However, he'd never seen the wife, and he couldn't help but pull his attention away from the crowd to take another look at her image. Stunningly beautiful. Very thin, yet with ample curvature at her hips. Her skin was fair, and her medium-dark brown hair fell in lofty waves, finishing below her shoulders. Bright, perfect and dark eyes, on a face that somehow looked both old-fashioned and exotic. A prominent Marilyn Monroe beauty mark sat on her left cheek, just outside her smile, a pièce de résistance to her radiant beauty.

He looked away from Huber's wife, took one more quick look at Huber's image, and then began scanning the crowd once more for the man.

And as he did, something pulled his eyes to the opposite end of the terminal hallway. A couple. Sitting along the edge of the hallway like he was, looking into the crowd like he was.

And he recognized them.

No. No, it couldn't be.

He reached into his jacket pocket, took out his stack of Polaroids, flipped through them frantically, found the right photo.

There they were. A grainy image within an image, the photo Pike had snapped of the television news report playing at the bus station back in Kentucky. A man and woman in dress clothes, standing together, facing one of Kendrick

Horn's neighbors, listening as the woman gave an animated speech.

Troy and Gibbs.

Pike had taken them to be Louisville detectives.

But if they were here in San Francisco, they must be feds.

"Shit," he said through his teeth.

Feds!

And here they were, at the airport.

In the correct terminal.

At the correct time.

They were waiting for Austin Huber as well.

Which meant that Pike would somehow have to beat them to Huber and get out of the airport without being followed. Icy panic sweat flushed over his body as he considered the logistics. It would be damn near impossible, and—

At the end of the hallway, the pair stood up and worked their way into the crowd, heading in his direction. Pike watched as they moved to the opposite side of the hall, where the tail end of a clot of incoming travelers belched out of a set of gate doors.

The feds slowed as they approached the gates, both of their stares focused on the center of the group.

Pike followed their sightlines to the center of the group.

But Austin Huber wasn't there...

Confusion scrunched Pike's face for only a moment. And then he saw her. A woman with shimmering brown hair, dark eyes, fair skin. And a beauty mark on her left cheek.

Huber's wife.

Pike did another quick scan of the incoming travelers. Austin Huber was nowhere to be seen.

The Benefactor had said that Huber's card was used to purchase a ticket that morning, but he'd assumed—and Pike had too—that it had been Huber himself. The notion that it had been Huber's wife hadn't surfaced.

At the other end of the hall, the feds stepped through the travelers and approached Mrs. Huber, whose hand went to her chest, eyes going wide. There was a quick exchange with both of the feds speaking to the woman, who gave short, bewildered responses. Finally, the man extended a long arm, gesturing down the hallway as though offering her a path.

The trio joined the crowd.

"Shit," Pike said again. He shifted his body to the left, turned his head, pulled the cap down lower over his face. It was an awkward plan, but there was little else to do. If the feds were *this* well informed, then they certainly would know Pike's face, and his mismatched eyes were a tell with which he could take no chances.

So he just stayed twisted to the side awkwardly in the uncomfortable plastic seat and waited, scanning the crowd from his peripheral. He couldn't see shit this way, but fortunately for him, he had an advantage—the male fed's height. The guy was easily six-foot-three.

So when someone in the crowd breezed past towering over the others, Pike hopped out of his seat.

And followed the feds and Mrs. Huber.

CHAPTER THIRTY-NINE

THE FOOD COURT was a semicircular swath of chain restaurants with a large area of tables packed with harried travelers and their ever-suffering luggage. People ate their food with the same unloving disregard and hastened pace with which it had been prepared by the less-than-enthusiastic individuals behind the counters. There was the smell of eight different deep fryers in the air.

They had pulled to the side, a bit of breathing room in the busy airport, and Mrs. Huber continued to give them a skeptical stare.

Gibbs held out her badge, and after studying it for a moment, Mrs. Huber's skepticism further deepened her brow.

"Well, it certainly looks real. But I don't understand... Florida? What does this have to do with my husband?" She pointed at Troy. "And who's this?"

"My bodyguard."

"Mmm-hmm..." Mrs. Huber said, eyes narrowing further as she scanned Troy up and down. Her eyes stopped at the book in his hand, which was turned out, revealing the author photo on the back. The woman's husband.

Troy had heard the name before, even read a couple of the books, but he wasn't a fan like Gibbs was, so they'd stopped at one of the airport gift shops and bought a paperback solely for the photo on the back. They didn't know that they'd be looking for the wife instead.

Mrs. Huber pointed at the book. "You have my husband's photo, but how'd you pick me out of a crowd?"

"I'm a bit of a fan," Gibbs said. "I've read all his books. A few of them multiple times. I keep up to date on his website. I've ... seen several of your photos there."

Mrs. Huber's shoulders went up an inch, a slight bristling. She raised an eyebrow. "Should I be jealous?"

An awkward moment passed before Troy's deep, terrible voice made both of them jump.

"Ma'am?"

Mrs. Huber stared at Troy in disbelief for a moment before replying.

"Yes?"

"Time critical," Troy said. "May we..." He swallowed. "Ask some questions?"

CHAPTER FORTY

SAN FRANCISCO, CALIFORNIA

Austin bounded up the steps of The Centurion Hotel, a home away from home in a city he frequented. Twenty stories of glistening glass and sharp angles, a prismatic sculpture of reflected light.

It bordered Justin Herman Plaza—an expanse of red brick with a massive geometric fountain on one end—and was, thus, right across from the Embarcadero and the Ferry Building, with the water and Bay Bridge in the background.

An ideal San Francisco location.

When Austin was two steps away from the all-glass entrance—with its revolving doors and views of the sparkling lobby area beyond—there was a shout from behind.

"Hey! Are you Austin Huber?"

Austin pivoted. A man trotted up the steps toward him, beaming grin on his face, hand already extended for a shake.

The man's appearance made Austin jump back on the granite step.

He was blond-headed, fit, and wore a nice suit that was

wrinkled, dirty, and soiled. The man's hair was tussled, and his face was pink, cheeks puffy, nose swollen to a shine and notched to the side. There were remnants of dried blood on his cheek—from what had clearly been an attempt at a rudimentary cleaning—and massive amounts of blood dried into his white dress shirt.

Austin reluctantly gave him his hand.

"Oh, man!" the guy said. "I thought it was you. I freakin' loved *Precise Directives*! Are they *really* gonna turn it into a movie?"

"That's right."

"Oh, man! That's awesome. I'm a huge fan." The man waved a hand toward the mess of his appearance. "Sorry, had a bit of an accident earlier. A bad fender-bender." He pointed to the Ferry Building on the other side of the Embarcadero. "Say, could I buy you a beer? Something to repay you for all the entertainment you've given me?"

Austin felt the pressure of his mission, the seconds ticking away. He forced a smile.

"Sorry, I don't normally get drinks with readers. Besides, I'm on a bit of a schedule."

"You're sure?"

Damn, this guy was persistent.

"I'm certain." Another forced smile. "Have a good one."

He quickly turned and rushed up the steps.

Encounters like this were getting more common for Austin. Though authors were, sadly enough, not regarded with the same esteem as other storytellers—and the trend seemed to get more disparate each year—when one became as successful as Austin had, one was bound to be recognized from time to time.

But this guy was probably the weirdest of all the weirdos Austin had encountered...

———

"That'll be great, thanks," Austin said as he signed the bill and hoisted his backpack off the polished marble counter and onto his shoulder.

The desk clerk—in his sharp navy blazer, red tie, and glistening gold name tag—gave him a smile and a card key.

Austin headed for the elevators at the back of the lobby, a cavernous space with tall glass walls looking out onto the plaza and the Embarcadero, lush tropical plants, and a coffee shop in the corner.

For the duration of the check-in process, Austin hadn't been able to shake the moments-earlier confrontation with the deranged fan on the exterior steps. The more he thought about it, the more he realized it wasn't just the broken nose and the blood that had unsettled him; it was the man's overall demeanor.

Something about him had been just … off.

A true lunatic fan.

As he drew closer to the elevators, a newspaper rustled at one of the decorative tables outside the coffee shop. When the paper lowered, a smiling face looked at him.

One with dried blood and a broken nose.

"How about a coffee instead?" The man reached into his pocket, pulled out a wallet, opened it, and held it for Austin to examine. "I'd love to have a word with you."

Austin looked at the wallet, and though he'd had no intention of breaking his stride, what he saw made him slow his pace.

Three large letters in the center of an ID card made his heart jump.

FBI

A golden badge sat on the lower half.

Austin's gaze traveled up to the swollen nose then down to the bloody shirt then back to the man's eyes.

"Posing as a federal agent?" Austin said. "You're ... you really are deranged, aren't you?"

Austin's heart pounded. He looked down the side hallway, past the line of elevators. At the very end was a stairwell door.

He bolted.

And immediately heard footsteps behind him, tapping on the marble.

He looked over his shoulder.

The man was behind him. Not sprinting but moving briskly. Still smiling.

Holy shit, this guy was truly insane.

Austin shouldered through the door and into a stairwell— a stark, plain-Jane contradiction to the moments-earlier opulence.

His footsteps echoed up the walls.

And then a bang from below. The door.

Austin glanced down. It was the bloodied man. Smile gone. Now a grim expression.

Austin grabbed the handrail, pulled himself up another two steps.

And felt something. On his back. His shirt being pulled to the rear.

The man had caught up with him blazingly fast.

Austin took a swing, and his arm stopped dead, like it hit a wall. The man's hand was wrapped around Austin's fist.

Another attempt at a swing, but Austin was already being flung around, arms twisted behind his back. And falling.

Pain exploded through his chest as he collided with the steps, stealing his breath with a wheeze.

Keeping Austin's arms behind his back, the man stood

over him, and a smile returned to his lips, though not big and gregarious as it had been before. This smile was patient but almost patronizing.

"It's only going to take two words to earn your trust," the man said. "Hard Sprint."

CHAPTER FORTY-ONE

SAN MATEO COUNTY, CALIFORNIA

GIBBS WOBBLED side to side in the bench seat, her shoulder bumping against Troy's thick, solid arm, as the train barreled down the track, everything creaking and squeaking.

Across from them, Mrs. Huber had just finished settling into her seat, and she took a deep breath, sighed it out, closed her eyes as sunlight flooded over her face and her shiny hair, pouring in through the dust-and-body-oil-smeared window onto which she'd let the back of her head drop. Tension seemed to flood out of the woman, but rather than evaporating, it stayed in her orbit.

The BART train—Bay Area Rapid Transit—was headed into San Francisco proper, all the way to the final stop in the city proper: the Embarcadero, San Francisco's famous bayside thoroughfare.

Mrs. Huber's brief respite concluded as she pulled her head back upright, opened her eyes, and squinted to look at the wall above Gibbs's and Troy's heads, where the station map was.

"Austin has a favorite hotel he stays at whenever he's in the city. 'Where dreams meet at the Bay,'" she said with a small, wistful sigh. "That's the best place to start. It'll be another several minutes."

Her gaze descended, finding Gibbs then Troy, eyes dancing between them for a moment.

"Talk," Troy said in the gentlest version of his growl

Mrs. Huber leaned forward, placed an elbow on her knee, and let her head drop again, this time into her palm, gazing at the grooved flooring speckled with litter.

"Austin's a difficult man, so I didn't immediately recognize that he was acting out of the ordinary." She shook her head, slowly, exhausted. "But he's never been cross with me before. Not like this. It's not in his nature. That's what clued me in."

"Mrs. Huber," Gibbs said and glanced left and right, checking out the neighbors. A businessman in a suit at the back of the train, speaking loudly into a cellular phone. A passed-out vagrant. A man buried behind a newspaper a few seats away. She continued in a lower voice. "There have been a string of murders across the country recently, and—"

"And Austin hired his private detective to investigate the people before they started dying. I know. And call me Lena, please."

"Okay, Lena," Gibbs said. "I know this will be incredibly difficult for you to hear, but there seems to be at least three people involved in the murders, and we believe your husband is one of them."

Lena nodded quickly, almost frantically. Tears suddenly welled in her eyes, and she used the back of her hand to wipe at them, smearing her mascara. "Yes, I've been thinking the same thing, that he's involved somehow." She stopped and looked up to the ceiling for a moment, exhaled "I spoke with the private detective, Otis Watts, and he agrees."

"What has Austin..." Troy said and swallowed. "Been doing lately?"

"He's gone from the house for long hours, longer than usual," Lena said. "On the phone constantly. Out-of-state calls." She hesitated. "And I found this."

She reached into her bag and took out a notebook—not a small notebook like Troy's PenPal, but a full-sized one—and reached it across the aisle.

Gibbs leaned into Troy, looked at the notebook as he opened it. The first page was covered with handwritten phone numbers, in groups headed by the names of the Hard Sprint survivors.

"I have no idea who these names are," Lena said as they looked at the notebook, "but those are the phone numbers he's been calling recently. I checked with our telephone company. There's more on the next page."

Troy turned the page. Gibbs leaned in even closer

It was a list of the Hard Sprint survivors and their locations, in the same handwriting.

TRISTAN PIKE - N/A
DONNIE LANGSTAFF - ???
ELLIOTT BELL - Breckenridge, Colorado
DEREK ARTIGA - Panama City, Florida
KURT HORN - Louisville, Kentucky
LYNN DAVIDSON - San Francisco, California

Troy glanced at her.

"Notice something?" he said.

Gibbs took another look. "No."

Troy stabbed the list with his index finger. "Who's missing?"

It took her a moment.

"Remo Milano..." she said.

Across the aisle, Lena gasped.

Gibbs looked up to find Lena's hand had returned to her chest, shaking badly. Fresh tears filled her eyes.

Troy turned to Gibbs again, perplexed concern painted over his strong features, before leaning forward, inching across aisle toward Lena.

"Remo Milano," he said and swallowed. "You know that name?"

CHAPTER FORTY-TWO

PIKE NEARLY DROPPED THE NEWSPAPER.

Remo Milano.

Mrs. Huber had gasped when the fed woman said the name, which meant that the wife of famed novelist Austin Huber recognized *one* Hard Sprint survivor's name but not the others.

What the hell was going on?

The BART train shimmied and squealed around a gentle curve, shifting Pike in his seat, jolting him back into reality. He reaffirmed his grip on the newspaper.

When he'd followed them from the airport, the assumption had been that Mr. and Mrs. Huber had planned their trip to San Francisco with separate means of transportation with the aim of meeting up in the city. Following the wife and the feds, then, would lead Pike to Austin Huber, Pike had assumed.

But since he'd positioned himself within earshot of their conversation on the train, he'd found out that the situation was much more convoluted than he'd imagined. Evidently, Austin's investigation of the murders had been not only bizarre but also something he was keeping a secret from his wife. Lena Huber had then taken it upon herself to chase after him to San Francisco. And somehow the feds had gotten the same intel that the Benefactor had and were able to intercept her at the airport.

All of this meant that no one on the train knew where Austin Huber was.

In theory, Pike was no better off than when he'd left the internet café. But now there was a revelation, one that might crack this whole thing wide open.

The woman somehow knew Remo Milano....

Pike pulled the newspaper in a little bit closer and leaned slightly toward the others, angling his ear toward the conversation.

Mrs. Huber hadn't spoken for a few moments after the big, growly-voiced fed had said, *Remo Milano. You know that name?* Just little shuddering breaths, audible over the screeching and rattling of the train.

Finally, she said, "Yes, I know that name."

Pike peeked around the edge of the newspaper.

Mrs. Huber sat on his side of the train, across from the feds. She was bent over, elbows on her knees, one hand propping her head up, the other clenching the opposite forearm. Tears trailed down her cheeks. She started to talk but could barely get the words out.

"'Austin Huber' was my husband's pen name before he did a full, legal name change. His original name was Remo Milano."

Pike's fingers tightened on the newspaper, crushing it, and he fought the urge to scream out, *YES!*

This was it!

He'd found the second-to-last Hard Sprint survivor. Lena Huber would lead him to her husband, Remo Milano; Pike would make quick work of the man, who by all accounts had gone from a military man to a fussy *artiste*; and then all that remained would be to find and eliminate Donnie Langstaff.

But he couldn't get ahead of himself. He couldn't get lost in his thoughts.

Focus, he told himself. *Focus.*

He peered around the edge of the newspaper again. The big fed's eyes had gone wide, lips parted, his brain clearly igniting with clarity as he processed the revelation with nearly as much shock as Pike had. He looked at the female agent then back to Mrs. Huber as he fished a small notebook from his pocket, pulled a mechanical pencil from the binding, and started to furiously scratch out a note.

His partner placed a hand on his, stopping him from writing, gave him an *I got this* nod, then turned to Mrs. Huber.

"Your husband isn't involved in the killings, Lena," the woman said. "He's the next man on the hit list."

Mrs. Huber wailed, drawing attention from the other people in the train.

Pike sank back behind his newspaper.

The mood in the train quickly turned to one of concern and discomfort. Whispers and hushed conversations from the travelers surrounding him.

The poor thing.

How terrible.

I wonder what happened to that poor lady?

And the more the commotion grew around him, the more Pike realized that the one man unaffected by the hubbub—the man so deeply consumed by his newspaper that his entire face was hidden—would stand out like a sore thumb.

He could sense the big fed's eyes upon him through the newspaper.

Every second counted now.

A plan had been tickling the back of Pike's brain. He'd need to implement it soon.

Very soon.

His body lurched to the side as the train began to slow. An automated voice came through the scratchy speakers mounted in the ceiling.

This stop: Daly City.

Perfect timing.

The doors on either side of the train squealed open, and people shuffled out of their seats, slowing as the human trickle clotted at the doors.

Pike stole a glance around the paper. The Huber woman and the feds were still in their seats. Mrs. Huber had said that they were going to stay on the train until the Embarcadero, which was far down the line.

He slowly pulled farther away from the paper's edge, trying to confirm his suspicion.

Yes, the big man was staring right at him.

Which meant Pike had no time left.

He threw the newspaper down, jumped from his seat, and pushed through the people in front of him.

Screams. Shouts.

The big man was out of his seat, insanely fast, loping toward him.

A girl of maybe twelve stared open-mouthed as Pike barreled toward her. He grabbed the child and shoved her toward his pursuer.

The big man caught her, and in that time, Pike grabbed Lena Huber by the wrist and pulled her out the door.

CHAPTER FORTY-THREE

SAN FRANCISCO, CALIFORNIA

THE TWO-WORD NAME that the man had just said flittered through Austin's head, doing loops, flashing past his eyes again and again.

Hard Sprint.

This bloodied, disheveled man before him really *was* an FBI agent, and he knew about Austin's investigation.

Austin's stomach tightened, and he ran his tongue over his dry lips, tried to say something, but all that came out was, "How?"

The other guy stood back up, took a relaxed posture, and grinned at Austin as he had before the confrontation. He offered a hand. Austin took it and was pulled to his feet.

"Let's just say someone was concerned about your recent activities," the man said, his voice booming off the stairwell's stark concrete walls.

Austin immediately filled in the blanks. "Otis ... He called the feds."

The other man nodded and produced the wallet he'd flashed moments earlier in the lobby, offered it to Austin.

"Go ahead. Check it out," the man said. "I don't blame you for not trusting me. I wouldn't have either, which is why I went the enthusiastic fan route at first." He pointed to the blood on his shirt. "Had a car accident earlier. No time to clean up before tracking you down. The situation is *that* urgent."

The wallet felt substantial in Austin's hands, weighty. The badge embedded within the bottom half glistened in the dim lighting. He read the name off the ID card behind the clear plastic band at the top.

"Special Agent Clive Booker..."

"That's right," the other man said and held out a hand, palm up.

Austin returned the wallet, heart thundering.

FBI...

Otis had called the damn FBI.

Austin was in deep, deep shit.

"Seven survivors from a military disaster," Booker said as he dropped the wallet into his suit jacket. "The primary officer seems to be killing the others off. And we believe there's at least one other person helping him out. And there's you—someone who hired a private investigator to look into these people."

"Listen," Austin said. "This is all a misunderstanding. I'm an author. I've written—"

"I know who you are." Booker's tone was now serious, the smile finally gone from his contused face. "And I'm sure you're about to give me the same story you fed Otis Watts— that you're researching the Hard Sprint survivors for an upcoming book, that it's a coincidence that the slaughter started shortly thereafter. But tell me, why are you in San Francisco? Why have you been making calls that—"

"I lied to Otis."

Booker nodded matter-of-factly. "Mmm-hmm..."

"I'm not researching anything. I'm trying to save the remaining Hard Sprint survivors."

CHAPTER FORTY-FOUR

DALY CITY, CALIFORNIA

AHEAD OF SILENCE, Pike dashed through the crowd, tugging Lena by the wrist. She looked over her shoulder, made eye contact with Silence, sheer terror.

Pike grabbed a trash barrel, tugged it over as he and Lena turned a corner around a metal and glass partition, then headed down a set of stairs toward the ground level.

Bang!

The metal container hit the concrete hard and rolled in Silence's direction. He leapt over it, but his shoe caught on the top, and he landed hard on the other side, stumbling forward, arms windmilling momentarily before he regained his balance.

He whipped past the partition, down the stairs, turned a corner...

To find a fist flying at his face.

Pike had waited for him.

In the moment before the impact, Silence saw Pike and Lena plastered against the rough-textured wall of the concrete staircase. Lena's eyes wide with fright. Pike's face determined, teeth bared.

Crack!

The impact shifted Silence's jaw to the side and sent a current of shimmering pain from his head down his neck and into his core. The travelers around them—coming and going from the nearby idling buses—gasped and screamed.

Silence stumbled back. And when his vision refocused, he saw a blur from Pike's arm again. Except this time he wasn't throwing a punch.

He was drawing a pistol.

No time to go for his own gun, Silence shot an arm forward, snatching the other weapon, jerking to the side in a front disarm technique that was so quick, Pike's hand was still in the shooting position when his eyes open wide, registering what had happened.

During his training with the Watchers, two of the qualities that Silence had most readily adapted to, despite his size, were speed and stealth. This often came to the surprise of scumbags like Pike.

Before the other man could react, Silence threw a jab, smashing his fist into Pike's eye socket, sending him reeling. Pike lost his grip on Lena's wrist and tumbled to the floor.

And as he did, his jacket flew up, sending a confetti of large squares fluttering into the air. The objects were so unexpected that Silence's mind didn't immediately register what they were.

Polaroid photos.

They twisted and skirted away even as Pike scrambled back to his feet. And even though he kept his wary eyes locked on Silence, he quickly swiped at the floor, gathering as many photos as he could and shoving them back into his jacket.

A figure appeared at the base of the stairwell, behind Pike.

Gibbs.

With one swift motion, she crouched down and brought her foot spinning to the side, a front leg sweep that brought Pike's feet out from under him.

Pike fell again, but this time he didn't go all the way to the floor.

Instead, he was headed for the stairwell wall, the back of his head on a collision course with a plane of rough concrete

Before Pike even had a chance to make contact, Silence was swooping toward him, fist drawn, ready to land another blow, one that would incapacitate the creep.

Then another flash of Pike's hand.

But it wasn't another punch.

Nor was Pike retrieving a gun.

This time Pike pulled something from his pocket. Silence caught a glimpse of it just before his downward movement carried him right into it.

A stun gun.

Pike thrust the weapon forward.

Silence had no way of slowing his forward momentum.

A blue-white fissure of electricity crackled between the electrodes—*ZAP!*—and then Silence's chest made contact with it.

Waves instantly surged through him.

And he was frozen.

His mind went to a memory, involuntarily, like something out of one of C.C.'s meditation techniques.

Training. Years earlier. When he became an Asset, a Watcher.

They'd had an incredibly compact window of opportunity to train him. Unprecedented. Only three weeks. Which meant that every lesson was condensed. And intense.

His trainer, Nakiri, had electrocution-proofed him in one hour. Starting with minor sparks that made him jump, and concluding with full-on electric jolts terrible enough to arrest his entire body.

This moment at the Daly City BART station felt more like the end of his training hour than the beginning.

Time—which had already slowed during the action, compliments of both adrenaline and a C.C. method of slowing his mind—came to a crawl.

Electricity meandered about his body, top to bottom. Contradicting sensations waged war inside him—swelling and slackening; rigidness and melting.

He was frozen, muscles fully contracted.

Then he was falling.

Gibbs, her mouth open, screaming something muted.

Lena, plastered to the stairwell, one hand raised, the other digging into the wall, fingers arched, nails scratching into the concrete.

Pike, teeth bared, arm extended, one blue eye, one brown, mangled Polaroids bursting out of his jacket pocket.

Then time began its gradual return.

Speeding up.

Faster.

Gaining more and more momentum as Silence descended.

A long concrete bench. Approaching. Fast.

The bench was near.

Fast.

Near.

Fast.

And as time fully returned, the corner of the bench grazed Silence's head, a dull pain overpowering the currents that had arrested his muscles.

Spots. Light.

And Silence collapsed.

CHAPTER FORTY-FIVE

SILENCE DRIFTED IN A WHITE MIST, a cloud. Floating. A nothingness so quiet it hummed.

Then voices.

And a lovely scent. Flowers.

No, perfume.

But something else, overpowering the sweet fragrance. Something much more potent. And pungent. Noxious, even.

Automobile exhaust.

He opened his eyes.

A face above him. Gibbs. She stared down from a field of long, straight lines—the corrugated metal of the train station awning. The voices were louder now, clearer. A small group had crowded around them. Sirens in the distance. Idling buses rumbled a few feet away, and Silence took in a lungful of the potent exhaust.

"What happened?" Silence said between coughs.

Gibbs had a hand on his cheek, and she stroked her thumb beneath his eye. "You took a few jolts."

Ah, yes.

The memory flooded back to him. A stun gun to the gut.

The warbling sensation that flooded his entire frame, arresting and tightening his muscles. Falling to the floor. Whacking his head against a concrete bench.

He touched the side of his head, barely grazing it before his fingers recoiled immediately. The pain had teleported, like an invisible claw zapping through the ether and into his fingers.

Then he remembered something else—Pike and Lena Huber.

Gibbs's hand slid off his face as he jumped to his feet. Gasps emanated from the small group surrounding them, and the circle widened.

"Where are they?" Silence said.

Gibbs shook her head. "I'm sorry, Troy. Pike has her. I couldn't catch them. I managed to steal his little toy, though."

She held up Pike's stun gun, gave it a small shake. Then she pointed into the distance, indicating the sirens, which grew louder and louder.

"We gotta go."

———

The air was cool, and while it wasn't laden with exhaust like the BART station, the smell of vehicles was still apparent. Gray concrete pillars stretched into the distance, and flickering overhead lights illuminated the shadows with the help of bright California sunlight pouring in through rectangular window openings along the walls.

The parking structure was a few blocks away from the train station, and it was the first place they'd found to duck in for a few minutes. They were still close enough that the sirens were loud, echoing off the concrete surrounding them.

A chance to catch their breath.

Even if doing so was pointless.

Because Lena Huber was gone, in the hands of the murderous lunatic that Silence and Gibbs had been hunting so doggedly. Silence never got completely hopeless, but sometimes a moment of despair flittered over him. This was one of those moments.

But, as always, he had something in his C.C. toolbox with which to tackle the issue.

Meditation.

He closed his eyes.

The smell of vehicles. Old motor oil festering in the concrete. A hint of antifreeze. Flowers in the planters on the window openings.

Sounds, too, not just smells. The sirens. A train somewhere in the distance. Traffic. Car horns.

He felt his touch points, where his body was coming into contact with reality. The hard concrete making itself apparent through the soles of his dress shoes. His feet, so tender, so in need of a soak. His body quivered slightly as a vehicle rumbled through the building one story below.

And this rumbling took him back to the train, an hour earlier, his body undulating with the vibrations as the train sped along the tracks, Gibbs beside him, Lena Huber across the aisle, her lips moving but no sound coming out, the memory keeping its secrets hidden.

Lena had said something that could be important, a throwaway moment, something that could lead to her location.

What had it been, C.C.? What did she say?

Search your memory, love. Follow your instincts.

Lena's lips continued to move soundlessly, just the rattling and screeching of the train.

He tried to remember the exact moment, the topic of discussion.

Focus, love. You'll find it.

They'd been talking about her husband's sudden trip to San Francisco, the reason she'd come to the city. She'd said something about how Austin made regular trips to San Francisco, that he had a favorite hotel.

But she hadn't given the hotel's name.

She'd said something else.

Words finally came from the lips of the phantom Lena.

Where dreams meet at the bay, the woman said with a wistful almost serene smile.

Silence opened his eyes.

And found Gibbs staring at him quizzically. He stepped past her, to one of the window openings. He looked out into the bright sunlight drenching Daly City.

There was something there, a tickle of familiarity tempting the analytical side of his mind.

Footsteps clacking on the concrete, and then Gibbs was beside him.

"What is it?" she said, leaning into his line of sight.

He kept staring into the distance. "Dreams... Bay..."

"Huh?"

"Where dreams meet..." He swallowed. "At the bay."

Gibbs scrunched her face, raised an eyebrow, and a half moment later her expression slackened. "Oh, wait ... Lena said that, didn't she? When she was talking about the hotel her husband visits in San Francisco."

Silence nodded.

But there was more to this, more than just his memory of what Lena had said. The sense of familiarity grew stronger, toying with him furiously.

It was something fresh. Something recent.

Very recent.

He suddenly thrust his hand into his pocket, retrieved the Polaroids he'd picked up at the train station, thumbing through them furiously.

"Um, Troy...?"

He stopped.

There it was.

The photo of Pike and his lady friend in front of Vaillancourt Fountain. The one with the goofy faces. Crossed eyes. A protruding tongue.

Behind them, past the fountain, at the edge of the photograph was the glass entrance of a tower. In stylized letters above the revolving doors was:

THE CENTURION
Where Dreams Meet at the Bay

He put his finger below the signage, turned the photo toward Gibbs. She didn't reply, just looked up from the photo with an open mouth.

"Justin Herman Plaza," Silence said and swallowed. He turned for the exit. "Come on!"

CHAPTER FORTY-SIX

SAN FRANCISCO, CALIFORNIA

PIKE'S MIND was telling him he'd never been to this place. But the Polaroid photo in his hand and a nagging sensation at his core were saying otherwise.

Justin Herman Plaza was a one-and-a-quarter acre expanse of brick, right off the Embarcadero, directly across the street from the Ferry Building, in the heart of San Francisco. There were the sounds of seagulls, automobiles, and ships on the nearby water. People in sunglasses casually strolled across the manmade plane, some carrying briefcases, others carrying shopping bags. Palm trees and other decorative landscaping traced the plaza's boundaries. In the back were steps leading up to a concrete stretch peppered with outdoor seating for several picture-perfect restaurants and cafés. Beyond this were glistening high-rise buildings.

An abstract fountain dominated the northern corner of the plaza. Square concrete tubes snaked their way through the fountain's design, some of which poured water through their open ends back into the green pool below. The feature was so massive that it accommodated concrete islands, hovering inches above the water level, allowing people to explore the artwork, going under and through the tubes and the falling water. Several people were happily traversing the islands—snapping photographs, all smiles, shouting at each other over the roar of the water.

Pike looked from the fountain and back to the Polaroid in his hand. He and Rita. In front of the same quirky urban sculpture, smiling just as much as the people he'd just seen on the islands. One of the square tubes was right behind his doppelgänger and the woman he knew to be Rita, water rushing from it, frozen midair, locked in photographic time.

That man in the photo was him. His eyes—one blue, one brown. His hair. His face. And the woman was Rita. Could he remember her? No. Not that smile. Not the gentle curve of her lips. But there'd been a laugh. A special laugh, different from her usual chuckle. Yes, he could remember that. A certain fluttering sound she'd made when she was at her happiest.

When she traveled.

When she snapped Polaroid photographs.

He could hear it, through the photograph, through the gentle curve of the smile he couldn't remember.

I love you, Tristan.

He shoved the photograph in his pocket.

And looked at the woman beside him.

Not Rita.

Lena Huber.

Her face bore that same terrified expression she'd worn since he'd first abducted her, hardly concealed by the sunglasses he'd commanded her to wear. A moist trail from a recent tear ran down her cheek, right past the beauty mark.

He turned away from her, let his eyes drift past Justin

Herman Plaza, ignoring the half-memory, the ghost of laughter, to one of the high-rise buildings towering over the plaza. He started at the top of the modern-looking structure—all glass and angles and perfectly placed beams of metal—and his gaze traced down the twenty or so stories to the entrance. Above the glass revolving doors, a prominent sign with aggressive, angular letter read:

THE CENTURION
Where Dreams Meet at the Bay

He returned his attention to Lena, and in the process, his eyes flashed over the fountain again, bringing the image back to his mind, the image on the photograph he'd just shoved back into his pocket.

He and Rita in front of the snaking concrete tubes.

Rita.

Snapping her Polaroids.

She was real. He remembered that he couldn't remember her. After this mission, after he eliminated the last of the traitors, he would get this figured out. He'd find her. He'd remember her.

But first, he had to finish the job.

Lena was shaking, fingers interlaced in front of her, twisting.

"Try again," Pike said.

Lena retrieved her cellular phone, placed a call on speakerphone. Immediately, a digital voice spoke.

Your call has been forwarded to an automatic voice message system. To leave a—

She pressed the END button. "I told you, he won't have his phone on. Whatever he's doing, he doesn't want me or anyone else involved."

"Then we'll wait. What *is* he doing, Mrs. Huber?"

"I don't know!" she pleaded. "Are we going to wait here all day for him?"

Pike grinned devilishly. "No, I have another plan."

CHAPTER FORTY-SEVEN

AFTER AUSTIN TOLD the agent about his self-imposed mission of saving the Hard Sprint survivors from Pike's string of murders, Booker cocked his head, more confused than skeptical.

"I beg your pardon?" the agent said. "It's only been the last day that the press has established for the public the connection between the murders. And what skin do you have in the game, anyway?"

Austin took in a deep breath and held it, releasing it slowly between his teeth. "I came here to San Francisco to find Lynn Davidson. I was too late. Now there are two Hard Sprint survivors that Pike hasn't yet attacked. Donnie Langstaff and Remo Milano." Another deep breath, another slow release. "I'm Remo Milano."

Booker's mouth opened in a gradual circle, and his eyes opened as well. A small puff of breath escaped his lips, a reaction that took Austin aback, not what he would have expected out of an investigating federal agent.

"*You're* Remo Milano?"

Austin nodded. "That's right."

"So 'Austin Huber' is a pen name?"

"At first, yes. Then I had it legally changed. Kind of a long, personal story, really. I was never proud of where I came from, my father, and—"

Booker held up a hand. "Just keep it 'long and personal,' all right? All I need to know is that you're the Remo Milano from Hard Sprint."

Austin nodded.

Booker shook his head and sighed, almost scoffed.

"Unbelievable," he said.

Austin couldn't decipher the small, inappropriate smile on the man's face.

"So, you see, this is all a misunderstanding," Austin said. "I had stayed in touch with one person I met at Hard Sprint. Elliott Bell, an Army JAG. At the time I was a fresh-faced Air Force A1C looking to separate and start his writing career, and Bell took me under his wing, helped me with separation, my name-change, some of my early contract work. Most of it he did pro bono. Hell of a guy.

"I hadn't talked to him in a couple of years, and then he calls me up out of the blue, asking *me* for help this time. He said that Derek Artiga—an Army buddy of his who was also at Hard Sprint—had been experiencing weird symptoms the last year or so. Anxiety. Paranoia. Headaches. And memory loss. He said he'd had the same symptoms and asked if I had as well. I told him, yes.

"Bell knew I used a private investigator to help with my book research, and he asked if I could have the detective track down the others from Hard Sprint. I said, *of course*. But as soon as Otis Watts, my detective, started searching, Pike started killing off the survivors. So naturally, it looked like I was connected to the murders.

"Bell and Artiga were the first to go, so my mission switched from locating the survivors in order to compare symptoms to finding them before Pike did. If I went to the police, they'd think I was involved because Otis's investigation predated the first murder. That's why I went on my own. But now that I know you're involved, let's pool our resources. Bring me onto the investigation as a consultant or whatever. There's still one person Pike hasn't attacked: Donnie Langstaff."

Another bizarre smile from Booker.

"No, Langstaff's in no danger. He's already dead. A year ago. Cancer."

Austin hesitated. Somehow this revelation hit him in the gut—even though he'd never known Langstaff. This nightmare had somehow given him an unspoken connection to the people who'd been at Eglin Air Force Base years earlier.

"What now, then?" Austin said.

"We get you and your wife somewhere secure. It's not safe at your house. And—"

A shrill sound made them both jump—a cellular phone chime, echoing harshly off the concrete walls.

Booker fished the phone from his pocket, checked the small screen on the front, then gave Austin a look.

"Excuse me."

He turned around, ascending a couple of steps. Some muffled, urgent words—*Yes. Yes. Where? I understand*—then he came back down, snapping his phone into its folded orientation.

"We need to go."

CHAPTER FORTY-EIGHT

SILENCE AND GIBBS moved into the massive stretch of red brick, bounded by concrete steps and palm trees and with the twisted geometric tubes and thundering water of Vaillancourt Fountain at the far end. Traffic on the Embarcadero hummed past on one side, and tracing the other side were soaring towers, including the glistening glass building that Silence recognized from the photo—the Centurion Hotel.

As he twisted past a group of tourists laughing and comparing cartoonish city landmark maps, a pair of people came into view. A man and a woman. One he hadn't seen since the previous day in Kentucky; the other he'd just seen in the BART train.

They were by the edge of the fountain, standing very close; likely Pike wasn't going to let her get more than a few inches away.

"Shit, there they are!" Gibbs said, hurrying to keep up with him. She pointed to the fountain, to the concrete island-pathway that hovered inches over the water, tracing beneath the tangled concrete tubes and their roaring waterfalls. "Do your creepy pop-out-of-nowhere thing and grab the bastard."

Silence slowed and pulled to the side, still several yards behind Pike and Lena. He eased to a stop, stared at them.

"What are you *doing?*" Gibbs said. "That's the man we've been hunting, the freaking murderer. He has Lena! What are you waiting for?"

Silence hesitated before answering.

"Listening to my gut," he said.

Something was about to happen. He could sense it, an energy rippling through the pleasant California air. Something that would change the dynamic of the situation. If he delayed for just a moment longer...

That's right, love, C.C. said. *You can feel it, can't you?*

Yes.

"Look!" Gibbs said.

Silence turned.

Another pair of people approached Pike and Lena, crossing over the brickwork from the Centurion.

Silence took off again, Gibbs rushing beside him.

Ahead, there was a quick exchange of words among the other four people, and with almost no hesitation, the two Hubers switched places, Lena going to Booker and Austin going to Pike.

A hostage exchange.

There had been so little friction in the trade-off that it all took place within moments. The only party who protested was Lena, first requiring a shove from Pike to get her moving, and then reaching desperately for her husband once she'd taken her place beside Booker. Her screams were lost over the thundering of the fountain, but her dread was evident even over the distance—tortured face with pink, tear-streaked cheeks.

The two newly formed groups exchanged a few words, Booker and Pike doing all the talking.

Silence couldn't be sure of what was happening, but what-

ever had just occurred during the exchange had deadly implications. Pike now had the next Hard Sprint survivor, Remo
Milano, in his control.

Which meant he'd take his prisoner somewhere far away
from the crowds of Justin Herman Plaza.

And execute him.

Silence had to move quickly. No time for stealth. No time
to slip through the island pathway twisting through the
fountain.

He reached under his jacket, took hold of his Beretta.

But before he could draw, Gibbs grabbed his arm.

"Wait! Look!"

Another pair of people approached the growing coterie at
the fountain.

The man in the back wore an immaculate black suit, dark
sunglasses, and the clear coiled wire of a communications
device traced the side of his neck. Mid twenties. He had the
appearance of a secret service agent, though the man in front
of him—while clearly the more important of the two—was
not a president.

The man was short but broad. Bone-white hair, neatly
combed, framing a bank manager face. Dark blue slacks,
white shirt, pressed and professional, strait-laced.

The younger man slowed to a halt, hovering behind as the
older man stepped closer to those by the fountain.

Pike's mouth fell open, and as Silence and Gibbs inched
forward, Silence was now close enough to hear the killer utter
the newcomer's name in shock.

"Colonel Noyer?"

CHAPTER FORTY-NINE

AUSTIN HAD WRITTEN plenty of novels in which kidnapped people were placed in harm's way. He'd always believed he was good at empathizing with the characters and then convincingly translating their plights to readers.

But now he quickly realized that nothing could have prepared him for what it *actually* feels like.

Still, he was proud that he'd strangled his own fear of death with something far less selfish. When the exchange was made—when he went to Tristan Pike and Lena went to Agent Booker—there wasn't even a moment of fear. Only relief. Somehow Pike had found his wife, kidnapped her, and inexplicably brought her to San Francisco. How and why, Austin had no clue.

He was just happy that his wife was safe.

Even if he now faced certain death.

Pike had been killing off the Hard Sprint survivors one by one. Now Austin was in the man's grasp. The future was inevitable and bleak.

Another notion that was somehow keeping Austin's mind off his plight was the storyteller side of his brain, forming theories as to who the new arrival was and how he factored into the plotline. When the white-haired man had suddenly approached the group, Austin's captor, Pike, was stunned into a state of open-mouthed paralysis.

Pike had called the man *Noyer*, and though Austin didn't recognize the man, he did recognize the name through Otis's detective work. Noyer was the colonel who'd been in charge of Hard Sprint.

Austin remembered the briefing room. On the doomed night. Years earlier. The space was dimly lit, only a single desk lamp and the projector providing illumination. Pike had been at the projector screen, laying out the details, the slides glinting off his mismatched eyes. While Austin and Bell and Artiga and all the others who went into the field had been in the chairs facing the projector, there had been one other person in the room.

Austin had needed to turn around in his seat to spot the individual, a man who stood half-concealed in the shadows at the back corner, barely more than a silhouette. The man never said a word. Austin hadn't been able to discern the letters on the man's nameplate, but he'd seen a silver colonel's eagle on the man's shoulder, glistening in the muted light.

Now Austin could see all of him. In broad daylight.

"Colonel," Pike said, looking desperately at Noyer, pleading, keeping one hand clenched hard around the back of Austin's arm. "What's going on, sir?"

Noyer stepped forward. "It's General now, son. I told you that a few days ago when we spoke on the phone, remember? No, of course you don't. EX391 has rotted that memory of yours. And your reasoning. That's why you've done all this. You're not well."

"It was you, sir?" Pike said. "You're the one ... the one who called me? I..." He trailed off. "Yes! Yes, I remember now. You told me about my mission, that the other survivors are spies, traitors, that I needed to hunt them down. Every one of them."

The older man shook his head, a sad grimace on his face. "No, son. You've concocted all that in your head. I told you to come to Fort Meade, that we'd help you."

"But ... I ..."

Noyer held out a hand, pleadingly. "The drug. It's got a hold of you. You don't know what you're doing. Let Remo Milano go, son. He's done nothing wrong."

The grip on Austin's arm strengthened, fingers pushing into his flesh hard enough to make him cry out.

"He's a spy!" Pike shouted. "A terrorist!"

Noyer shook his head. "You're wrong. Tristan, you were one of my finest young officers. A good man. Listen to your old CO. Let him go."

Austin peered to the side, stole a glance at Pike's face—oily, sweaty, covered in stubble, confusion in his blue-and-brown eyes. His mouth was open, breathing hard.

Noyer inched closer, still reaching out with a pleading hand. "Please, Captain."

"He's the last one," Pike said quietly. "I killed Bell, Artiga, Davidson. Maybe Horn, unless he recovers. And Langstaff is already dead."

Noyer looked at Agent Booker.

"That's what I told him," Booker said. "Enough lies. If you don't wrap this up, General, we're all in for a world of hurt. Pike's a liability."

He turned to Pike then.

"Don't you recognize me, you dumb shit?" Booker said. "I'm Donnie Langstaff."

CHAPTER FIFTY

PIKE COULDN'T COMPREHEND HOW, but he *did* recognize the man who'd moments earlier given him an introduction as Clive Booker.

Seventeen people had gone out that night at Eglin Air Force Base so long ago. Pike had met none of them before, but one of them had stuck out in his mind through the years because he was one of only two, including Pike himself, who had actually been stationed at Eglin. A young Army officer, a butter-bar spec ops guy. He'd had short-cut blond hair, clean-shaven. The man had said he had horrible shakes after coming back from the desert, one of the few who saw action in the 100-hour ground offensive component of the war.

Pike's eyes bounced across the people surrounding him, from Colonel Noyer—who was now a general and looked foreign to Pike in his civvies—to Remo Milano's stunning wife with her beauty mark and long hair shining in the sunlight to Donnie Langstaff and his scruffy-faced, bloodied appearance, so different from the soldier he'd met years earlier.

Booker grinned, a treacherous look that Pike couldn't

decipher. "I see. You *do* recognize me. Then I'll let you in on a secret. I've been the one chatting to you this whole time. I'm the Benefactor."

Noyer continued to reach toward Pike, the pleading father figure, inching closer. "Don't listen to him, Tristan. He's trying to confuse you."

Pike looked back and forth between the other two men. "But how would he..." He trailed off, processing, memories and thoughts colliding in his mind. "How would he know about the Benefactor?"

"Please," Noyer said. "Let Milano go. You've done your job, soldier. I'm going to get you some help."

The tumult in Pike's mind crescendoed. Flashes of memory. The explosion. The cocky, blond, sneering Army lieutenant. The fire.

And other memories too. Rita. Laughing. Snapping her Polaroids. At the Grand Canyon. Yosemite National Park. Times Square. Justin Herman Plaza in San Francisco.

"Please..." Noyer said.

And Pike complied.

He released Milano's arm, gave him a gentle shove in Noyer's direction.

Booker scoffed.

"Thanks," he said as he pulled a pistol from a shoulder holster under his suit jacket.

He fired.

The pain was instantaneous and blinding, a sphere pulsing through Pike's stomach. He screamed out, and for a moment, he was stunned in a sort of rigid paralysis.

The shouts from the onlookers, the roar of the fountain— all of it took on a disconnected, muted, echoing quality as a ringing sound grew louder and louder, overtaking everything else.

His vision went white. Sweat flushed his skin. He blinked, shuffled to the side, trying to steady himself.

And he fell.

He heard a woman's laughter, the click of a shutter and the whir of tiny plastic gears—a Polaroid camera ejecting a photo.

He remembered.

Rita.

Looking back at him as she scampered off down a cobblestone street, some old part of an old town they'd visited in New England. A glimpse of her broad smile, auburn hair, light brown eyes. The street in front of her was busy with tourists. She twisted through them, raised her Polaroid camera.

Flash.

A sterile office. A conference table. Rita across from him, not looking at him. A man in a suit beside her, manila folder resting on the table in front of him. Quiet words. Setting forth the parameters, who would own what. A tear fell from the corner of one of Rita's light brown eyes.

Flash.

A trail. Cool and moist. Massive trunks. The redwoods, the giants. All alone. Rita whipped around, grabbed him by the shoulder, pulled him close. She was surprisingly strong, all those yoga and pilates classes. On her tiptoes. He leaned his face down. Cheek to cheek. She held the camera in front of her, stretching as far as she could, giggling as she awkwardly managed to press the button on the inverted device, a photo of the two of them.

Flash.

The light blinded him. There was nothing but white.

And Rita's laughter.

Until everything faded away.

CHAPTER FIFTY-ONE

SCREAMS. People in suits and dress skirts, T-shirts and sunglasses, scattering in all directions. Lena looked through the twisting limbs, trying to find her husband.

The last she'd seen of him was when the agent had fired his weapon at the other man, the one with mismatched eyes, and pandemonium had erupted, people pushing around from all sides. The crowd had engulfed her line of sight, and she lost track of Austin, hadn't seen if the bullet had struck him as well.

The agent had sprinted off.

A large woman bashed into Lena's shoulder, sending her stumbling to the side, and Lena twisted her way through another pod of people as she got on her tiptoes, searched for Austin.

She nearly fell over, and as she reached for her knee, she caught a glimpse of him. They locked eyes. He was unhurt.

Her exhale was so pronounced that she heard it even over the chaos.

But then another wave of screams stole her relieved smile,

broke her visual tie to her husband. She followed the pointing fingers, the faces with their wide-open mouths.

Everyone was looking at a dark figure running behind Vaillancourt Fountain.

With a pistol in his hand.

Chasing after the bloodied federal agent, who had made it to the far end of the plaza.

The shadow figure was terribly tall, and as the person cut through the lines of concrete and streams of water, she couldn't get a visual on the man.

It wasn't until he burst out the other side of the fountain and chased after the federal agent that Lena saw who the man was.

It was Agent Gibbs's partner, Troy.

And he barreled across the plaza.

CHAPTER FIFTY-TWO

GIBBS HAD a visual on Troy as he sprinted toward the Embarcadero, a streak of motion, Beretta in hand.

And a wave of screaming people surged past.

She jumped to the side, redirected her attention to where she'd last seen Troy.

He was gone.

Out of instinct, she went for her gun. And remembered—it wasn't there. She'd gone to an airport two days earlier, embarking upon an unlicensed investigation.

No gun.

Hell with it.

She lunged forward, toward the spot where Troy had disappeared—

And she halted, her shoes scraping on the brick.

Because someone was moving in her direction, steadily, dodging the throngs of people all around him, finger to his ear.

It was the suited man who'd arrived with Noyer.

The man with the meticulous and trim haircut. Pitch-black sunglasses. And a coiled wire tracing his neck and ending in an ear-worn communications device.

A man in black.

It was finally happening.

From the moment Gibbs began digging into the facts back in Pensacola to the moment she defied Caldwell, her boss. Peeking through the drapes in her house, examining the cars on her street. Fleeing Troy at the Pensacola airport. Being abducted by Booker.

The entire time she'd felt, she'd *known* that she would face a man in black.

And now it was finally happening.

Another cluster of people streaked past, blotting the man from view momentarily, and then there he was, only yards away, head lowered, mouth tight, plowing right toward her.

Gibbs took off.

She rounded the edge of the fountain at a sprint, twisting through a group of fleeing Japanese tourists, and stole a glance at the Embarcadero.

Troy was nowhere to be seen. Vanished.

She was alone.

The man moved steadily toward her as the crowd rushed past him on all sides. Sunglasses zoned in on her.

Instead of going for the Embarcadero, Gibbs ran for the back side of the plaza—the cafes and restaurants.

She funneled past another pod of people, looked over her shoulder.

The man was no longer moving at a determined walk. Now he was running just like the others.

Gibbs gasped.

She sprinted harder, shoving her way past more people. A restaurant ahead—The Golden Hour. She couldn't go there. Too many people. Too obvious.

Another glance back.

The man was closer. Locked in on her.

Around a corner. A nondescript gray door off a hallway. A janitor's closet, door slightly ajar, a yellow mop bucket visible.

She bolted for it, pulled the door open, closed.

Darkness. Just a hint of light coming in from the gap at the bottom of the door. The smell of bleach and citrus cleaners and a stale mop.

Her own shuddering breaths overpowered the sounds of the chaos outside. She felt the door's presence a few inches in front of her and tried to lean away, her back squeezing against a line of brooms affixed to the wall.

Another breath came out of her, choppy and shallow. She'd been holding it, didn't realize.

A moment passed. The noises beyond the door lessened. The crowd was thinning, everyone clearing the area.

Gibbs was alive. She was going to get through this.

She exhaled.

And the door shot open, a shadow figure swooped in, and a powerful hand grabbed her by the throat.

CHAPTER FIFTY-THREE

DONNIE LANGSTAFF WAS a master at escaping.

It wasn't the first skill one would expect from an operative working for a secretive military contractor. But, then, there were a lot of misconceptions about the inner workings of clandestine bureaucracy.

When faced with the choice of engaging or escaping, the latter was often the preferred option.

After all, he'd just made plenty of noise by eliminating Tristan Pike in broad daylight in the middle of a crowded plaza in the middle of a large and significant city.

So instead of engaging the monstrous man chasing him, he would elude him.

Langstaff hadn't yet been able to identify the agency or organization to which the man calling himself Troy belonged, but at the moment, it didn't matter. All that mattered was that this man was one of the best trained individuals he'd ever encountered. The source of that training was inconsequential.

And to escape this man, Langstaff was using textbook misdirection.

He'd crossed the Embarcadero, and as he moved south on

the sidewalk, the Ferry Building was ahead of him, a colossal and stately two-story structure tracing a long section of the waterfront, a lofty clock tower at its center. Langstaff had no clue how old the building was, but it looked really freaking old, turn-of-the-century stuff.

It was a famous city landmark, and its reputation was what Langstaff needed at the moment. If Troy was still behind him, he would see Langstaff heading toward the building and assume that he was going there to take one of the many ferries out of town.

Langstaff stepped into the shade of the entranceway, heading for the glass doors, and immediately swooped to the side, positioning himself behind one of the massive pillars that lined the wide sidewalk along the Embarcadero.

He glanced to the street.

There was a decent amount of foot traffic at this time of day, but the crowd was by no means thick. And among the people that were out and about, there was no tall, exotic looking man with a dark expression and a designer suit.

Troy had fallen for the bait.

Langstaff grinned and stepped out into the sunshine.

He headed north, toward Justin Herman Plaza, doubling-back toward his actual destination.

He'd seen it earlier—Pier 1 1/2. A tiny finger jutting into the bay, two positions north of the Ferry Building. He'd spotted a pair of crude signs advertising scenic ferry trips. While Troy would search the more substantial lines at the Ferry Building, Langstaff would ride to safety on an oversized fishing boat.

Langstaff grinned broader.

As he turned onto Pier 1 1/2, he got a better view of the two signs he'd glimpsed earlier. One said *Beautiful Bay Tours* with a strip of paper pasted diagonally across it: *CLOSED*. A small red boat bobbed in the water to the side.

The other sign was black and featured a skull and cross-bones. In pirate-style lettering was, *Shiver Me Tours*. A black boat very much like the red one was beside this sign, and a captain waited at the helm.

He was a big dude, hunched over the wheel, his back facing the pier, wearing a pirate's hat and a long black jacket with theatrically perfect patina.

Langstaff stepped onto the boat. The captain didn't turn.

"I'd like a tour. The sooner the better."

In response, the captain grunted, deep and grumbling.

"Yeah, cute, guy. Arr, matey," Langstaff said. "Let's just go. I'm in a hurry."

The captain stood and shuffled to the side, dragging one leg, keeping himself in a ridiculously over-the-top hunched slouch. He began unfastening the rope from the cleat.

The time-consuming theatrics flushed Langstaff with a moment of annoyance, but as he dropped into the row of vinyl seats—which were hot from the bright sunlight—his frustration faded away.

Because he was safe.

He stared at the Ferry Building, its ornate walls, the looming clock tower. And grinned.

The captain continued with the pirate routine, head and shoulders hunched over, right leg dragging, as he went back to the front of the boat. And after he assumed the controls, they took off.

A pleasant breeze washed over Langstaff as the small boat scooted over the water, relieving any discomfort he'd felt from the hot vinyl seat. He stole another look at the Ferry Building, growing smaller in the distance.

Langstaff closed his eyes, leaned his head back, felt the warm sunlight through his shades.

And then his body jolted.

The captain had gunned the throttle, and the boat bolted off across the bay.

"Hey!" Langstaff shouted.

The boat rocked hard as the captain pulled it to the left. Wind hissed past Langstaff's ears.

"What the hell are you doing?"

The wake from a large ship was right ahead, frothy white on the crests.

And the little boat crashed right into it.

Bam!

Langstaff catapulted from his seat, striking the plastic floor of the boat hard, his palm digging into the textured footing, a puddle sloshing onto his pants.

"*Hey!* I said, *what the hell are you doing?*"

The captain suddenly pulled down on the throttle. The boat slowed, its receding movement jostling Langstaff on the floor.

The captain turned around, slowly extended to his full height, losing the hunchback, towering over Langstaff. He shook off the black jacket, threw the hat to the side.

It was Troy.

CHAPTER FIFTY-FOUR

GIBBS TOOK another swipe at the man's face, and he twisted to the side, almost casually, to avoid it, while tightening his grip on her throat.

He'd shut the door behind him when he'd barged in, but the sliver of light at the crack of the doorframe was enough to illuminate his features, his determined scowl half-hidden behind sunglasses.

This close to her, he was no longer a mythological shadow figure, a clandestine no-man, a man in black—he was a real, living, breathing human being. She saw the pores in his skin, smelled his perspiration. Maybe twenty-five years old. White. Lean, athletic build with dark brown, parted hair. His expression was blank, unaffected, and the dark lenses blotted out his eyes.

Squeezing even tighter around her throat, the man threw a jab to her ribs.

A jolt of pain, and Gibbs's knees buckled.

The man hooked her beneath the arm before she could fall, and he whipped behind her, getting her neck in the crook of his elbow. He squeezed down hard, his arms a pair of piston-strength scissors. His bicep bulged against her neck.

She gagged. The air in her throat whistled as it grew hot, stale, painful, horrible.

The man finally spoke, and his voice was as by-the-books, as anodyne as his expression. "This was not your battle, Agent Gibbs."

A vicious tug against her neck and another jolt of pain. Gibbs's mouth opened in a scream. Nothing came out. Her throat popped, eyes watered. She smacked at his forearm, dug her fingernails into his flesh.

Then she felt something.

The tiniest bit of pressure against her thigh. Something hard and foreign. For a moment, she thought it was a broom or a mop.

But then she understood.

She peeled her right hand from the man's forearm, plunged it into her pocket, her fingers skittering off the top of the object.

The man gave another violent yank to her throat, and her hand went back to his forearm momentarily before it returned to her pocket.

Her fingers brushed the object again.

Hard, cold to the touch.

Another wave of pain from her neck.

She wrapped her fingers around the stun gun, pulled it from her pocket, and swung it backward, jabbing it into the man's side at the same time she pulled the trigger.

ZAP!

The sound echoed harshly off the packed concrete confines. And it gave her a half moment of freedom as the man's body pulled away from her.

Cool air poured through the pain in her throat, funneling

into her lungs, and she gasped before jabbing the stun gun
into the dazed man again, this time under his chin.

ZAP!

The man spasmed in place, frozen in position. Drool fell
from his mouth.

Gibbs had a small window of opportunity.

It was all she needed.

She slugged the man across the jaw, and he stumbled back.
His force cracked a shelf, and a barrage of paint cans and
industrial cleaners fell on him. He shielded himself feebly, as
his foot slipped once, twice. Then he was on the floor.

Crack.

It was a terrible sound, much quieter than the bark of the
stun gun but twice as ominous.

Broken bone.

Gibbs gasped and retreated, hand going to her mouth.

The man was still, but a few cans rolled and shimmied on
the surrounding floor.

And then a bit more movement. Something glistening.
Fluid.

A puddle grew from beneath the man's head.

Gibbs stepped backward, her eyes not leaving the person
on the floor.

Completely motionless. Eyes open. Puddle expanding.

The closet was quiet again, and Gibbs's shuddering
breaths returned as the only sound.

She slowly crouched and put two fingers to the man's
neck.

Nothing.

Dead.

Immediately, her training kicked in, determining whom to
call.

But then she realized...

There was no one to contact.

Not for someone like this. Not in this situation.

Another shadow man lost to the shadows.

All she could do was leave him behind.

That was exactly what she did.

One more glance at the body, then she stepped over it, opened the door, and left.

CHAPTER FIFTY-FIVE

DONNIE LANGSTAFF—THE man Silence had known as Clive Booker—was a formidable opponent.

From everything Silence had gathered back at the confrontation at Justin Herman Plaza, the man was some sort of freelance operative under the employ of a deep-state contractor. Whoever he was, he'd not only had the balls to impersonate a federal agent, but had the means to create a nearly perfect set of fake FBI credentials.

Logic dictated that the man's physical prowess must be in line with his other resources.

A notable threat.

But as Silence moved from the small boat's bow to the seats along the back, a twinkle of fear flashed over Langstaff's eyes. Not only had Silence surprised him, not only had he gotten the creep isolated in the middle of the bay, but he'd also gotten into the man's head.

And it took a lot to break through a trained professional's facade.

Silence should know.

Minutes earlier, when he'd seen Langstaff heading for the

Ferry Building, he'd known the move was likely a diversion. And when they'd passed by Pier 1 1/2, he had a good idea of what the man's alternative plan would be.

That's why Silence hadn't gone to the front, main entrance of the building as Langstaff had. Silence had slipped away to the north side of the building doing so confidently, because Langstaff—as skilled of an operative as he seemed to be—apparently wasn't keen on recent Californian history.

Silence, though, spent his early childhood in the Golden State and kept abreast of goings-on in California.

From the 1950s until recent years, the Embarcadero had been a freeway running right in front of the Ferry Building. After the '89 earthquake, the freeway suffered significant damage, and in '91, after much discussion and debate, the freeway was removed, bringing the beloved Ferry Building back into direct connection with the city. San Francisco also took this as an opportunity to restore the building's former grandeur and revitalize the waterfront into a thriving commercial and transportation area.

But the project wasn't to be completed until the early twenty-first century.

Which meant that right now, the Ferry Building was as much a construction site as it was a tourist hub.

So while Silence wasn't sure whether ferry service had been reestablished, he'd known that the Ferry Building wouldn't be bustling with travelers as much as it would be overrun with construction crew. Spotting Langstaff inside would be no difficult task.

When Silence had stepped through the northside doors, staring down the long and magnificent nave—with the copious scaffolding and construction equipment promising even more magnificence in the near future—it hadn't taken long for him to recognize that Langstaff hadn't entered the building beyond the main doors.

So Silence had circled back to Pier 1 1/2, moving at double-time to outpace Langstaff. As with the hotel clerk in Louisville, a stack of cash had been enough to convince the pirate boat's captain to take "a quick break."

Silence asked him for the jacket and hat before the man left.

And now, having isolated the boat and shaken off the pirate gear, Silence approached Langstaff slowly at the stern. True, there had been a glimmer of uncertainty across Langstaff's visage, but this man had proven himself to be an undeniable talent. Silence would need to keep his guard up.

He raised his silenced Beretta, leveled it at Langstaff's chest.

"Slowly," Silence said.

Taking his meaning, Langstaff carefully reached under his jacket and retrieved his Glock, pinching its handle between his fingers, well away from the trigger.

Silence swiped his head to the side, a command, and again Langstaff took his meaning. Sneering but not breaking eye contact, Langstaff tossed the gun over the side of the boat. It disappeared into the water with a plop.

"Talk," Silence said.

Langstaff's sneer widened. "Talk, huh? Why? Because you know there's more to this, don't you? Because you don't believe the bullshit Noyer was spitting back there."

Silence nodded.

"Noyer's a conman. A politician in a uniform. He's the one who sanctioned the murders. Hard Sprint was his show, and when it all went south, he spearheaded the coverup. Kasperson never existed outside of a few tax forms. This is all high-level stuff. I don't know what the hell they shot in our arm that night. I just know that I've never been the same since.

"A few weeks after Hard Sprint, I started getting edgy.

Headaches. Anxiety. Memory issues. So I did my best to follow the chain of command, which is sorta tricky on a covert TDY. I figured the only place to go with my concerns was Pike. But I couldn't find the guy. Ended up he was medically separated only days after the incident. As far as anyone else at Hard Sprint knew, Pike was the guy running the show.

"But I was actually stationed at Eglin, unlike the others, and I recognized the colonel who'd been standing in the shadows at the briefing room. I went to Noyer. He let me in on the secret, told me he *knew* EX391 would have side effects. That was the reason for the NDAs, the secrecy. Noyer offered me a ground-level position with the organization that backed Kasperson. And since then I've been a contractor."

"Why kill survivors now?" Silence said.

Langstaff scoffed. "That's the million-dollar question, isn't it? Had it not been for the explosion, Hard Sprint would have disappeared entirely from the record as intended. But for a few years, it looked like everything had worked out on its own. Then Derek Artiga starts getting fresh symptoms, talks to his buddy Elliott Bell, and the two of them start asking questions. They were getting too close to the truth. We needed someone to eliminate them—not just Artiga and Bell, but all the survivors ... aside from me, of course."

He chuckled.

"Pike had lost his mind after Hard Sprint, and his life fell apart after he was medically separated. So we track him down, give the disgraced soldier a new mission, pump him full of more EX391 in case anything happens to him and they run toxicology.

"And that's why I killed him. Now that people are asking questions, there can be no survivors, no links back to Hard Sprint. But Noyer was going to let him go. And Milano, too. The man's a snake trying to save his own skin.

"If the truth comes out and people start looking into Kasperson, they're going to find my employer. I won't allow that. I'm going to finish what they started. I've already eliminated Pike. Now I'll kill Horn and Milano, and this will all be over." He paused. "But first I have to take care of you."

Langstaff climbed to his feet. The boat rocked gently with his movement. The sneer remained on his face, and he glanced at Silence's Beretta.

"Gonna shoot me right out here in the Bay, are you?" he said. "Without a suppressor? The sound's gonna carry over the water. They'll hear it all the way at Alcatraz. Then what? Police boats. Choppers." He pointed a finger straight up at the sky. "I don't know who you're working for, but I know you're a pro. And you're smarter than that."

Silence said nothing.

But he shrugged.

And holstered the Beretta.

Because Langstaff was right. He couldn't fire out here.

That had never been his intention.

There was a moment of stillness as the two pros stared one another down. Langstaff wore that glaring smile of his. Silence remained blank-faced.

Water lapped gently against the hull. The sounds of the city, muffled and softened by distance.

And then both parties exploded into action.

Silence flew at the other man, covering the distance between the two in a flash. But there wasn't the immediate collision he'd expected—their bodies didn't strike until a split second later than his subconscious had calculated.

Because Langstaff had reached to the side and grabbed a metal rod that had secured the front doors of a pair of side-by-side storage spaces.

The bar blurred toward Silence's face, matching his forward momentum, and with a reaction that had been burnt into the deep, natural, unthinking part of his brain via ruthless training, Silence's hand shot forward, stopping the bar, absorbing the force with the thick flesh of his palm, right at the point of impact.

Bam!

They collided and stumbled toward the stern, somehow staying on their feet, but only for a moment before Langstaff swept Silence's leg with a move Silence instantly recognized— a *kari-ashi*, a judo foot sweep.

But as Silence fell, he clenched one of his large hands entirely around the other man's hip, yanking him to the deck with him.

Silence's face smashed into hard plastic. He tasted blood.

Langstaff rolled on top of him, the metal bar between them, guiding it to Silence's throat. A feral scowl revealed the operative's teeth in a broad slash across his sweaty face.

Silence shot his free hand up, bringing it to the bar.

The length of metal hovered between the men, four hands strangling it. Silence clenched his jaw, putting everything he had against Langstaff's incredible brawn.

The bar quivered in Silence's hands as it shifted upward. Langstaff's monstrous strength was nothing compared to Silence's.

Confidence drained from Langstaff's eyes.

With a quick explosion of energy, Silence shot the bar toward Langstaff's face.

Thwack!

The impact was both wet and dry, soft and hard, the sound of crunching bone and torn flesh. Silence had pulsed the bar so hard that the collision with Langstaff's face sent it flying from his hands. It hit the deck and bounced erratically, loudly, skittering to the bow where it crashed into one of the chairs with a loud clank.

Langstaff summoned reserve energy and used the new

momentum he'd gained from the blow to the face to reposition himself at Silence's side, recovering remarkably fast from the impact. He pulled more skills from his bag of tricks—grappling maneuvers that Silence took to be *Shuai jiao.*

Strong arms and legs clambered all over Silence. He tried to pry his legs through Langstaff's, but the creep held on, summoning the desperate strength of a man who knew he was about to die.

Silence had seen many people call forth such reserves.

In the hands of a trained operative, those reserves were particularly formidable.

But as Silence had told the man in their pissing match back in the SUV, Silence had an impressive pedigree of lethal training on par with Langstaff's.

Silence swung his head backward and felt a satisfying crunch against the back of his head, through his hair.

He'd re-broken the man's broken nose.

Langstaff howled, and Silence used the moment to pivot his weight, clamping his long thighs over Langstaff's torso, swinging the man beneath him.

Silence clasped his hands around Langstaff's throat. The operative's eyes immediately bulged, and in their depths was not only fear but resignation. And something like confusion.

"Who the hell..." Langstaff wheezed, his voice tiny. A cough. "Are you?"

In response, Silence squeezed tighter.

There were a few more coughs. Some small kicks of Langstaff's legs, twisting in circles on the plastic surface, making scraping noises. A few gurgles from his mouth, sputters of bloody saliva.

And he was done.

Silence exhaled, slowly released his grip. There were clear-as-day white outlines of his hands in the angry red splotch covering Langstaff's neck.

Now he needed something.

Something heavy.

He looked to his right. The two doors from which Langstaff had grabbed the metal bar were slightly ajar, bumping with the now vigorous movements of the boat. They sat beneath the row of vinyl-cushioned seats, and apparently the bar was a jury-rigged solution, as both of the doors' handles appeared to be damaged. One of the doors bumped open again, revealing sandbags in the storage space beneath the seats.

Perfect.

Silence affixed the sandbags to the dead man, sliding them into position beneath his pants. After cinching them in with the man's belt, Silence opened the short door at the stern of the boat, pushed Langstaff over the two small plastic steps, and watched as he sank into the greenish-blue water.

Langstaff vanished.

Silence re-latched the door, went to the controls and took off, just one of many boaters enjoying beautiful San Francisco Bay.

CHAPTER FIFTY-SIX

LOS ANGELES, CALIFORNIA

THE WINDOWS in Otis's office had gotten dark, and the only light in the room was the small television set on his desk.

Austin had told him to watch the news, that doing so would answer all of Otis's questions.

Otis was glad he'd taken him at his word.

He watched, dumbfounded, as the latest story reached its end. The line of text at the bottom of the screen read:

*BIZARRE SHOOTING IN SAN FRANCISCO
INVOLVING L.A.-BASED AUTHOR AUSTIN
HUBER*

"...and police have informed Channel 58 that the victim was Tristan Pike from the small town of Sullivan, Illinois," the female anchor was saying. "While it appears Pike was a deranged fan of writer Austin Huber, it's still unclear why another individual fired on Pike. The unidentified shooter escaped into the crowd. He is described as Caucasian, average height, blond hair. San Francisco and state authorities are asking anyone with further information to contact them."

Austin and Lena appeared on screen, embracing, both of them draped with gray emergency blankets. Microphones and cameras crowded the edges of the frame, and the image jerked left and right as the camera operator jockeyed for position with contemporaries. Lena's cheek was on Austin's chest, and he rested his chin atop her head, eyes closed, neither of them acknowledging the chaos surrounding them.

Otis smiled.

The anchor returned, and she pivoted to face her male companion. "A bizarre and troubling situation, Clayton."

"And one we'll certainly be monitoring," the other anchor said, squaring to the camera. "L.A. City Councilors voted today on measures that would..."

As the words faded from Otis's perception, his insides were a maelstrom of conflicting sensations—relief wrestling with regret. The predicament was resolved, and he now knew that his friend and client was not the potential murderer he'd believed him to be. Rather, Austin had gotten himself involved in a deadly situation with a deranged fan.

A tidal wave of guilt drenched Otis. He'd contacted the FBI, given them information about Austin. He'd doubted a friend. He'd—

A shadow moved across the glow of exterior light outside his window.

Then a rattling at the door.

It flew open, and two uniformed cops stood there covering their guns.

"Hands up, sir!"

Otis complied.

The cops came in, patted him down, then gave him a nod, telling him to relax. He lowered his hands.

"Who did this to you?" the older one said—black, mustached, thick gut.

Otis thought back to what Austin had said.

Just remember that friends take care of friends.

He'd puzzled all night over the cryptic words Austin had said just before he left Otis locked in his office.

Now he understood.

"I don't know," Otis said. "Some teenage punk with a ski mask and a gun. Took my phone so I couldn't call."

He pointed to the empty phone jack.

The younger cop groaned as the tension melted from his rigid posture. "And yet the little bastard called it in anonymously. Probably some sort of dare." He stepped to Otis, scanned him up and down. "Are you hurt, sir?"

"No," Otis said, then pointed to the empty McDonald's sack on his desk. "But I could use a fresh Big Mac."

CHAPTER FIFTY-SEVEN

FORT MEADE, MARYLAND

BRIGADIER GENERAL STUART NOYER eased back into his plush leather chair and let a small smile form on his lips as he exhaled. Not because it was the end of a long day, but because of the way things had played out in the last forty-eight hours since the events in San Francisco.

Normally, a man in his position would have been the opposite of relieved. There had been a media firestorm. One of his former soldiers—an officer, no less—had gone on a killing spree, murdering fellow service members.

And Hard Sprint had been uncovered.

But the good news was that no one would ever know what really happened in the backcountry of Eglin Air Force Base. The press or the feds or NCIS or whomever could dig all they wanted. The paper trail had been burned.

Hell, the paper trail had never even existed.

And Noyer's only connection was the fact that he'd been there in San Francisco. What few records had been kept on Hard Sprint showed Pike as the officer in charge of a small training exercise pulling service members from different branches, from all over the country, to Eglin on TDY for what ended up being an ill-fated mission.

And Pike was dead now.

So let the little Sherlock Holmes wannabes swing their magnifying glasses in whatever directions they wanted. They'd get no further than Kasperson, Incorporated, a company that existed for less than a year and did so in name only.

As for Noyer, the image crisis he'd suffered—by having one of his former trusted officers lose his mind—actually amplified his persona. It was a facelift, not a black eye.

Because the public had seen him.

It was what he'd always wanted.

And it was happening now, so late in life, after he'd all but given up on the dream.

He stood from behind the desk and stepped to the closet in the back of the office. As he strolled past the window, outside the sky was black, and the base glowed from street-lights and building lights, all of it playing off fields of green grass, well-kept buildings, neat paths.

Meade was a nice post. Comfortable. Fitting with its mission, which had, through the years, become one of information—words and numbers and images. Meade was home to many information-based concerns including his own Defense Information Systems Agency as well as the Defense Courier Service, the Defense Information School, even the Army Band.

And, of course, the NSA.

As Noyer looked out his second-floor window, he could see the National Security Agency's two black towers in the distance at the edge of the base. Noyer had always loved the fact that they were black in color, so fitting of the agency's mystique. At night, they would disappear were it not for their all glass exterior glistening in artificial light.

Noyer had lobbied hard to get stationed at Meade, and he'd since worked his ass off kissing other people's asses to get himself aligned with the NSA. But still, while he spent a considerable amount of time over there on the other side of the base, he didn't stay there.

Here he was. In *this* building. Wearing a uniform.

Until very recently, he'd looked at these dark buildings on the far side of the base with a sense of almost painful longing. For his ascendancy to work in the way he had planned, he needed to be in that building. But tonight, he couldn't help but grin. Because it now appeared that he wouldn't need the NSA at all.

He was in the public's eye.

He could skip all the maneuvering and move right into politics.

He'd hoped for so long to use a climb through the military to get into a position to run for office. But life, as they say, caught up with him, and before he knew it, he was a career man like so many of the other poor saps who joined the military. He'd considered law school for a long time, and even tried it for a semester, but it was too difficult.

How else was someone like him going to get into politics if not by getting a high-level position within government? His best bet, he thought, was to use what skills he had and get an NSA slot, eventually climbing to the level of Director, which would ultimately put him next to the commander-in-chief.

This had been a plan he'd held onto for a long time. Too long, it would seem. His hair had gone white. He was fifty-nine, and it had appeared his opportunity had passed.

Until forty-eight hours ago.

The incident in San Francisco had been his godsend. He could now hit the television circuit. He could write a book.

And he could start his political maneuvers in a wholly different manner than his long-held plan. And he could do so *immediately*. Not years down the line.

He gave a final, almost derisive smile to the NSA buildings, grabbed his jacket, shrugged it on, and stepped out of the office, flipping off the lights behind him.

In the outer office, PFC Sharpe gave him a professional smile from behind her desk.

"Good evening, Private," Noyer said as he stepped past.

"Good evening, sir."

The professional smile remained on the young woman's face, but PFC Sharpe was the sort of person who wore her heart on her sleeve, and she couldn't disguise the fact that she was both relieved the day was finally over and perturbed that she'd had to stay so long.

But that unintentionally obstinate attitude of hers was actually a turn-on—the defiance in her brown Latina eyes. Noyer had long held the fantasy of making it with someone far below him in the chain of command. Sharpe had been in his thoughts, so to speak, many an evening in the shower before bed.

He gave her a final smile—professional, hiding what was in his mind—and left.

―――――

Home was a five-bedroom, four-bath, two-story, custom-built home in Odenton. Gourmet kitchen with quartz countertops and a butler's pantry. Vaulted ceilings and tray ceilings and a spacious foyer. A sitting room with a three-sided glass fireplace. Wine cellar. Movie room.

By the time Noyer had returned, Sally had retired for her nightly soak in the master bathroom. With any luck, she'd move straight from there to the bed, read a few pages from her latest paperback, and pass out before Noyer climbed in beside her. It had been a long time since he could even stand looking at the old hag, a reminder of his own aging process and a visual ticking clock.

Besides, PFC Sharpe was still fresh on his mind. He didn't need Sally's image spoiling it.

For now, he was in another office, his home office, equally as appointed as his space back at Meade but more comfortable. He strolled in from the kitchen area, shutting the glass door behind him, and eyed the tufted leather high-back, sipping a tumbler of bourbon.

He stopped dead in his tracks, his black dress uniform shoes screeching on the hardwood.

Someone in the corner. In the gloom by the window where an accent chair sat. A figure. A shadow within the shadows.

Noyer gasped.

"Who..."

His question puttered out of existence, unfinished.

The shadow figure rose from its seated position, going higher, higher, higher, well over six feet. Shoes tapped on the flooring. Then a *click* and the jingle of a tiny chain as the man turned on the small banker's lamp with the green glass shade that sat on the corner of Noyer's mahogany desk.

A faint glow spilled off the desk, enough to reveal the man in a verdant, eerie, up-lit radiance.

Chiseled features. Dark hair with big, choppy strands. Cold eyes. He wore dark gray trousers and a black, short-sleeved shirt. He was fit—taut lines in his forearms, thick cords of muscle splaying his collar—but he didn't look military, nor did he have the precision bearing of an agency man, nor the polished-over restlessness of a contractor. There was something different about this individual despite the fact that everything about him said *killer*.

Especially the suppressed Beretta in his hand.

Noyer recognized him—he was the man who'd chased after Langstaff at Justin Herman Plaza.

Langstaff hadn't been heard from since...

The tumbler shook in Noyer's grasp, ice cubes rattling. A horrible tell. And men like this were good at reading tells. So, with his eyes locked on the stranger, Noyer took a sip—a gulp, really, way more than he'd usually swallow at once—then moved toward the desk and set the tumbler down. It clacked loudly against the glass topper.

"A professional. In my own home," Noyer said, trying his best to use his command voice, failing miserably. "To what do I owe the pleasure? San Francisco?"

The man nodded.

"Talk," he said.

Noyer jumped. The man's voice was unearthly. Alarmingly so. Deep, crackling, destroyed.

Noyer's mouth opened, and it was a moment before the words came. "Hard Sprint. Yes, there was a coverup. Okay? No one wanted that press—seventeen men and women blown up. It was supposed to be quiet. Who would have dreamed that they'd trigger an old freakin' bomb buried in the muck? The seventeen were volunteers, all with strong Gulf War Syndrome symptoms. They signed NDAs. Took a TDY to Eglin, got a nice little bonus. We gave them an injection of EX391, an experimental drug, sent them out into the bush with unloaded M-16s, a staged patrol to test the effects of the drug in the field. See, EX391's side effects..."

He trailed off.

Because the other man had cocked his head, smirked. His chin lifted an inch, lowered, a fraction of a nod that said, *There's more, and you're not sharing. A lot more.*

Something in Noyer's mind clicked.

"You already know about EX391, don't you? Gulf War

Syndrome, the coverup."

The man nodded.

It was then that Noyer understood what was actually happening in his office at 8pm on a Monday evening. He realized what organization this man belonged to.

Which meant Noyer needed to come entirely clean.

"Hard Sprint was never about Gulf War Syndrome," he said. "That was just a cover, a failsafe to a failsafe should someone ever go digging into the operation. EX391 was a stimulant. Keep a soldier up all night, keep him wired, prepared, alert. But there were side effects. The same ones you're evidently already familiar with. The best lies stay close to the truth.

"At the time, we thought the worst side effects would be headaches or shit pants or suicidal thoughts. No one knew about the memory thing. So we pump the stuff into the poor fools' arms and send them out in the field thinking they're helping to find a cure for GWS. The NDAs were signed, and no paper trail was left. It was all clean until the assholes blew themselves up.

"Nonetheless, our failsafe worked for years. The few people who found out about Hard Sprint knew it to be an experiment for a GWS drug. Nothing sinister there. But then Artiga started suffering memory loss. He calls up his buddy Elliott Bell, and... Well, I assume you know the rest."

The man nodded.

Noyer took another sizable gulp of bourbon. His hands felt steadier.

"People get hurt for the sake of progress, don't you agree?"

The man didn't respond.

"Pike was a loser. The man was supposed to be the exercise's leader, for Christ's sake, and he's the one whose weak composition reacted the *worst* to the drug. Pathetic." Noyer scoffed. "And Langstaff was a nutcase, a glorified gun-for-hire, the perfect sort to pawn off on a secret contractor."

He ran a finger along his tumbler.

"I had failsafes to my failsafes. And then, when it all fell apart years later, I still had the perfect plan to clean up the mess." He paused. "And then you came along." Another pause. He studied the man. "And I think I know who you are."

His thoughts went back to his moments-earlier conclusion.

"A good portion of my work is with the NSA," he said, the quiet tone of his words matching the gravity of his thoughts. "Every now and then we pick up traces, little hints, tiny indicators that something is happening outside our control, beyond our view, people moving in and out of our system, stealing information. And we suspect that several of them are NSA employees. Spies. We have further reason to believe that this group has their own field operatives. Their own assassins."

The man said nothing, but the dark shimmer in his eyes was a confirmation.

"We've never officially launched an investigation," Noyer continued. "Or written a report. Or even sent a memo. But in-house we call them the Guardians. Because it seems as though their mission is to correct problems that have gone unfixed." He paused. "You're one of them, aren't you?"

The man didn't respond.

"Here to eliminate me, are you? To fix another problem?"

The man nodded.

Noyer gave a backward jerk of the head, indicating the other end of the house. "My wife's home. Even with that suppressor, she'll hear. Is that how you want this to go? Do you want—"

The man raised his gun and fired.

CHAPTER FIFTY-EIGHT

PENSACOLA BEACH, FLORIDA

THE NEXT DAY.

The sky was blazing blue, sunglasses-not-optional, and the sand was obscenely white. Silence had visited many beautiful beaches all over the world—some with rocky cliffs, some that traced the edges of thick jungles, some with mountain back-drops—but none had sand as white as the Emerald Coast.

None.

The famous Pensacola Beach sign proudly proclaimed, *World's Whitest Beaches*.

This was no exaggeration.

Pure white. Sugar sand, as it was known. Like a long strip of unmeltable snow gleaming in the sun.

Silence was at a beach grille-and-bar just off the pier, at a table by the open windows. It was the kind of place that served lots of burgers, seafood, and umbrella-adorned frozen drinks and had a clientele of no less than fifty percent tourists, fluctuating depending on the season. A warm breeze tussled Silence's hair, and the sound of crashing waves threatened to lull him to sleep as he sat in the sun waiting for his companion to arrive.

A cackle to his left suddenly averted any unintended naps. It was a laughing gull. This one was living up to its species's moniker, squawking its heart out a yard or so away, its webbed feet half-buried in the sugar sand. If the white sand hadn't signaled that Silence was home, the chuckling avian certainly did the trick. He'd just completed back-to-back missions where most of his time had been spent in California. Laughing gulls, however, were a strictly east coast bird.

He loved those noisy little huggably-cute bastards.

As he took another sip from his condensation-dappled bottle of Heineken, the plastic sack on the table rustled in the breeze. He tied the loops in a loose knot, and the gull cocked its head, hoping for a handout. Out-of-towners were notorious for feeding them—despite signage and personal pleas to the contrary—and the gulls had gladly warmed to the custom.

Silence made eye contact with the little guy. Shook his head. And the bird moved on.

He pulled the magazine from beneath the sack—the latest issue of *Entertainment Weekly* featuring a full-cover image of a brooding Johnny Depp, head propped by a forearm adorned with an assortment of bracelets, chin cocked just so, eyes penetrating the reader. Among the cover's splashes of bold text, in the bottom right corner, was a single line that read, *THRILLER AUTHOR THRILLED.*

Silence flipped to the table of contents, then to the correct page. A tiny article discussed Austin Huber. Silence assumed the article's brevity was because the magazine had just gotten wind of the story before publication.

New York Times-bestselling author Austin Huber was caught in a situation straight out of a plot line from one of his novels when a pair of crazed fans attacked both him and his wife in San Francisco. Huber—whose novel, *Precise Directives*, is soon to be a major motion picture—and his wife both emerged rattled but unscathed and are safely back in Los Angeles, where Huber has requested privacy so his family can recuperate and he can resume work on his latest novel, *An Abuse of Power*.

Silence closed the magazine just as heels clacked on the weather-kissed wooden flooring beside him. Gibbs breezed past and pulled out the other tall chair on the opposite side of the table, which was an upturned barrel with a plexiglass-adorned circle of wood on top.

"Sorry I'm late," she said as she settled in. She cocked her head to the side, much like the gull had moments earlier, and studied the plastic sack, whose contents were vaguely visible through the thin plastic. "Um ... is this some sort of strange goodbye gift?"

The sack contained a P-trap, pivot rod, a short length of PVC, and thread-sealing tape.

Silence shook his head. "Plumbing work."

He hadn't wanted to keep Mrs. Enfield waiting any longer. He'd returned from Maryland the previous evening and promised Mrs. Enfield he would finish fixing her kitchen sink as soon as possible.

Gibbs grinned. "Well, don't work too hard." She hooked a thumb over her shoulder toward the waves and the sand and the laughter. "Try to enjoy yourself for a while."

Silence nodded.

The waitress appeared—a college girl wearing microscopic, frayed-edge jean shorts and a green T-shirt bearing the restaurant's logo—and took Gibbs's drink order: a strawberry margarita.

With a skeptically raised eyebrow, Gibbs took another look at the table. She pointed at the magazine.

"You're a coverboy now, huh?"

Silence blinked.

"Well, you *do* look a lot like him. And you don't strike me as the *Entertainment Weekly* type."

He opened the magazine again, slid it to her, poked the article with his index finger.

Gibbs's eyebrows slowly rose over the top edge of her sunglasses as she read the short piece. "'Deranged fans,' huh? Guess the powers-that-be can work super quickly when they need to erase something from the record."

Silence nodded.

Gibbs closed the magazine, slid it back to him, and interlaced her fingers before she looked out to the beach, chewing her lower lip.

"Which means they can do whatever they want, however they want, and whenever they want," she said, her voice now quieter. "I'm always going to be looking over my shoulder. They could get me anywhere, at any time, and—"

"No. My organization..." Silence said and swallowed. "Will protect you." Swallowed. "From now on..." Swallowed. "We'll watch over you."

Yes, the Watchers would be watching Gibbs. Forever. A sphere of protection would follow her wherever she went. If any harm was done to her, her attackers' blood would be spilled.

Gallons of it.

Silence would see to it personally.

She turned back to him, and even with her face half concealed by the large sunglasses, he could see genuine relief. She'd never known what he really was—nor would she ever truly know about the Watchers—but she understood enough to know he was serious.

"Thank you," she said, then turned around in her seat, observing the Gulf for another moment—the glass-clear water with choppy waves, happy beachgoers, carnival-colored umbrellas.

"Caldwell took me off administrative leave," she said as she turned to face him. "My first act was to contact authorities in Louisville. Kurt Horn has a long recovery ahead of him, but he's going to live."

The waitress arrived and placed the margarita in front of Gibbs, who gave her thanks.

Gibbs glanced at the glass for a moment before tracing a finger along its edge, much like she had with the wine glass in the Louisville hotel suite.

"So, with Horn recovering and the Hubers safe, I guess that's the end of it," she said, her voiced slowed by hesitance, almost disappointment.

Silence nodded. "Yes. After this, if..." He swallowed. "We see each—"

Gibbs waved a hand. "Save your throat. I understand. You live in Pensacola. I live in Pensacola. If we ever see each other around town, you're going to act like we never met."

Silence nodded again.

"Well," Gibbs said and tapped the side of her margarita glass, "will you enjoy one final drink with me?"

"Of course."

Gibbs smiled. "I want you to know, too, that I called my brother. Dean. It was ... tough. But I'm meeting him next week. And I wouldn't have done it without your advice. Thank you."

Silence bowed his head.

Gibbs took a big sip of her margarita, then removed her sunglasses, folded them, and placed them on the table. She looked at him then with a slight grin. And something in the eyes.

Something he'd seen on her face before.

The look.

Except this time it wasn't drunken, and it wasn't quite as sensual. There was something else there, something deeper, as a slight grin teased the corners of her lips and her eyes went side to side, scanning his face.

She stood up.

And stepped to his half of the table. Placed her hands on his shoulders. Leaned toward him.

Silence winced and jerked back.

"Gibbs..."

She stopped her forward movement. "Don't worry. I took the hint before. I'm guessing you have someone. But just give me this."

She resumed her progression.

Silence moved farther back.

When she was a few inches away, her path averted, going to the side. She gently kissed his cheek.

Her hands retracted from his shoulders, and she quickly circled back around the table and dropped into her chair.

She lifted her margarita, inviting a toast.

Silence tapped his beer bottle against her glass.

"To bittersweet goodbyes," Gibbs said with a smile that matched her sentiment.

Silence gave her a smile in return.

"Cheers," he said.

ACKNOWLEDGMENTS

For their involvement with *Tight-Lipped*, I would like to give a sincere thank you to:

My ARC readers, for providing reviews and catching typos. Thanks!

Dad, for technical information and a research errand.